GAIL IS GAEA

ARTHUR BUTT

Cover Art:
Michelle Crocker
http://mlcdesigns4you.weebly.com/

Publisher's Note:
This is a work of fiction. All names, characters, places, and
events are the work of the author's imagination.
Any resemblance to real persons, places, or events is
coincidental.

Solstice Publishing - www.solsticepublishing.com

Gail is Gaea
A Novel by
Arthur Butt

Dedication

As always to Susie, my loving wife.

Chapter One

G ail ran.

Wet grass under a sullen sky stretched before her. Farther on, a forest rose in her vision. She slipped, scrambled to her feet, and dashed off again.

Help. I must find help.

"OH-MY-GOD, OH-MY-GOD, OH-MY-GOD."

Field ended in woods. Gail hit the tree line and paused, the dim sunlight shaping the dark forest into menacing shadows. Where was a road?

The gasps of her breath, the hammering in her head, drowned out any noise of traffic. She gulped air again, trying to calm herself, and listened. *Nothing.* She plunged into the forest.

It looked—spooky. Not like the woods around her home. She slowed, kicked through vines, until she jogged in a park-like expanse with towering tree trunks. Gail stopped. "Hello? Anybody there?" Her words disappeared in the gloom.

She began walking.

An hour later she dropped, dirty, sweating, and exhausted onto a fallen tree by a spring. A light mist fell; steam from her body rose in the air.

Should'a taken that membership in the gym. Lips tightened, bile rose in her throat—the muscles of her legs throbbed. *I am so out of shape.*

The last hours blurred in her mind. Partying, drinking, and dancing. She and Ted jumped in his truck—then nothing.

She'd run the wrong way—she knew it. *Lousy sense of direction, always getting lost.* Not only had the road vanished, but the forest stretched on forever—and the trees. She'd never joined the Girl Scouts, but knew what a pine was, could tell the difference between an oak and a maple. Woods like this didn't grow around her home.

How did she always fall into these messes? Where were the cops? Her parents? She wanted to go *home*.

Tears dripped down her cheeks, mingled with the rain, and fell on her legs.

Gotta get a hold of myself. This isn't helping. Gail scrubbed at her eyes and assessed the situation.

They couldn't have driven so far off the thruway in this forest. She must have walked in circles for hours. She didn't have the faintest clue what time it was. Her phone was in her purse. Her purse was in the car. *Of course. Damn, why didn't I call 911?* She stood to retrace her steps to the field.

"Oh, great!"

Which way had she walked? The trees were all the same.

She was lost.

She groaned and yanked off her sweater. She was dying. Glasses were jammed into her pants pocket—they weren't needed. She'd bought this pair for the hipster look.

Gail regarded the muddy spring with disgust, a trickle of water bubbling out of the earth, wandering a few feet, and vanishing again.

"I gotta have a drink," she mumbled to herself. "I don't care if there's bugs, germs, or whatever." She sniffed under her arm. "And I stink!"

Gail sat, kicked off her sneakers, and shoved her feet in the water, splashing the cool liquid over her head until her dark hair was dripping wet. With a sigh of relief, she cupped her hands and drank as much as she could hold. She searched around, hoping to remember some landmark. If anything, the grim forest appeared more foreboding than ever. She strained to hear the swish of traffic, the blare of a truck's horn, anything to tell her the direction of the road— nothing, except the chirp of birds and the scurrying of an unseen animal in the treetops. Slowly, the full weight of her predicament descended like a heavy stone.

An invisible hand clutched at her throat, threating to choke her. "Why do these things happen to me?" Gail wanted to scream, or hit something. Instead, she wrapped her arms around her shoulders and cried.

She was still feeling miserable when she heard a low growl.

Standing across the stream, not ten feet away, was a wolf, a monster the size of a pony. Muscles bunched as teeth curled in a horrid snarl. The beast took a cautious step forward and glared at her, the rumble in its throat rising to a higher pitch.

"G—good puppy," Gail stammered, standing in slow motion and snatching her shoes and sweater at the same time. "You looking for a drink, boy? You want water? Here," she gestured to the spring, "it's all yours."

Gail set one foot behind the other, retreating, as she placed a tree between her and the animal. All the while she repeated, "Nice doggy, sit—you stay there," trying to remain as calm as possible and not freak out. She kept creeping backward until she withdrew a hundred feet, and then turned to run—and slammed into a man stalking up behind her. In reflex, he clutched her shoulders in a tight grip glaring into her face.

"Oh!" The tension slipped away from Gail's body. "You scared me." She smiled up into the stranger's eyes. "I'm lost." She twisted in his arms and gestured behind into the trees. "Ted, my friend. He's hurt. Can you help me? Oh—" She remembered the wolf. "There's Dogzilla or something wandering around here. You'd better be careful."

"Tu me ella, La-tan!" the man snarled. His dark eyes narrowed. He broke into a grin, revealing blacked teeth, and glowered at her. His hands tightened with bruising force on her arms.

"What?" The words sounded like Spanish, but not the Spanish she'd learned in high school—and he was hurting her. The coldness of wrong flooded her stomach again. "Hey, let go, you're gonna break my arms." She tried twisting away, unsure whether to attempt running, or if her instincts were mistaken.

The man issued a roaring yell and a second stranger emerged through the trees, followed by a third. All wore swords strapped to their sides, carried bows, and appeared no more eager to help than the stranger clutching her was.

The first man repeated, *"Tu me ella, La-tan. Choma ya."*

The coldness in her belly flowed through her body, making it hard to talk, and threating to overwhelm her senses. To calm her rising apprehension, Gail stammered, *"Me llamo,* Gail?"

The man shouted to his companions, and increased the pressure on her arms to the point where Gail thought her bones would crush, as he discovered the wolf approaching. One of the others notched an arrow and shot between the trees. The wolf dodged and disappeared. Someone had hunted it before. The archer laughed and snarled a remark at Gail.

Fear welled up inside her, a tightening sensation that reached into her chest. She struggled helplessly to yank free. She whimpered, "P—please will you help me?"

Her captor stared at her with a puzzled expression, sending a questioning glanced to his companions. One swaggered over to Gail with an arrogant smirk and seized her face in a vice-like grasp, gazing deep into her eyes.

A crawling worm sensation danced across Gail's scalp. Her brain burnt and she felt dizzy.

"Hey, you're hurting me! Stop it—let me *go.*" Whoever these guys were, they hadn't arrived to help her. She brought her knee up into her captor's groin and tried to run.

4

A moment later she found herself on her stomach, face pushed into the leaves, with a heavy knee in her back.

"Damn you—leave me alone!" she screamed as the man grasped her arms and jerked her hands up behind her. Gail gritted her teeth at the pain and twisted, attempting to throw him off. His leg pressed harder and she felt leather thongs wrapping around her wrists, and then he hauled her to her feet.

She tried to get her emotions under control. "What are you going to do with me?" she grated. *Not that, please, not that.*

The three ignored her and fell into heated debate. Gail knew she was the center of the discussion by the glances and fingers aimed her way. Two of her captors urged the third into some course of action. The man was adamant in his refusal, and emphasized his point by slapping his right fist into his palm, uttering a word that could only be an oath in his trilling language. He gestured to Gail.

The two men grumbled. One stepped forward and seized her by the back of the neck while the other disappeared. He returned leading four horses, three saddled, and the fourth loaded with packs.

Gail's eyes darted from the animals to the men. This wasn't real, no, not ten miles from her home. Stuff like this happened in other places, to different people, not her.

"Please, don't hurt me mister," she begged. She sniffed back tears. "I didn't do anything to you guys."

The three ignored her. They muttered to each other in low voices and acted as if she didn't exist.

Who were these guys? Gail examined their clothes. Besides the bows and swords, each wore capes, baggy colored pants, and tunics below their knees. They operated as if they were drug dealers.

She'd heard tales of Mexican gangs on television. Was it possible she'd wandered into someone's crazy pot farm by mistake? Gail tried one last time to make herself understood to these people.

"Look," she addressed the leader, trying to remain calm, "if you're planning to kidnap me, you know the cops will be all over you, right? They're out searching now," she lied. "If you release me, I promise I won't say a thing about what happened here, or what you're doing. I'll tell them about the car accident and how I lost myself in the woods and all." She smiled pitifully. "Let me go, okay?"

The leader knitted his brow and stared back at her, incomprehension on his face.

Gail knew they spoke some English, even if they were foreigners. This was New York, America, people didn't wander around without speaking the language. This bunch acted as if they'd landed from another planet.

Her first captor collected her shoes and sweater, stuffing both into his saddlebag. He mounted his horse and hauled Gail up into the saddle before him. The party rode off in the direction they'd appeared.

After a half-hour's ride through dense trees, they exited the forest and emerged into amber plains with mountains sketched against the sky. Gail quickly checked the area, sure she'd see a house or store she recognized, Maybe even the road.

If I can make it there, flag down help, anyone.

A small herd of dome-headed, humped-backed elephants grazed in the foreground, their long curved tusks gleaming in the sun.

Gail did a double take. "What the—?" she exclaimed. She said to her captor, "Where did they come from?"

She received a cuff on the head.

A few miles on, they encountered a pride of feeding cats, their long incisors gleaming in the sun. The foul odor of the rotting carcass the creatures feasted on drifting to her long before she saw the huddled animals and swarms of flies. Her mouth dropped as the riders circled wide around the snarling beasts.

"No—no—NO!" Gail moaned with dawning dread. This couldn't be real—it couldn't. Mammoths are extinct, so are sabertooth tigers. *Where am I and who are they guys?*

She sat in her saddle the rest of the day, frozen, her mind a riot of confusion. Had she stumbled into a super-secret government breeding lab? Genetic testing? Abducted while unconscious and whisked off to God knew where? Or was she stretched out, under sedation, in a hospital bed because of the car wreck?

Whatever it was, she must escape, and make her way home. She didn't understand what these people wanted with her anyway. She was a nobody, a weird little nerdball, who spent most of her time reading in her room, or on the computer. A guy in high school told her that. He then picked her up, dumping her in a garbage can in the cafeteria.

She kept track of her surroundings, hoping to discover a way of escape. They couldn't watch her all the time. The sun passed it zenith, settling behind the mountains, maybe tonight while they slept.

Let's see, the sun rises in the east and sets in the west, or was it the other way around? Gail focused on the landscape, estimating the path the star took, so in case she did free herself, she'd know which way to run.

As the day ended, and they entered the foothills of the mountains, a greater problem faced Gail. Her stomach growled horribly and her bladder felt ready to explode from all the water she'd drank at the spring.

She snarled under her breath to her captor, "We'd better stop soon or neither one of us is gonna be happy." She wiggled her bottom to emphases her remark.

The rider understood her meaning. He barked an order and they made camp for the night.

Maybe now. If they turn their backs for two minutes while I go—I'll go.

Her captor yanked off a long cord from the horn of his saddle and looped the rope around her neck like a leash. Untying Gail's arms, her guard cuffed her toward a clump of bushes and watched while making comments to his companions. Gruff laughs followed her as he hauled her back to the campfire where strips of dried beef jerky along with a small, hard brick of fruit and nuts was thrust into her fingers. Gail sniffed. The food emitted a faint rancid odor making her queasy stomach feel ready to erupt. It reminded her of a granola bar gone bad.

Gail sighed. The three kept an eye on her, scrutinizing every movement she made. *Maybe later, when they're asleep,* she thought.

The food didn't appear appetizing, but she ate it all, even licking her fingers to catch the last crumbs. When done, her captors allowed her to drink from a skin waterbag shoved into her face. Afterward, they tossed her sweater and shoes at her feet. She struggled into her clothes, and her captors retied her hands. After that, they left her alone, sitting by the fire to wondered and speculated on her fate.

She hadn't been molested, which was a good thing. In fact, except for a few cuffs on the head, she hadn't been hurt at all. They'd fed her, let her pee, and given her something to drink. Maybe this *was* a government research facility, or, a private game preserve of an eccentric tycoon. The more she thought about it, however, the lamer those explanations sounded, even to her. The antiquated weapons, lack of English, and strange clothing, weren't something you'd find at a government agency, and she would have heard rumors of a daffy billionaire years ago.

As Gail sat thinking, she gazed at the hills fading into the starry night. One mountaintop glowed red like the tip of a cigarette in the dark, gray smoke bellowing to the sky, long fingers of ruby running down the sides. She stared at the peak, wondering if the top was on fire, and then realized what it was: an active volcano spewing lava.

She wasn't in New York anymore.

Chapter Two

"I tell you, we have the wrong girl!" snapped Goth to his companion. He glanced at Gail from the corner of his eye, trussed and sleeping across the fire from the two. "This La-tan is supposed to be a blonde, not a brunette."

Sir Hosen grunted and continued to wolf down his travel rations without looking up, but after a few moments, he slowed his chewing long enough to reply, "Sir Grey said she is the one. Who am I to argue with him, I am his liegeman."

Goth continued in a lower voice, first handing their leader a sideways look to verify their conversation wasn't overheard. Sir Grey rolled over in his sleeping blanket, low snores issuing from his mouth. Goth bent forward and said *sotto voce,* "His argument the girl has dyed her hair to escape detection is ludicrous. Where would she buy dye out here in this wilderness? And her mind was closed to him— he knows nothing of her true identity."

Sir Hosen finished eating. He wiped his mouth with his sleeve. "What would you have me do?" he complained. "Try convincing him to release this one return into Bethish territory and continue our search for another girl? You must be mad."

Garth jabbed a finger at Gail. "Look at her clothes. Those are not Bethish, nor Ambosian. I have never seen their like before. I tell you, she is not the one."

Sir Hosen shrugged and stifled a yawn. "And I keep tell *you,* it is not our concern. Sir Grey claims to have seen her once in the capitol. I never have, you have not either. Any fault will sit with him. We are but carrying out his orders."

"But the duke," protested Garth, casting another

glance at their sleeping leader. "What will he do with us if we fetch him the wrong girl?"

The fire burnt low. Sir Hosen tossed another branch on the embers and stretched out to sleep. "We are obeying orders—who can fault us for acting as our liege commands? Besides, Sir Grey may be right. Tomorrow we cross the Little River and trek to Duke Ledo's palace. After that, it is his and the duke's problem, not ours."

The next morning Gail awoke to the prodding from Sir Grey's boot. They fed her, watered her, and led her into the bush for policing. As Gail squatted, she was watched carefully, but as her hands were untied, Garth wrapped the leash about her neck again.

"Why won't you talk to me?" Gail pleaded as he bound the tough leather throngs around her wrists. "I haven't done anything wrong." Her voice choked in fear and frustration. "At least tell me what's going on, where are you taking—*ahhh!*"

Gail jumped as something long and black slithered between her feet and disappeared into the grass. "Snake!" She danced backward to the harsh guffaws of the three men.

Gail hated snakes, and mice, and anything creepy and slimy. It was okay to read about gross animals, she supposed, or see reptiles and rodents on a television horror show, but to have one wiggling between her feet? *Almost touching her?* The thought made her skin crawl. A spider once fell on her keyboard while she was doing homework in her room. She refused to sleep in her bed for two days until her father sprayed bug killer into every corner. She wished he were here with her now, wondered if Papa Bear was even searching for her.

Sir Hosen grunted a harsh command and shoved Gail toward his horse.

"All right, I'm going." She surveyed the grass taking short, mincing steps, much to the amusement of

Hosen who mounted and waited for her. "Well, you're wearing boots!"

Sir Hosen hauled her up in front of him and they set off again.

As the day wore on Gail passed into a stupor. Her back ached from the car wreck, she was stiff all over from sleeping on the bare ground; she was so filthy her odor rose about her like a dead mouse in her pocket.

The three horsemen spoke little except for mumbled grunts and pointed fingers when some prowling danger presented itself, and to Gail not at all. The landscape was desolate, etched shaded lines in an endless sea of amber. Gail kept hoping to see anyone who might help her. As the morning faded into the afternoon, she decided escape would never be possible. These men would slit her throat and leave her body in a ditch, wherever this place was, she amended. No one would look for her, no one cared, not even her parents.

Their party approached a wide sluggish river overhung with drooping branches. On the banks, someone had built a dock with a large brass bell attached to a pole. A heavy chain fastened to an eyebolt led from the dock and disappeared into the water. Sir Grey dismounted, rang a signal, the clanging echoing over the watercourse and into the hills beyond.

From across the river, another bell answered his call. A raft launched from the bank and approached, pulled by two men heaving on the chain. The craft docked and a hurried conversation occurred between the raftmen and the leader of their party.

Sir Hosen dismounted and jerked Gail from the saddle, walking both her and his horse onto the raft. The two sailors handed her curious glances, but said nothing, as they began hauling their craft back across the river.

Gail stared intently at the sailors. *Call the cops, please. Can't you see I'm a prisoner? Tied? Aren't you interested?* She kept shifting her eyes from the raftmen to her captors, hoping the two would understand what she was thinking. Fear of saying anything aloud kept her from shouting, even though the desire to scream surged up inside her. She was afraid if she said anything aloud, her captors would kill all three of them on the spot.

The raft docked at a hamlet, dilapidated buildings lining the shore. They remounted, Gail casting another forlorn look at the two sailors hoping they understood her unspoken plea and would send help.

No pursuit followed. Gail watched apathetically as they rode up a dry canyon and proceeded into the stark mountains.

Two day's travel brought their party to the outskirts of a city. Sir Grey was in a jovial mood. He waved to the estates they passed, with tiled roofs jutting up over the high walls and declared, "A baronetcy for this! You see this place?" He gestured to a townhouse larger than the rest, "Before today is finished that could be mine!"

Gail picked up a few words of this strange language, and every time Sir Grey stared at her, and the crawling sensation ran its fingers over her scalp, she discovered she knew more. They were riding to someone in authority, and as the palaces grew larger, she figured it must be someone important.

The longer they traveled, the more excited she became. They must have an interpreter, or someone who spoke English. She could explain her story, tell these people whatever they thought she'd done, she hadn't meant it. They would have to release her. She was a kid. The authorities would notify her parents and they would arrive and pick her up. Everything would be fine. When they reached an imposing building, with a massive stone wall surrounding the outside and an iron gate for the entrance, she was positive it was a matter of hours before this mess was straightened out. Her mom and dad would drive up in their old car to take her away.

Along the way, she kept a vigil, searching for the police, or anyone to help her in case she was wrong. People were in sight, but none near. They dressed in tunics and baggy pants, the same as her captors, and kept their heads averted as Sir Grey and his party rode by. What was even stranger, no cars drove on the cobblestone boulevards, not even a bicycle riding on the streets. To her amazement, a few carriages and sedan chairs operated on the roads and passed the other way.

"Announce me to Duke Ledo," Sir Grey bellowed to the sentries at the palace gates as he vaulted from his saddle. He reached up and dragged Gail to the pavement next to him, shaking her at the startled guards. "Tell him Sir Grey has caught the fugitive girl he seeks!"

After a hurried conversation, one of the sentries dashed away. He returned accompanied by an armed soldier who escorted the four through a labyrinth of corridors to a throne room. A red carpet led up to a dais where a man with blond hair fading to silver lounged.

Sir Grey towed Gail, wrists tied, with the throng around her neck, along behind him to the base of the throne. He dropped to his knees, jerking her down, until her head rested on the floor.

"Rise, Sir Grey," the duke intoned. "Where is the daughter of Senator Tasab-tan?"

"Why—this is she, m'lord," stammered a confused Sir Grey, scrambling to his feet. He tugged Gail up and pushed her forward, pointing. "See? As you ordered."

Sir Hosen and Goth read the expression on the duke's face and tried to make themselves small behind their leader.

The duke's mouth worked soundlessly. He glared at Sir Grey as if the other lost his mind. *"Imbecile! Fool!"* he thundered, half-rising from his throne. His face darkened to red as he jabbed a shaky finger at Gail. "That is not La-tan!

This—this," he sputtered, lost for words as his rage mounted. The duke finally blurted out, "She is not even blond, you idiot—what have you brought me?"

"I—I—you...." stammered Sir Grey, looking at Gail, bewildered, "Your message said she crossed the border and was in the hinterlands of Bethand," he started, "How many young girls could be wandering alone in the jungle out there?"

"YOU HAVE BROUGHT ME THE WRONG GIRL!"

"B—but...."

"You were in the council chamber when she addressed the lords, were you not?" accused Duke Ledo, livid, his rage mounting. *"Did you even look at her?"*

"Y—yes, yes I did," whimpered Sir Grey, taking a step backward and stumbling into Goth, "but I was way in the back—I could not...."

"FOOL."

Duke Ledo bolted from his throne and took a menacing step forward toward Gail. "Who are you? Speak up, girl! What is your name?"

Gail tried to follow the conversation with rapt attention. Something was wrong, that was for sure. The man on the chair was incensed with fury and screaming. Sir Grey faded to a colorless shade of pale, and cowered. Now the angry old man was yelling at her for some reason.

Gail was addressed several times on the trail as La-tan, and she'd heard the term applied to her here again. She figured it must be some sort of formal address like "Ms." or "Mr.". She replied in a hesitant voice, "La-tan?"

"WHAT! WHAT NONSENSE IS THIS?"

Gail jumped back at his blast. *Oh, geez, screwed up again. Maybe he wanted my name.*

"Gail?"

"GET HER OUT OF HERE," screamed the duke. He squeezed his eyes shut. "IMBECILS BRINGING ME

IMBECILS—*OUT. OUT.*"

"Yes, Duke Ledo! Certainly, m'lord!" Sir Grey swung around so quick this time he slammed into Sir Hosen who was on his knees cringing in fear. Still bowing, and dragging Gail by the leash around her neck, Sir Grey stopped at the entrance of the throne room and asked, crushing his eyes together, "What should we do with her, sire?"

Duke Ledo settled back on this throne, breathing hard, his face scarlet. He waved a hand in disgust. "I do not know. Take her to the docks and sell her for all I care!"

Gail didn't know what was happening. This hadn't gone the way she thought it would. Where was someone who understood her? Where was help? She tried shaking Sir Grey's hand off and lunged toward the chair, shouting in a desperate attempt to make herself heard, "*Hey, please, I didn't get to ask….*"

"*OUT.*"

"*But I didn't do anything.*"

She was hustled away by her captors, who scurried from the palace to their mounts throwing terrified glances over their shoulders. The guards, hearing the tongue-lashing, jeered the trio as they collected their horses and ran out the gates.

"I tried to tell them—I tried to tell them," Goth kept repeating to no one, as he shot venomous looks at Hosen and Grey. He shoved his hand to his mouth and said in a hoarse tone, "The duke will have us hung by our thumbs."

Out on the road, Hosen, Goth, and Grey stopped to regroup, shooting horrified looks toward the palace. Sir Hosen took a deep breath, his voice lowering to a hiss, and asked Grey, "What now?"

"Now? You heard Duke Ledo," snarled Sir Grey, a shudder running through his body. "You two take the girl to the docks and sell her." His face was deathly white. "If you need me, I will be in the nearest tavern, hiding. After

16

you dispose of her I advise you to do the same, before the duke remembers he has not punished us yet." He vaulted onto his horse and dashed off.

The Goth and Hosen glanced at each other.

"He is right," said Goth, his eyes shifting to the gate as if waiting for guards to march out and arrest them both. "Let us do this quick and make ourselves scarce for a while. Maybe we will be lucky and the duke's wrath will fall on Sir Grey alone."

Gail looked from one man to the other in total confusion. Why did they bring her here? What happened? She strained her limited vocabulary and asked Goth, "What...now?"

"No time, girl." He scowled at her, raised his hand as if to strike her again, and changed his mind. "We must go." He mounted his horse and hauled her up in front of him.

The river leading up to the city bustled with traffic. Recently dredged, for the first time in years, deep-sea ships called at the city dock. The pier was crowded with sailors, stevedores, and merchants loading and unloading freight.

Goth and Sir Hosen hitched their horses and wandered among the busy people in confusion. Gail on her leash was towed behind Goth, wondering what would happen next.

She finally decided she was about to be released. Of course, this was why the angry man was yelling! He realized her captors made a mistake and ordered her returned home. It was only a matter of time now.

"Do you have any idea where we should go?" Sir Hosen whispered to Goth. Sailors and merchants swirled around the three like bees, hustling about their business, or standing in small groups gossiping.

"We must locate a slave factor," said Goth shrewdly, scanning the pier. "But I do not know where...." He studied the stalls lining the dock. "Wait!" He shoved

Gail into Sir Hosen's arms. "Hold her. I will be right back."

Goth sauntered over to an open-air lunch counter, a few customers stood around drinking and wolfing down food. He waved to the server, who was busy at the opposite end of the bar collecting empty bottles, until he received the man's attention.

"Excuse me," Goth said to the counterman, "where can I find the slave factors?"

The counterman shrugged and gestured along the pier. "Down that way, but ya jus' missed 'em, mate. Held their auction and left fer the day an 'our ago." He wiped his counter with a dirty rag while scanning the bar. "Why?"

Goth shifted his eyes to Sir Hosen and Gail. "I have a girl the duke ordered us to sell."

"Hmm…" The counterman searched the faces of his customers. "Maybe I can help yah." He cupped his hands and shouted, "Hey! Capt'n Herros. Gotta minute?"

A dark-skinned man dressed in oilskins, with a pegged leg, glanced up from a group of similarly dressed sailors clustered together talking. The counterman waved him over. "Gotta fella might 'ave somethin' you're interested in," he yelled and nodded to Goth. "You talk to 'em," he grunted to Goth, pointing to the man. He hurried away to the far end of the counter to help a customer.

Captain Herros wandered over, the *clip—clip—clip* of his artificial leg resounding on the stone of the pier. He took in Garth's measurements with one swift glance, and stuck out his hand. "Capt'n of the *Evening Star*. You sellin' something?"

Goth surveyed the seaman dubiously. "I have a girl Duke Ledo wants me to sell. You buying?"

"Maybe," the sailor admitted. He shoved a finger in Gail's direction. "This one?"

Goth waved Sir Hosen and Gail over. "Yes. How much will you pay us?" Gail hung back, unsure who this man was, or if he were the one to take her home. Her sense of wrongness tugged at her insides. Sir Hosen yanked hard on her leash, jerking Gail forward until she stood in front of the sailor.

Captain Herros walked around Gail, studying her from every angle. He saw a dirty, frightened, half-starved girl in her late teens, wrapped in a foul-smelling sweater. She might clean up nice, though, and he had a use for a young woman such as this. He hadn't discovered what he wanted in his price range at the slave auction today, and these soldiers didn't appear to have any hint what a slave sold for. He might pick up a bargain.

"Three silvers."

"What? You must be out of your mind!" sputtered Sir Hosen. He had no idea what a girl servant cost, but the price certainly seemed low.

The captain studied the two men, saw the uncertainty and desperation in their eyes. "The Duke is rich enough already," replied Herros with a hoarse laugh. "'e doesn't need my money." He paused, and pretended to considered Gail again. "Tell ya what—trading's been good. I'll make it four."

Sir Hosen glanced at Goth—the other raised his thumb. "One gold piece."

Herros laughed. "One gold piece? I wouldn't pay that much for the duke's daughter." A thought dawned on him. *What were these two doing trying to sell a slave anyway? The duke had people for that. Something was wrong.* "You have papers on her?"

"Why no," stammered Sir Hosen, not sure what papers Herros meant. "The Duke said...."

"I thought so." Captain Herros stared at both men. "Four silvers and not one bronze more. Otherwise wait for the factors ta open tomorrow, but I don't think they'll touch 'er without papers." He spun on his heel as if to go.

The two men whispered at each other. "Sold!" said Sir Hosen. He thrust the rope acting as Gail's leash into the captain's hand before Herros could walk away, and shoved her roughly toward the captain. "You—him!" he ordered.

Captain Herros chuckled, fished out a leather pouch, and counted four rounds of silver into the waiting hands of Sir Hosen.

Gail's former captor examined the rounds, and with a shrug, pocketed the coins. Without a backward glance, he and Goth mounted their horses and galloped away.

When Gail saw the transfer of coins to Sir Hosen, and her leash to this stranger, she got the idea through her head she was not being rescued. They had sold her like some animal in a pet store. She didn't know why, or what she'd done wrong, or what would happen next. A sense of loss and dread seized her, and she took a step to follow, her small world crumbling.

She hated Sir Hosen, Goth, and especially Sir Grey, for holding her prisoner, but at least they were a stable force in this new world. Now they had gone. She looked at the man holding her bond and wondered what he would do to her.

"Well, girl!" Herros boomed, "Let's haul ya aboard ship." He took off her leash, and withdrew a knife. Before Gail could react, he spun her around and sliced the leather thongs binding her wrists. "I don't think ya'll be needn' those anymore."

She was free, just like that! She was wrong—her ordeal was over. Gail stood and regarded the world as if she never saw it before. "Thanks Mister, I don't know why those two men grabbed me—I didn't do any wrong. Are you going to bring me home now?"

Captain Herros scowled and shot a stream of words at her in the same funny language she didn't understand. A tentative smile of gratitude washed over Gail's face and she rubbed her wrists. "I don't understand, maybe if you spoke slower…"

"What kind'a gibberish are ya talking, girl?" Herros

said. "And while ya at it, take off that wrap, too—it stinks. We'll find ya some clean clothes when we climb aboard. Here, I'll help ya."

Gail froze as the man stepped toward her and shrank back as the captain reached out, jerked off her sweater in one swift motion over her head, and pulled her shirt halfway up in the process. She yanked her blouse back into place, startled, and wrapped her arms around herself. Coldness stabbed her. He wasn't here to help, she wasn't free, the brief elation at the thought of rescue vanished in a heartbeat.

Her eyes darted left and right. Should she try to make a break for it? She decided no. The pier was crowded with people; she would never escape. She didn't understand the language, had no idea where she was, or where to go. Gail tried to convince herself whatever was about to happen was better than it was. It must. After the stranger removed her sweater, he made no move to hurt her, and appeared more puzzled than angry. Gail's hopes rose. Maybe things would work out; at least she wasn't tied up.

Herros flashed a reassuring smile, and without appearing to do so, took her by the back of the neck, not hard, but enough to let her know she couldn't go anywhere. He gestured to a ship. "This way. What's your name, girl?"

"Gail?"

"Gael? So? Is that supposed to be a name?" Herros swung her around to face him and studied her face and dress closely for the first time. "Where are you from? And none of your stupid talk—speak right."

Gail raised her hands hopelessly and shook her head, feeling dumb for not knowing how to communicate with this man. She knew he asked a question but didn't have the language to reply. An idea occurred to her, she pointed to her mouth and said, "We. Don't. Speak. The. Same. Language."

"What the —"

The crawling sensation crossed the top of her head again. She brushed at her hair without results.

Herros scowled. "It appears our friends sold me something not right," he rumbled, rubbing his grizzled chin as he fumed inside. "Maybe those two got the better of the deal after all."

Cursing under his breath, Herros escorted her up the gangplank of the ship. "In you go, girl," he said with a gruff tone, pushing her along to a door on the main deck. He swung the hatch open and shoved Gail into a small piano box size cabin. "This is yer new digs fer now. Make yerself comfortable and stay here," he ordered. "We'll get to the bottom of this after I'm underway." Herros slammed the door, giving Gail a thin-lipped shake of his head in bewilderment before he did so.

The sudden change of attitude scared Gail. Wrongness without understanding what had happened swirled around her head. Something this man planned hadn't gone the way he wished, and it was her fault—and she didn't know why. Nothing was going right, mounting emptiness engulfed her, and for a moment, she slumped on the small bunk fighting back tears.

This isn't getting me anywhere, she thought bleakly. She realized for the first time since this ordeal started, she was alone—escape was possible if she hurried. With renewed purpose, she rushed to the door, wiggling the latch in an attempt to open it without making noise. The hatch moved a scant quarter of an inch and stopped, chained from the outside. With a sigh, she swung from the door and surveyed her new prison.

Gail long ago gave up any expectations of comfort. Shoved and pushed around, sleeping on the bare earth and sold, left her with a cold sense of detachment to her physical surroundings.

Now, with the dubious change in her status, she gazed around the furnished room in awe. The cabin was equipped with a small port. She hurried over and peeked out. The dock and strangers lay beyond. *Escape to where?* She rubbed her raw, bleeding wrists tenderly, touched her neck where her leash chafed her, and released a whimpering sigh of despair.

One wall held a small drop-down shelf for sleeping. Gail released the latch and sat, then stretched out with a groan, curling herself into a small ball on the thin mattress. Her throat tightened as she thought how unfair the world was treating her.

I don't give a damn. I'm away from that mess and good riddance. As long as this guy doesn't try any funny business, I'm happy to be leaving with him. Maybe someday someone will come along and I'll return home.

Chapter Three

Gail awoke to the gentle rolling of the ship under her. For a moment, she couldn't recall where she was, and lay on her bunk, staring at the cabin ceiling, trying to orientate herself. Then she remembered. She was at sea! She perked up and sprang to the tiny port, threw it open, and gazed out. Grey water under a sullen sky spread to the horizon. The tangy scent of salt water, dead fish, and pine tar flooded the cabin along with a cool breeze.

She'd never been on a real ship before. In her dreams, she thought of taking cruises, flying off on jets to far distant places, maybe living in a foreign country one day, but this was actual.

Reality slapped her in the face. Her stomach growled, she itched all over from not bathing for two weeks, and she was a prisoner. Still boiling with the excitement of going somewhere, Gail marched to the door determined to do something about her situation.

"Hey, anybody there?" she banged and shouted, *"Let me out."*

A rustling on the other side of the door answered her. The hatch opened, accompanied by a blast of cold, wet air. An old man peered in. He spoke in that trilling language she didn't understand and squinted at her inquiringly.

"Food. I'm hungry." Gail pointed to her mouth with a chewing motion and rubbed her stomach. As an afterthought, she raised her arm and sniffed, screwing up her face. "Soap—water." She rubbed her hands together in a washing motion.

The oldster bobbed his head in assent, mumbled something, and slammed the door behind him. Minutes

24

later, he reappeared carrying a tray with a bowl, basin, and pitcher. He placed all three on a small fold-down table, and with a crackling smile, left.

Before the door closed, Gail was wolfing down the food, some fish chowder with a chunk of dark bread to soak up the broth. She splashed water into her mouth from the pitcher, and was about to strip off her shirt to take a quick scrub when the door banged open again.

"Well, girl, appears as if you're settled in."

Captain Herros stood framed in the hatchway.

She wrenched down her shirt and retreated a few steps, watching him. *Here we go.* "Gail?"

The captain nodded impatiently. "Gael, yeah, I understand—but how come ya don't know how to speak?"

She stared at him in silence and shook her head.

The captain sighed. "Well, let's see what'ca can learn." He dragged a crude stool over and pointed to the bunk. Gail nodded, sat, and the captain tapped his chest. "Herros."

The word held no meaning for her. She didn't know what he wanted, and then decided he said some type of personal identification, maybe his name. He was trying to communicate. Gail was never good at languages, although she squeaked by in high school Spanish. She listened carefully and repeated, "Herros."

"Good," he beamed. "At least you're teachable. Now, let's try this," the captain pointed to himself, "Capt'n Herros."

Gail was an eager student. Her driving force always in the back of her mind, the need to know where she was, how she arrived there, and above all, what she must do to return home. The captain encouraged her enthusiasm to learn with an occasional cuff on the head. It rarely went this far though—the impatient tapping of his wooden peg on the deck was enough to spur Gail's memory.

Herros named the world Tierra. When their lessons

progressed far enough, he brought maps revealing oceans and the distribution of lands around the globe. Gail recognized the Earth, but a mutilated planet, distorted by ice sheets reaching fingers from the Artic into Europe, Asia, and North America; lowlands abounded she'd never seen before. Dominating what she thought was the Atlantic Ocean, was a strange new island he called Mu.

"Mooo?" Gail repeated, as she and Herros poured over one of his maps during a language session.

Captain Herros roared with laughter. "That's right, Gael, *Mooo.*"

Gail studied the map again. "But this is—past." One of her favorite subjects was history. She spent many long hours at her computer at night, reading about ice ages, cavemen, wars and kings.

"It can't be, though." She shook her head in disbelief while gazing at the map and tracing the new coastlines with an index finger. "Mu doesn't exist. In my time this is all water." She slammed her palm on the new continent. "But we have legends—"

"You tell some tall tales, don't you?" Herros stopped and a serious expression spread over him. "Well, maybe it's true. We Muians have legends also. They say our ancestors reached this land from the stars." He gestured to the ceiling of the cabin.

"What!"

The captain shrugged. "Who knows?" He broke into a chuckle. "Glad I'm a seafaring man, though. If Mu is gonna sink under the water I'll be aboard the *Evening Star.* At least I'll have a place to hang my cap."

This was too much for Gail to absorb all at once. Could Mu be Atlantis? These people traveled from the stars? They looked human, not like the aliens she always thought of, and if this was Atlantis —?

She traced the continents with her hand. "How did I get here?"

26

Herros stood and sauntered to the port, gazing out to the ocean and the low coastline they sailed along. "If'n your story is true, hard to tell." He stroked his beard.

"You must have some idea." Gail said. She still couldn't believe she existed in a far, distance past. "Can't you at least take a guess?"

"Hmm…. I was never much for schooling, didn't study the mysteries—received most of the basics out here on the sea from my father."

"Where was your mother?" Gail asked.

Herros was silent. When he spoke, he stared at the deck, his voice bleak. "Mother died when I was five; don't know what of. My father took me on as a cabin boy and I've been shipboard ever since."

Gail bit her lip. "Oh, I'm sorry." She was. She couldn't imagine losing a parent and having to go out to work for the rest of your life at the same time.

He swung away from the port with a shake of his head and said to Gail, "No matter, but back to your question, out here on the water we see strange things. Ships disappear on calm seas. Sometimes we discover boats in perfect condition, but with no one aboard. Jus' one of those things, I imagine."

Gail remained confined to her cabin and studied, but even with all the new information she learned, she possessed long periods when there was nothing to do. A few times she asked to take a walk up on deck. During the day, her small cabin grew stifling hot, and the small port let in hardly any cool air. Herros replied with, "Don't think it's a good idea, Gael, leastwise not when it's light and the crew's about. The men—" he gestured out the door, "—they're kinda nervous a woman's onboard, superstitious lot, but—"

"Nighttime?"

"We'll see," Herros replied, rubbing his chin as he thought over what she asked. "Now let's get back to ya lessons."

When the captain did bring her on deck, Gail would stand by the railing, gaze up at the stars as the cool ocean breeze blew through her dark hair, and make a wish on the first one she saw. Her prayer was always the same. *"Let me go home."*

***

The old man, "Cooky" continued to fetch meals to her, and Captain Herros stayed late in her cabin, telling tales of the sea, the different cities of Mu, and their history.

"Bethand is the richest," Herros jabbed a spot on his map. He traced a line along the coast. "Here's Ambos." A callous finger stabbed the north shore of Mu.

"Which country is this?" Gail pointed to ragged peaks marked off in the center of the parchment. Someone scrawled a name there, maybe the mapmaker, but she hadn't mastered the script of Mu.

"This? Name's Carago." Herros leaned back on his stool. "Big war brewing between Bethand and Carago. Don't do any trading with Carago," he mused. "They're landlocked. Only river big enough to sail there is the Little River and Bethand controls the mouth. That's what the war is all about."

Gail studied the map, tracing the watercourse forming the border. "Why would it cause a war?"

"Carago wants a port," he explained. "Once they got one they can start trading on their own. Right now everything gotta be transported by land, or they pay high tariffs to Bethand. Can't have no merchant marine fleet either, the Bethish won't permit it." He shook his head. "Don't know if'n I'd like the Caragons trading or not; more competition."

"Yes, but—war?"

"Oh, well." The captain chuckled and raised his shoulders in a shrug. "Ya have trading ships, ya need a navy, right? Bethand is afraid of the competition, too. And they control the bay," he traced an inlet on the map, "the Caragons want."

Other marks caught her eye, but Gail was confused. Etched in the middle of the water, clustered around lowlands not present in her age, were small figures of people.

"How about these?" she pointed. "More cities?"

"Them? Well, yes and no," Herros smirked, glancing over Gail's shoulder and the area she indicated. "Those are the lands of the sea people."

"Sea People? Who are they?"

"You know, *Sea People*." He made diving motions with his hands. "The natives who live in the ocean. Don't tell me ya never heard of those folks?"

Mermaids? "Ah—individuals say they've seen human-like creatures living in the water, but most think they're a joke, people telling a story."

"It's rare to see one," the captain agreed. "Shy. But if you can make friends, it's good trading, or so I've heard."

"Do you think we'll see any?" Gail asked. She fought the urge to rush to the port and start scanning the water. "If we do can I please go on deck and look? Pleassse."

The captain pursed his lips in thought. "Don't think we'll see any this trip, too far north," Herros replied at last with an indulgent smile. "But if'n we do run across a pod I'll fetch you."

Gail forgot about her confinement. Trapped in the past, no hope of returning to her own time, the cabin became her home. The ship developed into a place of safety and refuge against the ordeal she'd encountered during the last weeks. When she wasn't learning the new language, she kept poring over the maps, her small world growing larger. She accepted the stark reality of her life. She was in the past—it all made sense. Somehow, she traveled back in time. It was impossible, but it all fit; the continent, which later disappeared into the middle of the ocean, the prehistoric animals, people who appeared human, instead of hideous monsters out of a movie.

A month into the voyage, Gail was hard at work, bent over her map, learning the new coastlines of the world. For the last few days, the weather had grown warmer, more humid, and Captain Herros became an infrequent visitor. She'd heard him on the forecastle, bellowing orders to the crew, his peg leg thumping on the deck. A sense of foreboding filled her. Something was about to happen.

In her heart, she knew this voyage couldn't continue forever. Although always paternal and friendly, the captain was becoming more distant as the days continued. Herros bought her for some reason, why, he never said. When she heard a knock on the door, Gail was on the verge of exploding with anxiety.

Herros poked his head in and entered. Gail looked up quickly and asked, "Captain Herros? Where are we going?" Her stomach twisted, afraid of the answer.

"Sailing, Gail, sailing!" He strode over to the map and touched the faint lines indicating the continent of Mu. "I've traveled from Bethand to Ambos," his finger traced along the coast, "that's where we picked you up." His hand moved across the narrow sea to the west coast of Africa. "I should be sailing there, the wild lands, to drop off manufactured goods and pick up raw materials, but on this trip, I'm cruising here," his finger continued down the coast of Mu, "to Zarbin."

Herros stabbed at a small dot on the coast. "Doin' a favor for a friend, mighty lucky I am, too. Ya need a permit to dock at their port. If'n I make a profit on my cargo, and the people there like me, I'll be able to add it to me regular route." His face clouded over and he stared at his boots. "You'd be part of the freight."

"What?" the premonition of change she'd felt for

days shot into her body with an urgency she couldn't deny. It was what she thought. The twisting inside her belly swelled into her chest. She felt like he slapped her in the face. "What do you mean?"

"I'm the captain of the ship, not the owner," Herros rumbled. His voice edged with inner conflict, as he glanced up and approached close, a serious look on his face. "Me and the crew work for shares of the earnings, ya understand. Every port I stop at, I gotta show the company I'm making money."

"Couldn't you tell them I was a...." Gail began. She tried keeping her features composed, forcing herself to remain calm, inch by inch along her trembling body, while suppressing the churning inside her.

Herros waved a hand and rushed on, "The people who pay me employed spotters in the port I bought ya. If word leaked out I brought you aboard ship without ya appearing on me manifest and showing a profit, I'd be outta a job. As it is, I'm gettin' a lot of heat from me crew. You're cargo, plain and simple."

"But I thought—I'd hoped...."

"That I'd take ya with me?" Herros smiled. "You don't know anything about ships, and shipboard living ain't no life fer a young girl anyway. And I can't drop you off in some port, what would you do? How would you live?"

He frowned and sat on the edge of the bunk. "No, girl, this is the best thing fer you, and the best thing for me. If things were different, but—" his words trailed off and he shook his head. "I'm sorry, but that's the way it gotta be."

Wetness ran down Gail's cheeks. She choked out, "And when exactly am I supposed to be—*sold?*"

Herros stood and moved toward the door, refusing to look at her. "We'll be makin' port in three days." He turned with a half-smile. "We'll clean you up good. I have an idea, you'll see. I'll take care of ya as best I can."

"I guess I don't have much choice, do I?" she

mumbled. She concentrated on her hands to stop the trembling. "I'm your *slave*. You can do what you want with me."

"Now, Gael, don't say that," Herros's voice held genuine regret. "It'll be all to the good. You'll see."

Gail sat in shock. The feeling of safety developed over the last month vanished in a heartbeat. She fooled herself into believing she belonged, that this cabin, the ship, would be her new home. The nightmare was starting again. *Sold—a piece of meat—into what?*

***

The *Evening Star* sailed up a broad jungle river to the city of Zarbin. For this occasion, Herros allowed Gail on deck to see her new home, but first insisted she scrub to the point of redness with rough yellow lye soap. He provided her clean clothes, and a forest green cloak. The cool morning breeze felt good after confinement in her cabin; but even at this early hour, she knew it would be a hot and sultry day.

The ship swung into a channel flanked by marsh grass and veered around a bend, revealing floating docks and a city stretching through the swamp.

Logs driven through the water into the soft earth to the bedrock below supported a framework of rafts on which buildings sat. In some parts, the inhabitants paddled between the structures along canals where streets would have stood; in others, waterproof rock rested over the platforms to form a solid base for roads and houses. The whole city reached inland for mile.

Captain Herros strolled over and stood next to Gail. She asked, "Why did they build in a swamp? Wouldn't it be easier to put the city on dry land?"

Herros chuckled. "Easier, yes; safer, no. Besides, there is no dry land. This whole place rests on a bunch of submerged islands. Did their best, I suppose, couldn't construct it anywhere else. This marsh extends inland for miles," he waved to the distant mountains, "and once you wade in that far, there's creatures you wouldn't want to meet, believe me."

"But why be here in the first place?" Gail asked. "This place is so—" she swatted at a swarm of mosquitos buzzing in her face "—nasty."

Herros signaled to his helmsman and pointed. "They started as a religious cult somewhere up by Bethand way. Trekked down here after a flood to start their own city."

The captain gestured to the buildings as they drifted closer to the docks. "I've made port here twice, like I said, ya need a special permit, but it's the one place I'll trade for certain spices and drugs. This one stop could be worth as much as the rest of my trip."

Gail listened to what he said with her lips twisting down into a scowl. "You're going to get that much for me?" She saw the coins exchanged hands when Herros bought her. No wonder he was anxious to make a sale, he must be making a bundle.

Captain Herros guffawed. "I wish, lass!" He sobered, "But if the people I take you to like what they see, ya could be worth your weight in gold in the future."

"I guess that's good for you."

"I told you I'd try to do right, and I will," Herros replied with a shake of his head. "Maybe for the company too." He rubbed his hand over his face, wiping sweat away. "I don't know what the future holds, but I think the Gods loaned you to me. This is for the best. Now down to your cabin, girl, we need to dock and unload."

Gail spent the balance of the day alternating between fear and hope. She kept scurrying to the small port, peeking out, and sitting, only to leap up again. This was where she belonged, on the ship, not in some strange city, alone among strangers. Maybe Captain Herros would change his mind. She knew he like her, he said as much. If she convinced the captain to keep her with him, she would show him what she knew and could do.

Gail lay on her bunk far into the night trying to figure out a way to keep herself on board, while the sound of freight unloading and the yells of sailors rang in her ears. When she fell asleep, she still hadn't figured out a way to hold off an unsure future.

***

Captain Herros woke her at dawn the next morning as a red sun rose and hurried her into the heart of the city. He disregarded the hawkers and smaller businesses lining the streets, and with grim determination kept marching for an ornate building set in the middle of the town.

"This is the temple of Moack, the patron God of Zarbin," Herros whispered to Gail as he swung ornate cedar doors open and hustled her into a large atrium. "We're gonna see the high priest. These people run this city. If he likes what he sees, you'll be set for life. If not, I gotta sell you on the open market to one of the slave factors. Try to impress this man. Your life depends on it."

I have to trust him. He's never lied to me—Oh, God, what will happen to me?

"Why are you shaking?" Herros patted her on the shoulder. "Scared?"

"Y—yea. I guess so."

Automatically, the captain squeezed her arm lightly. "Don't be. Everything is gonna be fine."

The captain snagged a purpled-robed priest who strode out to meet them and said, "I'm Captain Herros, off the *Evening Star,* to see the priest Eros. I was here yesterday and he know I'm coming, he's expecting me."

The priest scrutinized Herros, shot a fleeting glance at Gail, and waved them to walk behind him.

Their guide escorted the two along a marble hallway adorned with strange pictures of men with bull bodies, women with catheads. Gail gasped when they

34

passed a serpent whose eyes tracked their progress.

The priest stopped before two bronze doors and swung the portals open, revealing a darkened room where a wrinkled old man with parchment skin sat on the floor. Incense perfumed the air. They entered and the doors swung soundlessly closed behind.

"Sit." The voice was warm and serene. The old priest waved to the empty space before him.

Gail's fear washed away. Peace and tranquility radiated from the ancient before her. With more calm than she felt in many days, she squatted and made herself comfortable. Herros did likewise with a grunt.

"This here's the girl I was telling you about," began the captain. "Do you—"

"I see," replied Eros with a tight nod. A full penetrating gaze fell on Gail. "Do not be afraid, child. You are a maiden? Unbroached?"

"What?" The neutral tone he asked this in caught Gail completely by surprise. Under other circumstances, she would have blushed red by a question such as this, and didn't know what answer he expected. She decided the truth was the best response. She replied while studying her hands, "Yes."

"Good. If we take you it will make your training easier."

Herros put in, "Yes, sir, and she tells a story about arriving from a place in the future, and her mind is—unusual."

Gail glanced at the captain. What did he know of her mind?

The priest drew back slightly, shooting a questioning glance at Herros before returning his gaze to Gail "Hmm… Do not be afraid, girl. Gaze into my eyes."

After the last time it happened with Herros, Gail never experienced the crawling sensation again on her brain, and she'd forgotten all about the odd touch across her skull. Now Gail fell into those eyes with the identical creeping feeling across her scalp she'd felt before, but magnified a hundred fold. Vertigo, like falling into a black hole with no end swept over her, and she thought she would scream until it stopped; she was back on the floor, sitting.

"Interesting." Eros lips twitched up in secret delight as if he'd unearthed a diamond in a slab of clay. He swung to Captain Herros and raised his voice. "How much did you say you are asking for her?"

The captain cleared his throat and glanced at Gail. "I'd mentioned to your man ten gold round, sir; but I'm as concerned what will happen to her as the price."

"So?" replied the priest, amused. "This is admirable of you, Captain, but if I pay ten gold rounds, I can do with her as I please." He tugged at the sleeves of his robe with a look of contemplation and replied seriously, "To ease your mind, however, I will tell you. I think this one can transcend into the ranks of priestesshood in time. We will see, I make no promises, but not for ten rounds."

A smile spread over Herros's face. "A priestess!" He issued a low whistle and winked at Gail. "This is your lucky day."

"About the gold, Captain—"

"Ahh—" Herros studied the other's face with a shrewd look. "Well, if you think you'll turn her into a priestess, I could settle for—eight?"

"Seven."

Herros frowned as if he'd bitten into something rotten. He swung to Gail, shrugged with a smirk and said, "Seven it is," he sighed.

Eros flowed upward and strode to a table. Picking up a quill, he scrawled a receipt on a piece of parchment and handed the letter to Captain Herros. "Here, take this to the priest in the atrium. You will receive your money."

Herros accepted the note, hesitated and asked, "Ah, about that permit I was askin' about. Do you think…?"

"Hmm..." The priest's eyes shifted from Herros to Gail and back again. "I think a license can be arranged." He withdrew another skin and wrote something. "Take this to the city magistrate. You will be issued your permit." The priest paused as if thinking. "Next time you dock at this port, if you find any more like this one, bring her by," he said. "You bring interesting cargo."

Gail listened to his conversation with building humiliation. *What am I—a piece of fruit to bargain over?* Listlessly she listened to the men discussing business, picking up most of the conversation. She perked up some when the priest mentioned the captain returning. *Maybe I can sneak aboard and stowaway without anyone knowing.* When Herros mentioned the word "priestess" Gail perked up more. Were they going to make her a nun? She supposed prancing around in black robes and praying all day wouldn't be too bad. Then she remembered she was still a slave, being sold and deserted again. Her face hardened into bitterness.

Herros took both parchments and stuck out his hand to Gail. "Well, I guess this is it..." He saw her expression and dropped his arm to his side. "Sorry." He left without looking back.

As the captain disappeared and the door swished shut, her world crumbled again, Gail swung to the priest. "Sir?"

Eros's calm expression turned harsh. "You may call me Master."

Chapter Four

G ail sat on the floor in the lotus position. She was learning telepathy. The crawling sensation she felt all these months were people scanning her mind, trying to communicate or read her thoughts. To her this was better than the college education she would never receive, and Master Eros was teaching her the way. As soon as Captain Herros left, the priest commanded, "Look into my eyes."

"Y-yes, Master." Gail wasn't sure what he was up to, but she was too frightened to argue. Taking a deep breath, she gazed at him.

Vertigo hit her again, this time with a bombardment of words, and noise. It felt like he was laying her soul bare and scribbling a book on her brain. When he released her mind from his grip, she discovered herself slumped on the floor.

"I have imparted the *Shaddard,* the Muian language into your brain," the priest informed her in his serene voice as Gail pushed herself upright into a sitting position.

She stared at him without comprehending. Master Eros explained, "I transferred concepts to your mind." Gail nodded tentatively, understanding the sounds, but not what he meant by his words. "For now you are dismissed," he continued, folding his arms with a nod to the door. "You will be shown a room and we will proceed with your training tomorrow."

Her education progressed. First mind reading, which all educated Muians could do, to more exotic fields. After the first day, Master Ho, a short, jovial priest with a perpetual grin and short black hair, took over her education. To her relief, she found most of the people in the temple to be as kind and considerate as he was.

The bane of her existence, however, was the high priestess.

After her interview with Master Eros, Gail followed another priest to a comfortable room, a pure white robe of a novice thrust into her hands, new sandals tossed at her feet, and was instructed to wash herself.

Gail regarded the cloth in her hands stolidly for a long second, trying to fathom the rapid turn of events. *It's all going to work out. I'll become a priestess, have a place to live. Even if this isn't my time, or land. I'll make a home in this place.*

Gail gazed around the small compartment and picked up a bar of perfumed soap from a small table with a sponge, washbasin, and pitcher of water. The room was five times larger than the cabin aboard the *Midnight Star*, almost as big as her bedroom back home, furnished with a carved, wooden dresser and small writing table. *Better than the ship,* she admitted to herself with approval.

Gail stripped and worked soap and water into the sponge. She held the sweet-smelling suds to her nose and inhaled the flowery fragrance. *This is going to be better than a nun, anyway. Priestess. It's a start, and someday....*

She finished giving herself a sponge bath and sat on the bed when she heard a noise behind her.

"Humph."

Gail swung around and discovered an older woman with iron-blue hair and a long nose glaring at her from the doorway, arms crossed, lips drawn down with disapproval on her face. "Well, hurry up girl! Don't stand there gawking!" Her bony foot tapped on the floor with impatience.

The imperial voice and sheer arrogance of the woman grated on Gail the wrong way. She narrowed her eyes as her temper flared. "Who are *you?*"

The woman's brows rose. "*I* am the Priestess Helena—High Priestess Helena to you, girl—and remember it. I am in charge of you. Now, come along, I will show you your new duties."

New duties? She just got here. *These people don't allow a girl much time, did they?* The woman's expression told Gail the high priestess wasn't a person to tangle with in an argument on her first day. Gail bit back a flippant remark and stood, throwing the robe over her body, and hopped behind Helena trying to put her new sandals on as Helena stalked down the hall.

The high priestess approached two swinging doors, shoved both open, and let the entrance slam behind her without checking to see if Gail trailed. Gail managed to squeak through the portal before it slapped into her face. She found herself in a refectory. Women and men hustled about, most clothed in the robes of novices as she was, cooking food and sweeping floors.

Helena surveyed the busy scene with a light smirk. "From now on, you will study with the priests during the morning, work here and serve food in the afternoons and evenings," ordered Helena over her shoulder. She snapped her fingers at a fat toad of a woman dressed in priestess robes who sat sweating on a stool.

"This one is yours for the afternoons, Colops. Put her to work." The high priestess acknowledged Gail with scowl of distaste. "She has an attitude."

The matron looked Gail over with the same expression as Helena, acting as if another charge was the last thing she needed, and shouted to a novice who set tables. "Palma, over here, now. Take this one and show her what to do, and do not be slow about it."

A skinny girl with dirty blond hair hurried over. "Yes, Ma'am." She grasped Gail's hand and tugged her away from the two priestesses as if the women excreted vitriol. "Come on," she said in a low voice, keeping her head bowed. "I'll show you what to do."

With Gail in tow, the girl scurried back to the table

40

she'd left, and picked up plates, napkins and silverware. Gail glanced around, spotted more dishware stacked on a smaller table, and snatched up an armful. She rushed behind Palma setting places.

"My name's Gail," she whispered to the other girl, watching the arrangement of knives and forks and placing her tableware in the exact same manner.

"Palma," the girl muttered out of the side of her mouth, not looking around. "Don't worry, you'll get the hang of this place. It's not so bad."

The smell of cooking food awoke Gail's hunger. Breakfast was far in the past and the aroma of frying meat wafting from the fires made her mouth water. "When do we eat?"

"More work and less talk, you lazy novices." Colops glared at the two girls from the stool she perched on with diligence.

Gail and Palma dropped their heads lower and hurried up setting the tables, after a minute Palma peeked around to see if anyone watched. Colops was busy reading a scroll. She whispered back, "In the kitchen, after everyone else has finished."

Gail spent the rest of the day, and well into the night, helping cook, serving the other priests and priestesses, and cleaning up afterward. She copied Palma's attitude and ignored the comments, yells, and occasional threats of mayhem Colops leveled at the girls. After all her elders ate and left, she wolfed down a quick meal with the rest of the novices, and hurried back to her room, exhausted.

In the mornings Gail flourished. Master Ho didn't yell or threaten, and although her work in the kitchen was easier, she pushed herself to the limits to absorb whatever her teacher set before her. Each session with the priest was a continual delight and wonder.

"Master Ho, what if I can't learn this?" Gail wailed

one day. The previous night Helena gave her dark hints of what her fate was if she couldn't grasp the abilities of her new trade.

"Let us not dwell on might-be's," the priest said with confidence, "but what will be. Your mind has special qualities to it, wherever you traveled from, your ancestors must have achieved things we dream of today."

"Master Ho? Where did I come from?" Gail waved to the air. "I think I'm in the far future, but how?"

The priest sat back on his haunches, sighed, and said, "I cannot be sure, but if what you say is true, it appears to me like you traveled through a time rift."

"Time rift?"

"A rip in the fabric of time." He made a tearing motion with his hands. "Sometimes during deep emotional stress, a storm, or battle, they appear. No one knows why. Like lightening, you never know where they will strike, and fissures in time or space disappear as quick. I think you fell into one and passed through."

The storm we were driving in. Gail nodded. It was possible, but if this was Earth's far past, and she dropped through a time hole, how come no one did telepathy in her time? That was something people wrote about in science fiction books. "But we can't read each other's minds in future. No one knows how."

"Knowledge gets lost," replied Ho. "Perhaps in our future the human race forgot how." He clapped his hands together. "But you, my girl, have the ability, and it is my job to extract it from your mind."

The idea confused Gail. Losing something like telepathy was the same as losing a hand. Maybe it would happen to one person, but a whole race?

"How could we forget something as important as telepathy? It's the same as seeing, or speaking." People couldn't lose the memory of how to do mind reading. There had to be some different explanation.

Master Ho's sharp eyes focused on her and he sighed, scratching his chin while he thought of an explanation Gail would understand. "Of course we can. Even in this time, some of the things you will learn are guarded secrets. Everyone has the ability to do these things, but not everyone is taught." He thought for a moment. "Think of soap."

Soap? What had soap to do with the brain? You cleaned with soap. Although, Gail thought, smiling to herself, someone like High Priestess Helena probably scoured herself with a rock to see how much pain it would cause. "You wash with it, scrub stuff. I don't—"

"And if all the soap makers disappeared?" Ho replied, studying her face to see if she followed his reasoning, "Where would you find soap? Do you know how to make it yourself?"

"Soap? Of course not."

Master Ho nodded slowly. "You see? This is the fate of the human race, sometimes. Everyone *can* make soap, but if a few stop doing the manufacturing and no one is taught how, the art of soap making is lost, humanity goes dirty, until the knowledge is regained again."

Gail thought about what the priest said. He was right, she supposed; soap, glass, metal, even making fire, depended on a few people who knew what they were doing. Without specialists, much of what humans achieved would be lost, but this would mean an awful big disaster sometime in humanity's past. "But—"

Master Ho saw the dawning comprehension of Gail's face. "Enough." He clapped his hands together. "I think you are keeping me talking about the mysteries to get out of doing your lessons. First, you must learn to walk, girl, and we are here to make sure you will."

"Maybe." Gail didn't see how it was possible.

It took her two weeks of hard work and tears, but by the end of the second, she caught thoughts and sent them as if she'd been doing it all her life.

"Enough!" Master Ho announced. "I am finished with you." For this last test, he brought Gail to the open air market of the city where groups of shoppers, vendors, and deliverymen all mingled together, haggling, or hawking their wares. From a distance of three hundred yards, Gail blocked out the noise and other distractions to pick out the priest's thoughts. He walked back to her and laid his hands on her shoulders. "You have learned in fourteen days what others take a lifetime to absorb. I turn you over to Master Eros now to discover your other talents."

"As easy as that?"

Ho issued a sigh and patted her shoulder. "You will add nuances, pick up little tricks as you go along, but yes, once you have someone to show you the way, it is as easy as this." An impish expression passed over his face. "Wait here, I will be right back."

He strolled over to a stall selling clothing and purchased a long purple scarf. He carried it back to Gail and handed the fabric over. "Here, a present, and do not let the High Priestess Helena see it, but this will look good on you one day when you wear the robes of a priestess."

Gail held the scarf in her hands, feeling the softness as she ran it through her hand, and gave a happy smile to the priest. "Gee, thanks. I don't…"

"Enough," Ho said, holding one hand. "I have kept you too long and it is time for you to work in the kitchen. I am staying here, but you must leave. We will talk again."

Gail left and rushed to the dining hall of the temple, beaming. Colops, in charge of the refectory that day, scowled at her for her lateness, but Gail didn't care. She'd passed the first hurtle toward priestess-hood, and now she was privileged to work with Master Eros himself. She stuffed the scarf Master Ho gave her inside her robe, grabbed a handful of silverware, and began laying spoons and knives out on the tables.

Her new friend, Palma, more advanced than she, picked up a stack of napkins and hurried over to Gail, placing each next to the knives and spoons.

"You look happy today," the girl murmured, glancing at Gail out of the corner of her eye. "Good news?"

"The best," bubbled Gail in a whisper, first checking to see if Colops watched. "I get to work with Master Eros tomorrow." Soon she would no longer be the serving girl, the drudge.

"Good luck." Palma smirked, folding a napkin. "I've been studying with him for five months, and it's been the hardest time of my life." She sighed and brushed her hair out of her face. "Sometimes I wish I'd never been sold here."

"Golly, is it that hard?"

"Okay, you two." Colops yelled at the girls from her chair. "Less socializing, and more work." With a grunt, she stood up, glancing over her cleaning supplies, and waddled over to the pair, carrying a mop. "Here—" She thrust it into Gail's hands "—start cleaning." She wagged a gnarled finger at Gail's nose. "I want this floor to shine before people start arriving."

As she swung away to her stool, Colops spied the scarf Master Ho presented Gail sticking out from her robes. With one swift motion, she jerked the cloth out and examined the fabric with interest. "Well, what do we have here?" she sneered at Gail, holding the present up for the whole dining room to see.

"It was a gift." Gail tried to snatch the scarf back, but the older woman held it out of her reach.

"A gift is it?" A frown creased Colops features. "And who gave you this gift?"

Before Gail could think, she blurted out, "It was from Master Ho, for passing my test. He said I could start studying with Master Eros tomorrow."

Colops nodded, her eyes narrowed with cruel intent,

and leered at Gail. "Gifts from the priests, no wonder you succeeded in your first test so fast."

The dining hall grew quiet. Gail blushed as what the priestess implied sank in. and stammered, "I—I never…"

The matron threw the scarf back into Gail's chest. "Here, take your prize. I guess you worked hard to earn this thing, but I shall inform the high priestess of what you received." She chuckled lightly, glancing at the other patrons of the dining hall. "Do not think you will earn your priestesshood from Master Eros in the same manner. That trick has been tried on him before, and by prettier ones than you."

Colops spun with a chuckle and shuffled back to her chair, shouting to the novices, "All of you return to work."

Blushing scarlet at her humiliation, Gail picked up the mop and started cleaning the floor. Palma snatched a broom and swept before her. "I know you didn't do anything wrong," she whispered. Her eyes lifted toward Colops. "She's jealous, the mean old witch, because no one would want that bag of suet if you paid them, that's all."

"Thanks," Gail murmured back.

Palma shot her a smile. "She's right, though. Master Eros is one tough old bird. There's only one present he may give you."

Gail managed a small smile back. "What's that?"

"A cloth to wipe your tears away after your lessons," Palma replied with a smirk. "Maybe."

As Gail returned to her room that night, fear, anticipation of the morrow, mingled with the mortification of Colops remarks. *Is this how it's done around here? Have the other novices? Do the priests expect me to?* Even as far back as high school, she'd heard rumors of girls who were overly friendly with the teachers. Gail always thought the snide whispers in the bathroom were complaints of students too lazy to study. Why, someone even tried spreading rumors about her.

Gail slipped into her bed and stared at the ceiling in the dark. *I will do this. I know I can without any tricks. Try. All I have to do is try.*

***

The next morning Gail learned how hard lessons with Master Eros were.

She was lead to a darken room, the sole illumination, a brazier with glowing embers, which rested on the middle of the floor. The ruddy light cast flickering shadows in the corners. Her teacher waited for her in the deep purple robes of Moack.

"Sit, Gael." Eros rested in lotus. Gail copied him and waited nervously with her hands folded in her lap.

"We are going to study the art of Prophecy, seeing—searching the futures for possible outcomes," he said, leveling a stern look. "This is never easy and often what we see is not always what is—but this is what we do here." He leaned toward her. "First you must seek someone's future, and then you must discern the possible from the improbable, and of the possible, learn to see which is the most probable."

Gail's eyes went wide. "Master Eros, I'll never be able to do that."

"You will, girl." His eyes narrowed dangerously and he snapped, "If you wish to be a Priestess of Moack, you will, even if I have to beat the knowledge into you with a stick."

She gulped. "Yes, Master."

"Now," he continued calmly as if nothing happened, "first things first. Let your mind go blank. When you have, reach for mine as if you were going to read it—but do not. Hold it and feel the thoughts running in and out."

This was harder then it sounded. Gail tried and discovered the effort impossible, like trying to pick up a bar of slippery soap with rubber gloves on. By the time her first morning lesson concluded, sweat covered her body, her head pounded as if she had a headache, and was no closer to her goal than when she started. That night, she found herself trying to pick up bubbles without popping each while she did dishes in the dining hall.

Weeks passed into months. Helena and Colops continued to dog her every movement, yelling at her and issuing commands when she wasn't in class. Master Eros pushed harder, before she completely grasped one lesson he would start on the next. At night, Gail would fall asleep mumbling to herself, "What do they want from me?" *They don't give me a chance.* "It's not fair."

By the time Gail realized she was able to cradle a mind, separate out the possible futures, and decide which were the most important, she progressed far beyond that.

As she discovered she could use her mind to probe eternity, a new and exciting world opened to her. Up until this time, her personal life revolved around school, her friends, and then capture. Now the might-bes of any event she cared to focus on were revealed before her eyes to scan as she wished. Long after lessons were over, Gail would sit in the darkened room, concentrating, until an aggravated Helena called her away to her refractory duties.

Halfway through her training, Eros added healing. This was the exact opposite of seeing. She learned to narrow her vision, plunge into the wild world of cells. She saw germs, bacteria, and infection—blood pumping through arteries and veins. With her mind's fingers, she could destroy the wrongness with her thoughts, regrow new tissue, and bone given time.

Master Eros provided few indications of how she progressed, other than an occasional "Better," or, "You are coming along." His most common expression was, "Go back and try again. This time I want it right."

"You're doing great," Palma assured her one night as they swept and mopped the dining room floor. "I've talked to the other girls. They told me it takes about a year to become a priestess. At the rate you're going, you'll be there in six months. We'll receive our purple robes together."

Gail brushed hair out of her face and wrung out her mop, glancing around to make sure Colops wasn't in earshot. The matron was busy reading a scroll and chuckling to herself. Gail whispered out of the side of her mouth, "What then? Do you know—no one ever told me what a priestess does. Do we help perform ceremonies, or what?"

Palma glanced at her in surprise. "Why, the same thing we're learning now." She swept up sand and crumbs, dumping them into a bucket. She surveyed the floor with grim satisfaction. "This is how we serve Moack, that's the way the temple supports itself. I thought you knew."

Gail hoped her training would finish soon. She was arriving at the point where she felt she must explode. Every day Colops grew more demanding, less easy to please, but, she thought with a shudder, then she would fall under total supervision of High Priestess, Helena. Dealing with the old witch day in and day out was no prize, not with her haughty looks and caustic remarks. Gail had taken to giving the priestess wide berth, running the opposite way when she saw the other approaching, and once, even resorted to hiding in a closet to avoid falling into the sight of Helena. Gail hoped the older woman forgot their initial meeting, and her attitude was a reflection of how she handled all the novices. When circumstances forced her into contact with the high priestess, Gail remained indifferent to her remarks, kept her mouth shut, and tried to do her best. She kept the thought in her head. *Soon it would be over.* She would become a priestess with all the respect and honor due the rank.

Gail wondered how her best friend, Palma, always stayed so happy and willing to help. She acted as if the temple was the best place in the world. After a half-hour tirade by the high priestess on the proper way to scrub the kitchen stoves, Gail heard Palma humming, her lower half hung out of an oven, while the upper dug crusty drippings from the bottom.

Gail snatched a bronze scraper and pushed in next to Palma, grimacing as her hands and arms became coated with black sludge. The girl wiggled over until the two brushed shoulders.

"Palma? How did you get here? Did someone capture you and made you a slave, too? Was it bad before you were sold to the temple?"

Gail heard the faint echo of a laugh before the girl answered. "No. Well, I guess my life wasn't the best," she said, startled by Gail's question. She backed out of the oven, straightened with a low groan, and swept her filthy hair out of her face, leaving more dark smudges along her face. "I sold myself."

Gail slid out next to her, refusing to look at herself. *"What?* I must have misunderstood you."

"My father was a hunter and collector of plants in the outback," Palma explained, throwing a hasty glance at Colops who glowered back. The priestess jabbed her finger at the stove. Palma dove back into the oven while Gail hastily grabbed a rag and mopped the greasy muck in front of the door with her face averted. "One day he didn't return," Palma murmured from inside the oven. "My mother needed money, I've got two younger sisters, so…" Palma poked her head out quickly with a smirk and gestured to the refectory.

Colops waddled past. "The dining hall is closing for the night," she said. "I want this stove shining in the morning when I return." She leveled a stare at the two girls. "Good night. Remember what I said."

"Yes, Priestess Colops," the two girls answered and hurried scrapping the oven until the doors swung shut behind the old matron.

Gail gave a hurried glance to the room. The place was empty except for her and Palma. "Couldn't you find a job in the market, or something?" Gail protested. She blinked in disbelief. "I mean, you're not a stupid person. You should have…"

"I should have what?" A small smile touched Palma's lips. "I grew up in the outback. I don't have any skills tradespeople need, no man wanted me for a wife, not ones I would marry, anyhow. My mother and I decided this was for best."

"But how could you agree to do *that*?" Gail had a queasy vision of an evil mother, a Helena, abusing her children.

"Oh, it wasn't her idea," Palma hurried to explain, "It was mine." She swept the little piles of sludge she made into one large pile. "I wanted to work here. I started as a servant, and Master Eros saw my potential. Soon I'll be a priestess and send money back to my family." She nodded tightly to Gail. "I've got a job. I'm out on my own. Sometimes life isn't what you dreamed it would be, but you have to learn how to deal with it, right?" The girl glanced dourly at the burnt bits of food, scooped up a dustpan, and swept the scrapings in. "I survive."

Palma dumped her pile into a bucket and stood with a grimace, wiped off her hands on her robe, and bend down again to pick the pail up. Gail sprang over and snatched the container from her friend. "No, I'll take this," and carried the pail outside to empty it. Gail wondered if life was as simple as Palma made it out to be.

Chapter Five

T he day arrived when Master Eros allowed her a grudging nod. He strolled to a closet in his office and withdrew the purple robe of a priestess.

"We have traveled as far as we will go for now," he said, one of his rare smiles flickering across this lips. "It is time you earned your keep. You are a student of Priestess Helena for the time being." His face cracked into a genuine grin, the first Gail ever saw from the old priest. He handed over the garment to her. Gail clutched it tight to her and smirked back in happiness. "Work your trade well and you will be rewarded."

"Thank you Master Eros," she replied, weighing the fabric in her hands, drawing it through her hands, and gazing at the deep rich color. "I'll try to do my best."

The next morning Gail was belting on her new robe, draping the scarf Master Ho gave her around her neck, when she found Helena watching with distaste from the doorway of her room.

"So girl, you are my problem now." The priestess's cold brown eyes sized Gail up and down critically. "Well, hurry up and dressed yourself," she snapped. "I don't have all day—we will see what you have learned. It takes more than a purple robe and a scarf to make a priestess of Moack." She spun on her heels and stalked down the hallway, Gail hurrying after her, trying to tie her robe around her waist and listen at the same time.

"First we must purify ourselves," the priestess said over her shoulder. "You are clean, have washed your body?"

"Yes, High Priestess," Gail squeaked, trying to keep up and remain calm.

Helena's hair bobbed up and down in front of Gail.

"Good. No one wants to talk to a priestess who smells." She stopped at a door and swung it open. They entered a smoke-filled room—three other priestesses sat chatting on benches. When they saw Helena and Gail, they stopped talking and hurriedly left.

The high priestess ignored their hasty departure and said, "Sit, relax, and let you mind grow blank." She rested herself on a bench. The heavy scent of incense covered the room from braziers set on pedestals. Gail sat herself and let the smoke curl over her, permeating her clothes with its sweet odor.

"Are you calm? Free of loose thoughts?"

"Yes, High Priestess." *The smoke must have some drug mixed in with it.* Gail's muscles loosened, her cares drift away from her body, but she retained sharp clarity of mind.

"Follow me." Helena rose and entered another corridor. This one with heavy velvet drapes covering the entrance. She sauntered to one and pushed the curtains aside, ushering Gail ahead of her as if herding a cow.

Gail glanced curiously around the room as she entered. Since she started in the temple, she'd never seen one like this before. The cubicle was small and cramped, with beaded curtains covering the other entrance, the furniture a deep-bottomed brass plate sitting in the middle of the padded floor. Helena made herself comfortable in tailor position on one side of the bowl and impatiently tapped the floor for Gail to sit next to her.

"Do as I do," announced the older woman. "It won't be long."

They didn't have to wait.

A young man dressed as an apprentice merchant pushed the beads aside, saw the two women, and entered. He peered first at Gail, hesitated, and then his eyes settled on the high priestess with relief.

"Uh—Seeress?"

"Sit," commanded Helena, waving to the empty space before her on the opposite side of the bowl. "You have tithed freely to Moack?"

"Y-yes. I have a problem—ah, a request," began the young man.

"So?" Helena gave him a level stare. Gail tried to copy her manner. "What is this request?"

"I—I need to know how to receive a promotion from my master to obtain a better position. Right now, all he has me do is—"

"ENOUGH!" Helena swung to Gail. "Let us see how good you are, girl. Search his future and solve his problem."

The apprentice said in apprehension, "Seeress, I did not want…"

"SILENCE."

Helena said to Gail, "Proceed."

Gail startled at the abruptness of Helena's actions. She glanced at the young man, gave him a reassuring smile to relieve his apprehension, and blanked her mind. Concentrating, she saw two possible paths for him once he left the temple. In one, he was happy, patted on the back; but his face was drawn from hard work, his shoulders slumped, and he was missing three fingers from his left hand.

In the other future, the boy was older, a man, with a smooth round face. He wasn't happy, but he wasn't unhappy either. He whistled to himself while carrying a bale of cotton.

Gail opened her eyes and studied the anxious boy.

"If you wish to succeed in your occupation," she began, "you must work relentlessly, and do as your master bids. It will be hard, you will suffer much pain, but in the end, you will receive your reward. If you do not, you will not be unhappy, but you will never advance in your career."

Gail glanced at Helena who nodded imperceptibly.

"Th-thank you." The boy withdrew a leather purse. "Who...?"

Helena pushed forward the brass bowl sitting in front of her. The young man dropped a few silver coins into the bottom and hurried away.

"Not bad," commented Helena, glancing in the bowl, "considering." She glared down her nose at Gail. "But you should have got more."

"More?" Gail said, perplexed. "More..."

"More silver, girl," snapped the high priestess, pointing to the coins. She picked up the brass plate and rattled the coins in Gail's face. "I will show you how at the next patron."

An old man entered. His hair was gray and he walked with a limp.

"Sit."

The man grimaced, but managed to ease himself to the floor. "I wish to hear the future," he stated with a grunt, looking at Helena and ignoring Gail.

"You have given to Moack?" She asked in her commanding voice.

"Yes, yes," the man brushed her question aside.

"Tell me your request."

"I have two sons, twins," the man said heavily, "and I wish to retire, but I do not know if I should divide my business between the two, or appoint one over the other. They are both good lads, but I fear if I allow each half of what I own, it will not be enough for either to live on. What does the future hold?"

An otherworld expression passed over Helena's face. At first, she said nothing, but presently she began rocking back and forth and moaned in a low voice, *"I see pain and anger, hatred and suffering! Blood is upon his hands as he raises a knife! I see—ahhh!"* She wailed and slumped.

"What? What is it? What do you see?" The old man

rammed his hand into his pouch, withdrew a handful of silver, and scattered the coins in the bowl. "TELL ME."

The high priestess roused, placed a hand to her head as if she'd awoken from a bad dream, and muttered, "I see one killing the other in a jealous rage if he is placed under his brother," Helena continued in a dry rasp, "but in another future I see both laboring together as partners. Divide your property equally and caution your sons to work with each other as friends. They will prosper." She opened her eyes. "That is what the future holds."

The old man's face had turned white, so did Gail's.

"Thank you, Priestess." The old man pursed his lips, nodded thoughtfully, and bowed his head to Helena. "I know what to do now." He reached into his pouch, pulled out more silver and a few gold rounds, and tossed the coins in the bowl. He pushed himself to his feet with renewed vigor, tipped his head to both the high priestess and Gail, and left.

"And this is how it's done, girl." chuckled Helena, emptying the contents of the plate into her palm. She dug around in her hand, extracted a small worn silver piece, and dropped the coin back into the pan. The rest she stuffed into her pouch. "Some for the Priests of Moack, some for the High Priestess," she nudged the bowl with her foot toward Gail, "and something for you."

Helena rose to her feet with a yawn. "Practice girl, Practice. There is more to the art of seeing than predicting the future." With a swirl of robes, and a chuckle at Gail's startled face, she disappeared.

It didn't take Gail long to learn the economics of the temple, or while they might serve Lord Moack, they also worked to line their own pockets for spending money. Tithes paid by the faithful went for the maintenance of the building and the support of the staff. Donations for predictions, healing, and other services, went to the priests, and priestess, as gifts for the good luck their seeing brought.

Gail and the other junior members of the temple, received stipends for their work, and paid over most of their takings to the senior members. She learned a good prediction brought a bigger tip (and more money in her purse) than a bad one—a dramatic presentation to a patron even more. Within a month, Gail had people asking for her by name. She'd waitressed at Lake George after school and summers for two years. She knew the routine.

Gail thought the High Priestess Helena would be happy with her performance, and the money Gail handed over, but she was mistaken. After a few weeks, the woman strode to her cubical and stood watching while Gail was with a customer. When she finished the man threw a gold round into her plate and left. Gail beamed at him and turned her smiled on the high priestess.

"So, you think you are so smart?"

"Who, me?" Gail said, taken aback by Helena's remark. She received a good tip from the petitioner and she knew it, and bestowed a prediction she hoped would make him a lot of money. If he did so, he would return, and tell his friends about the excellent prophecies of Gail.

"I don't understand what you mean, High Priestess," Gail stammered.

"It is this, little girl," sneered, Helena. "If you think bringing work into the temple will manage you special privileges, or boost you up the ranks of the Priestesshood faster, you are sadly mistaken."

Why is she starting in on me, Gail wondered to herself. "High Priestess, I'm doing what you said to do," she sputtered, not knowing why Helena was upset. "I thought you were happy with my performance. I'm trying the best I…"

Helena's eyes narrowed and her voice assumed a bitter tone as she glared down at Gail. "Remember, there is only one high priestess here, and it is me. Understand?"

The hint of cold hatred in the older woman's voice made Gail's stomach twist. She stared at her bowl, unable to reply, and afraid anything she said in way of apology would make the high priestess madder. She hadn't done anything wrong. Why was Helena always so mean to her? In a choking voice she finally mumbled, "Yes, High Priestess, I understand."

"Good, see you remember it." Helena pushed the curtains aside and stomped away in a huff.

After she was finished for the day, she sought out Master Ho. She hadn't seen him more than a few times in the hallway since she'd become a priestess, but he'd always been good to her and given advice when she asked for his help when question arose about this strange new world she lived in.

She located him in the foyer outside the dining hall, going to supper, and grabbed the sleeve of his robe before he disappeared behind the doors. "Master Ho, I was wondering if I could ask you a question." She stood anxiously, hoping he was not too busy to talk to her.

The priest swung around in surprise and beamed at her. "Gael, I have not seen much of you lately since you earned your robes. How have you been? Is Helena keeping you busy, I hope?"

"Master Ho," Gail said, "Yes, I've been busy. I was wondering if you could help me, maybe give me some advice."

His smile vanished, replaced with concern. "I will try, what is the matter?" He took her by the shoulders and moved her out of the way of the door back into the hallway.

Gail wondered if the priest would think she was being a crybaby over nothing, but she had no one else to turn to. She plunged in. "It's the High Priestess Helena. I've been working so hard to be a good priestess, and she accused me of trying to steal her job." Gail felt her throat contracting as the memory of Helena's remarks returned. "I don't know where she got the idea, and I certainly don't want anyone mad at me. What should I do?"

The young priest's lips shaped a silent "O" and he issued a grunt of understanding. "The high priestess is a strange case, Gael," he replied with a gentle pat on her arm. "When she was young, everyone praised her for her abilities. Then another novice arrived, became a priestess, and soon surpassed her. Helena was no long first, and in time, the young woman was made High Priestess."

"Oh, that's terrible. Was Helena disappointed?"

Master Ho nodded gravely. "Yes, very. Three years ago, the old high priestess died and Helena finally received her chance for the top position. She may be feeling, ah, insecure about another young priestess coming along."

"But I'm not—I would never..." Gail stammered. She stared at the floor and said in a small voice, "What can I do?"

Some slight difference in the priest's voice caused Gail to cringe. "There is nothing you can do," Ho replied sadly. "Anything you say will make her more insecure. Keep your head lowered and do your work as best you can. Once Helena settles into her job, she will be more assured in her position and perhaps her fears will diminish."

Gail's eyes opened wide and she nodded. She understood how Helena must have felt all those years of disappointment, and in what way the priestess must view her, a know nothing who, let's face it, was starting off in the trade.

"Thank you, Master Ho. I'll try and do as you say." Gail threw her arms around him in a quick hug.

"If you two are quite through with whatever you're doing, the dining room is ready to close." It was Colops, watching them from the doors of the refectory with a nasty smirk spreading across her face. "If you want to eat, you had better hurry up."

"Of course, Colops, we would not want to miss any

of you good cooking," Ho shouted back with a chuckle. He said to Gail, "I hope I have helped you."

Gail tried to do as Ho told her, but more than the high priestess's attitude nipped at her mind, problems bothering her she was sure the priest couldn't solve with a friendly word of advice.

She was required to stand with the other priestesses during daily morning ceremonies. After this, the most senior of the seeresses, Helena and her close friends, lounged around, gossiping, while Gail and the other young priestesses hurried off to their cubicles for work. Gail doubted if the high priestess labored more than an hour a day.

"It's no fair!" Gail stormed at Palma one night after their shift was over. She stalked around Palma's room, picking up items from tables and banging them down. "I squatted for twelve hours in lotus, serviced twenty patrons, one break, and this is all I earn?" Gail waved Palma's hairbrush in the air with one hand, and reached into her pouch with the other. She held out four silver rounds for her friend to see. "Helena took the rest. I understand the priests receiving a cut. They conduct services and teach, but Helena and her cronies? They do nothing." Gail jammed the coins back in her purse in disgust.

Palma rescued her brush from Gail's grasp, ran it through her hair, and dropped down on her bed lying on her back with a sigh. "I know it seems unfair, hon, but you have to look at it from their point of view. They've done the same thing we're doing for years. Helena and the rest of the senior priestesses feel part of our tips are their right, they've earned it." She shrugged and rolled over onto her stomach. "Maybe they had a greedy high priestess when they were younger, I don't know, or this is how it's done. Who can tell?" The girl put her brush away. "Tomorrow we have the day off. Why don't you go shopping with me? I want to buy some new clothes."

Gail flopped down next to her, and rolled on her side, supporting her head with her hand. "I suppose so," she sighed. "I need a new pair of sandals." She frowned at the worn pair she wore. "Besides, it will be good to get out of this place for a few hours and see what's new in town."

After she vented her anger to Palma, Gail strolled back to her room to prepare for bed. Being a servant of Moack was not what she thought it would be. She never dreamed there would be so much infighting. Yeah, she received food, shelter, and a job, sure, but after what she'd been through, she deserved something better. *My life should be different. I wasn't meant to spend the rest of my existence sitting in a small cubicle, wasting away until I'm old and bitter like Helena. I need happiness, too. I'm so miserable. I wish...this world is rotten. I want to go home.*

It was wrong. Being a priestess of Moack was not what she thought—everything was a lie.

Gail's performance, and her tips, dropped. Why should she work her tail off and not receive any of the benefits? Helena hated her no matter what she did. Why bother?

While not rebellious, she did her job by rote. Criticism by Helena and the older priestesses she disregarded with a quick nod of agreement. It didn't matter, what could they do to her, other than consign her into the hell she already lived now. Every night before she fell sleep her mantra was, *I hate this place, I hate this place.*

***

It was the beginning of the feast of Moack. The temple shut its doors and a celebration ranged throughout the streets and concentrated in the city square. Gail and Palma dressed in their best robes, but took no part in the festivities. The senior priests expected the junior priestesses and priests to mingle with the crowd and sing the praises of their God to all who would listen.

This was the first festival Gail attended, and she

was eager to see all the events the occasion reputed to have. Rumors circulated for weeks within the temple about the new amusements the city fathers brought in for the entertainment of the mob. Farmers and trappers from the outback traveled to the city, conveying their wares in hopes of selling enough to the throngs of people who were out on a holiday to provide needed necessaries they were unable to make for themselves. For one week during the year, they might earn enough hard cash to last them for months.

Gail and Palma greeted patrons they knew, or fawned on the rich who they wished to know better, and wanted to draw into the temple as patrons. At noon, a hush fell over the square. The two girls pushed their way into the crowd surrounding a stone platform to see what all the excitement was.

"Oh, Gail, is that Vernes?" Palma pointed a finger to a young girl clothed in a white robe standing on the platform surrounded by priests. She was a novice who attended the temple longer than Palma, and repeatedly failed her testing, although she never appeared distraught about her lack of capacity to learn. Gail rose on her toes and waved. "I wonder what she's going to do up there?"

"Whatever it is, let's hope it's not too complicated," Gail quipped back with a smirk. "You know Vernes. She's liable to predict the coming of Moack in twenty minutes, and when he doesn't show, laugh about it."

Palma frowned, but then her lips twitched upward. "Gael, that's not nice to say. It would probably be thirty minutes, and afterward she'd look confused." The girl put her hand up. "Wait, the priests are giving her something."

The young novice accepted a goblet of wine handed to her by Eros. She held the cup skyward for the people to see and drank the contents down in large gulps, spilling fluid over her chin and her white robe.

The crowd roared approval.

The priests marched around her, waving a silver

censer filled with burning incense and banging on drums. Vernes began a slow sway to the beat, her eyes closing, the goblet dropping from her hands. The drumming grew louder, the sound quickened. Gail thought the novice would do a dance until she slumped and four of the priests lifted her up by her arms and legs.

This is becoming weirder by the minute. "Oh, Let's move closer." Gail seized Palma's wrist and struggled her way to the front of the crowd, stepping on feet in the process. A few spectators shot the two nasty glances until they saw the purple robes and commanding looks the two priestesses threw around at anyone who refused to move out of the way. The people parted to allow the girls to pass.

The priests laid the girl onto a stone table in the middle of the platform.

The drums beat faster.

"Palma, what is Master Eros doing?"

The high priest stood behind the prostrated girl holding a bronze knife. He drove it into her stomach and ripped upward as the crowd gasped. Plunging his hand into her chest, he ripped out her still beating heart.

Eros intoned, "Lord Moack, accept this gift for the coming year. Let the smell of this smoke perfume your nose." He dropped the heart into a burning bowl of coals.

The crowd cheered.

Vomit rose in Gail's throat. She bent low and shoved herself out of the throng with Palma's arm around her.

"I thought you knew," Palma whispered as Gail's stomach released. "Didn't anyone tell you what would happen?"

"You knew about this?"

"It usually doesn't happen this early in the festival," admitted Palma, as she held Gail around the waist and held back her hair, "and I didn't think they'd choose Vernes. She's..." Another shudder ran through Gail's body, "not the type they'd pick."

People leveled the two strange looks. A few spoke in low voices to each other and pointed to Gail and Palma. Palma took this as a signal they should leave before Gail's reaction became common knowledge. She led Gail down the street toward the temple.

"Why?" Gail sniffed back tears as they walked along the road.

"Our Lord Moack demands it—it's—it's part of our religion."

"But why her?"

Palma started to cry, too. "I don't know." She wiped the corners of her eyes. "Oh, stop. Now you have me doing it. They had to choose one of us, but she always seemed so nice—slow, but willing to help. I thought the sacrifice would be one of the new novices. They always were in the past."

The dark entrance of the temple loomed before them. Palma yanked the door open and guided Gail inside and along the hallway to the priestess quarters.

"I talked to her yesterday." Gail shuddered as they entered Palma's room and sat on her bed. "She couldn't have known, did she? She was happy."

"Of course she knew." High Priestess Helena entered the room behind them and lounged in the doorway with a cruel grin. "Silly girls. She understood what happens to novices who fail to become priestesses," Helena glared at Gail, "or those who displease Moack. We all serve in our own measure. If we cannot do our duty in one manner, the God will find a way for us to perform in another." She spun with a swirl of her robes and yelled over her shoulder, *"Remember this."*

After the sacrifice, Gail forgot all about her long hours and the pilfering of the tips. She stopped complaining, kept a smile on her face at all times, and jumped to do the bidding of the senior priestess whenever they commanded her to do something, no matter how stupid or repugnant the task was. In every way, Gail became a devoted priestess of Moack and tried to be happy with her life.

It was the end of a long day. Gail squatted in her cubicle, hoping for a last client to impress Helena with her diligence. An old woman tottered into the room, dressed in a tattered robe and toting an over-large handbag at her side.

"Sit, Mother." Gail gestured to the floor opposite her. "You have given to Moack?"

"Yes." The woman bobbed her head up and down, fidgeting as she stared at her hands. "All I have."

"What is your request?"

"It is my son," whispered the woman, tears leaking down her wrinkled face as she bent forward. "I am a widow, and he is my sole support. He is a fisherman, he is, and sailed out two days ago, but never returned." Her voice choked. "Is he safe? Will he return?" She gave Gail a pitiful look.

A tingle of pity clutched Gail's chest. She patted the woman's hand and said in a soft voice, "Don't worry—let me look."

Gail concentrated on the possible futures and images appeared.

"Your son has returned," she said, not using any of her dramatic voices. "The boom of his boat hit him on the head and knocked him overboard. A trading ship rescued him and is returning to shore now, but he has lost his memory. Go to the pier and wait until the boat docks. The sailors will give you your son. Nurse him back to health." Gail pushed her bowl forward. "Go now."

The woman broken out in smiles, but when she saw Gail push the plate in her direction, her face shaded red. "I tithed all I have to Moack," she whispered in shame. "I have nothing left to offer."

Gail read the truth in her words. "That's okay,

Mother," she said with pity. "You contributed to the temple, this is all which matters."

"Wait." The woman opened her bag and withdrew a large sleeping kitten, a dirty piece of cloth wrapped around the cat's paw. The small animal yawned, sneezed, and glanced around. "I was planning to heal him, and try to sell the poor baby in the market," explained the woman. "I found him lost in the swamps while searching for my son. He is yours." She placed the kitten in Gail's bowl. "Thank you." She rose and hurried away.

Gail stared at the retreating figure of the old woman in amazement, gawked at the kitten as if still not believing what happened, and then picked up the tiny cat, cuddling it as her look of astonishment transformed into joy. "Oh, you are beautiful," she cooed. The cat possessed a light yellow coat, brown spots circled with black in a chain pattern.

"Mew?" said the kitten and began gnawing on Gail's hand. The feline next tried ripping the bandage off its paw. Gail hugged the little animal close to her. "You're adorable," she whispered. "I'm going to name you Amber."

"WHAT IS THAT?"

It was Helena coming to check up on the novices. The high priestess stepped into the cubical and towered over Gail, her eyes flashing in rage.

"It's a kitten." Gail clutched the animal closer. "The woman who left—she gave it to me—as payment."

"What?" The High Priestess's face shaded to red. "What are you going to do with this animal now?"

"Why—keep it." Some of the other girls owned birds as pets. One even kept a rabbit. "His name is Amber."

Helena's face burnt purple.

Gail pointed to the bandage on his front paw. "He's hurt, I have to heal him. I've never fixed an animal before—it'll be good practice," she finished in a rush.

"All right," Helena gasped at last, "but make sure you clean up after him, and *you* pay for his upkeep."

Helena picked up Gail's bowl and emptied the contents into her pouch. "Let me clue you in, girl—" She tossed the bowl at Gail's feet— "this is an *Oslo* kitten. At full growth he will be as big as you and eat twice as much."

"Yes, High Priestess."

Helena glared down her nose at Gail, sniffed, and left.

Gail returned her attention to the kitten. She unwrapped the cloth on the paw and the cat immediately started licking.

"Come on, you, cut it out," Gail chuckled, pushing Amber's head away from the wound and holding the paw gently between thumb and forefinger. "Let me take a look, too."

The laceration was long and ragged, but she couldn't detect any broken bones. Gail was raised with cats, and knew that left to himself, the animal would keep the gash clean. Her main concern was any infection setting in and traveling through the body. She narrowed her concentration and searched.

She saw bacteria and germs clustered around the opening—the cat's antibodies massed to repel the attack.

The infection around the cut she melted away out of hand. Germs in the bloodstream she destroyed as she could. Gail concentrated on the cat's immune system and sped it up. As she watched, the edge of the wound puckered and closed.

The kitten purred and kneaded its paws in Gail's lap, settling down to take another nap. Gail petted the small creature with tears in her eyes.

Amber was the companion Gail needed. At night, when she returned from work, the cat would dart out from under her cot to tangle her legs and give her a hug. When the time arrived to go for walks, he nipped at her feet, bounded for joy, and dragged her down the streets on his leash, poking his head into every doorway they passed out of curiosity.

Amber proved to be good advertising for Gail. During the day, she kept the Oslo in her small cubicle. At first, petitioners seeking predictions gave him dubious looks, and questioned the presence of the cat. Gail would reply in a mysterious voice, "He is my spirit guardian in the netherworld. He helps and protects me on my journey to discover your future."

This drew smiles from some, nods of awe from others, but Gail noticed the ones who looked the most fearful were the ones who returned often.

On her walks, townspeople who heard of Amber would greet Gail or point and wave. Her client load boomed from morning to night, everyone requesting "The Cat Priestess."

"How do you do it?" Palma asked one night at supper. Two of the older priestesses, who heard Palma's remark, wandered over and sat at the same table.

Gail smiled and shrugged. "It must be Amber," she said. "People like him."

Another reason for Gail's uptick in attitude was her adoption by Palma's family. Once a month, on their day off, Palma met with her mother and younger sisters, who traveled from the interior to visit. Palma would hand over to her mother what money she saved from her tips. Afterward, the four would make a day of sightseeing. On their second trip to the city, Palma invited Gail along. She reluctantly agreed.

"Are you a priestess, too?" Palma's two sisters, twins, goggled at Gail in her purple robe.

"Yes," Gail replied. They strolled in the market gawking at all the items for sale. Gail stopped and bought two purple scarfs like hers, and presented the garments to the girls. "Both Palma and I," she said in a deep voice, "serve the great Lord Moack."

By the end of the day, Gail discovered herself

officially one of the family. Palma's mother called her, "My other daughter," and the twins titled her, "Aunt Gail."

"I've never been an aunt before," Gail remarked with a giggle that night to Palma as they lounged in Gail's room. "I feel old."

Her renewed enthusiasm for her job, and the presence of Amber, caused an upsurge in pets among the girls, also an increase in revenue for the priests and senior priestesses—but not for the junior girls, and not for Gail. She resumed her complaints to the others.

"It's not fair. We do all the work, they take all the money." Gail flashed five rounds of silver, and showed the coins to the young women who crowded into her room to gossip.

"I made over thirty silvers today and four gold— and this is all I get?" Gail rattled the coins in her hands. "Helena grabbed my money and ran away so quick I thought she needed to use a chamber pot."

The girls exploded into laughter and Gail added, "She left me with this and thinks she's doing me a favor."

A newly promoted novice said, "Well, she is rather old —" with a mischievous grin.

"Let her retire," Gail retorted, not at all amused by the comment.

The rest of the women nodded.

One of the priestesses remarked, "You know, you're right. I never thought about it, but we *are* doing all the work around here. I wish someone would complain and say something about the troubles we're having."

The mutterings of the younger priestesses became widespread, led by Gail. One day, High Priest Eros called her into his office.

"Gael, sit." Eros paced back and forth in front of his desk, his hands clenched behind him. "High Priestess Helena informs me there is a problem in the lower ranks of girls, and you are behind it." He fixed her with his eye.

"Well?"

Gail studied her feet, trying to decide what to say, and then blurted out, "It's not just me. *Everyone* thinks the same. But, uh—it's unfair, Master Eros." She took a deep breath. "We work hard, you know we do, and receive nothing back in return. Couldn't you see your way to talk to the high...?"

"No, I cannot," he replied wearily. Eros sat behind his desk and waved to the walls. "All of this was built on the sacrifice of the previous generation for the Lord Moack. When our ancestors first fled here, nothing existed but swamp. Our people constructed this city with bare hands, afterward their children assumed the task. Each generation strove to make our state bigger and better so their parents could rest."

Eros studied her to see if she understood. "Thus it is with the senior priests and priestesses," he continued. "If I were to break this trust now, how could I face my descendants?"

Gail knew a refusal when she heard it—but she tried one last time. "Master, even one or two more..."

"No." Eros stood, his face stern. "We will speak no more about this subject." He waved her to the door. "Remember, you were bought and you can be sold," he warned, his eyes grave. His voice lowered and he added, "There are worse things than being a Priestess of Moack."

The next day Gail discovered fewer clients then usual waiting for her, which was a welcome relief from her usual workload. However, in the following days, she had still less. Gail remarked on this one night to Palma as they knelt on the floor of her room playing with Amber.

"I sat for two hours today and one client showed his face," Gail complained, tossing a ball across the floor for the cat to chase.

"Really?" Palma scooped up the ball before Amber could catch it and rolled the toy back to Gail. "That's odd. I

70

was busy all day." She cooed to the cat, "Maybe your magic is wearing off." She glanced at Gail. "You needed a break anyway. You're always moaning about how hard you work. Enjoy it while you can—this break won't last long."

"I suppose you're right," admitted Gail. "I've got money saved, and I don't need anything. I guess a few slack weeks won't kill me."

Her slow time grew. Gail took longer walks with Amber. On one of her evening strolls before the Feast of Moack, she ran across one of her former clients.

"Well, Priestess Gael—how have you been?" She recognized a merchant who visited her once a month to learn about market conditions. "Are you feeling better?"

"Better?" Gail replied, confused. "I'm feeling fine, Merchant Bock. Whatever caused you think I was sick?"

He peered at her through the gloom of the night and said, puzzled, "Why, the last two times I visited the temple they told me you were not well." He gave a wary glance to Amber. "Do not stay out too late. You'll need your sleep for tomorrow."

So, she thought as continued to walk Amber, mulling over what the merchant said, *this is how it's going to be from now on, huh? No clients, no money, in the end, no job.*

Lost in her thoughts, Gail hardly realized her wanderings took her down by the pier, the few ships tied up showed signs of activity. To her surprise, one was the *Evening Star,* unloading freight under a blaze of lights. She perked up and directed her steps in that direction. When she walked close enough, she heard a familiar voice bawling orders to the sweating seamen. "Let's haul this cargo up, my boys—a tankard of wine to the one who pulls the hardest."

"Captain Herros!" Gail waved. "I never expected to see you again."

The sailor peered through the light of the torches

and broke out in a hearty laugh. "Well, if'n it isn't Gael!" He balanced on a boom lifting cargo from the ship's hold. "I didn't recognize ya in that purple robe. What do you have there?" He pointed to Amber.

"An Oslo, my pet," Gail exclaimed, smiling at the Captain. "Are you in port long? The temple is closed tomorrow for the feast, but the day after, it's open. Come down and ask for me, I'll give you a prediction. I'm a priestess now, you know."

"I see." He nodded his approval. "I always felt bad about selling ya. I'm glad everything worked out all right." He stroked his beard while pursing his lips. "I wish I could stay around, but we sail at the lighting of the last candle. Can't miss the tide—gotta keep a tight schedule, you know."

Amber pulled on his leash, tugging Gail along the pier. "Well, good sailing." Gail wiggled her fingers at Herros and smiled as the cat dragged her farther along taking in strange odors. "Good luck."

When Gail walked back to the temple, an anxious Palma waited in her room, wringing her hands, eyes red from crying.

"Oh, Gael, it's terrible." The girl threw herself on her friend, voice choking as she tried to speak. "How could they?"

"What's the matter?" Gail took Palma by the shoulders and shook her gently. "Calm down and tell me what you're talking about."

"It's you," Palma wailed. "You are the sacrifice for *tomorrow.*"

Coldness shot from Gail's stomach into her chest. "It's a mistake—it has to be," she denied, fearing Palma was telling the truth. "Explain to me what happened."

"I—I was passing Helena's room after dinner," sniffed Palma in a whisper, wiping her eyes. "The door was ajar. Master Eros was in there with her. They were

72

discussing—you." Unable to control herself, she started crying again.

"What did they say?" Gail asked, a sinking sensation in the pit of her stomach.

Palma took a deep breath, getting ahold of her emotions. She said in a low voice, "M—Master Eros was reluctant, kept insisting you were the best of the young priestesses, said how you brought so many more clients into the temple, and might become High Priestess one day."

Gail's eyes flew open in surprise. "He said that about me? Why in the world would they want to...?"

Oblivious to what Gail said, Palma kept talking as if reciting from a book. "Helena kept pointing out how you were a troublemaker and always complaining, upsetting the rest of us with your notions of how they should be treated. She said you'd been talking to some of the younger priests, too, trying to coax them onto your side, and..." she stared at her hands, "saying you weren't acting virginal, shall we say, doing it." She shrugged. "When Master Eros heard that, he agreed to sacrifice you." Palma sniffed back tears. "What are you going to do?"

"Why, the lying old crone," Gail exclaimed. Sure, she talked to the younger priests, all the priestesses did, but she never voiced her opinions to any of the men. As for saying she... Gail's mind raced. Should she go see Master Eros, and tell him Helena was making up stories, trying to get her into trouble? Wouldn't do any good, Gail decided. Helena was the High Priestess—Eros would never believe her, and even if he did, Helena would make her life unbearably miserable. Palma still looked at her, eyes red, wondering what she would do. "I don't know. Run away I guess."

"Go to my mother," Palma exclaimed at once. "She'll hide you. The priests could search for a hundred years and never locate anyone out there in the swamp, if they didn't want to be found."

Gail thought about Palma's offer and dismissed the idea at once. "No. They know we're friends—this'll be one of the first places they'll check. I don't want to place your family in jeopardy, and if they suspect I'm in the outback, you know the priests can force the information out of your mother and sisters." She stared Palma in the eye and held her shoulders tight. "They're going to quiz you too, you know. You have to return to your room and bury your thoughts, this conversation. You can't let the priests know you talked to me, understand?"

Palma threw her arms around Gail's neck. "Oh, I am so sorry. I'm going to miss you."

Gail's throat tightened as she patted Palma on the back. The sense of loss she felt when she left the *Midnight Star* flooding back, threating to overwhelm her senses. "Me too. Now go. Hide this in your mind. Everything will be alright."

"Are you sure?"

"Yea, everything will be fine. Go."

After Palma left, Gail sat on her bed. She hadn't realized it would come to this. Of course, she'd complained, everyone grumbled once and a while, but kill her? Rip her heart out? What would she do now? What *could* she do? Palma's mother's place was out of the question. They would search there for sure. To travel inland by herself and try to make her way over the mountains was suicide. Between the quicksand, bogs, and animals, she would never survive the trip.

She must escape by sea. She owned no boat, didn't know anyone who kept one. Then she remembered Captain Herros.

Would he take her though? She had her tip money, but would it be enough to buy passage on his ship? Gail hurried to her dresser and jerked out a drawer, reaching far into the back and dragging out a bag hidden behind. She poured the coins onto her bed and counted the money she stashed away—two massive gold pieces and a handful of silvers. It had to be enough, she decided. It must be.

Gail emptied her savings into a pouch and gathered what few possessions she owned into a handbag. Amber watched with interest, curled up on her pillow.

She couldn't leave the Oslo, no matter what. "Don't worry, you're going with me." Gail pushed the cat onto the floor with a scratch behind Amber's ears. "Now get off of there, I have things to do."

Gail stuffed her pillow under the sheets, and for good measure, a spare blanket. *Maybe*.

She didn't know what would happen, what was to become of her, and then a sudden thought occurred to her. Calming her mind, Gail peered into her own possible futures.

In one, she saw herself on the sacrificial table, a knife poised over her chest, the surrounding crowd screaming in bloodlust.

In another, not as strong, she saw an old woman, dressed in the robes of the high priestess, walking the corridors of the temple alone.

Hidden in the shadows, lurking in the background obscured by the other images, she discerned a third future. Her and a man, danger and hardship, war and death, sorrow was theirs. Happiness shone there, too, joy and love. Gail determined to make the third future come true.

She grabbed Amber's leash and peeked out into the hallway. The corridor was deserted. She hurried, slipped out a side door, and sped along the dark street to the docks, dragging Amber with her when the cat stopped to sniff.

The pier was dark and deserted, the stevedores and workmen long since finished for the night and fled for home. One ship blazed with the light of oil lamps. Gail breathed a sigh of relief. The *Evening Star* was still in port. Her keeper, the old man, Cooky, was up top, parchment scroll in hand. Otherwise, no one was in sight. Gail hurried to the gangplank and waved.

"I need to see Captain Herros," she said. "Quick, please, before someone discovers me." Gail shot a nervous glance up and down the dock.

Cooky stared at her, eyes widening in recognition with a nod of his head, and jabbed a gnarled finger to the shadows of the gangplank. "You go, wait there," he ordered and disappeared.

Gail made herself small in the tiny space beneath the ramp, concealed herself and Amber as best she could, and clutched the cat tightly when the animal tried to break free. A few moments later, she heard the *clop, clop,* of the captain's wooden peg above her.

"Gael?"

"Captain Herros."

Gail crawled out of concealment, dragging Amber with her, and raced up the gangplank. "I need your help. I have to escape."

"Get up here." Herros seized her arm and hauled her aboard the ship, pushing her into a cabin and latching the door behind him. His eyes locked onto Gail's. "Now what is this all about?" he demanded.

Gail told him what the high priestess Helena said, and what would happen if she remained in the temple. "You see," she concluded, "I can't stay, it'll mean my death."

Herros gave a low whistle, rubbing his whiskered chin with a worried expression on his face. "You're a slave, and a Priestess to boot." His voice dropped to a low whisper. "If they learned I gave you passage, they'd yank my license, confiscate my ship, and string me up by my thumbs."

"Please, Captain Herros." Gail laid a hand on his sleeve. "I have gold, I'll pay you, but I'm going to be sacrificed tomorrow and have to leave now. The priests will rip my heart out and offer it to their God because I asked for decent treatment. You can't let this happen." She added desperately, "You said you felt bad about selling me. Now is your chance to make it right."

"Ahh… of all the nonsense." Worry swept Herros's face. "Does anyone else know you ran away from the temple? You said you have money?"

"No, no one saw me leave, and yes," Gail rattled the coins in her purse, hugging him fiercely, "all yours if you wish." Amber sniffed his boots and purred.

Herros untangled her arms with a bitter scowl flashing across his face and pushed Amber away with his foot. "Get below deck and hide in yer old cabin and lock the door," he ordered. "Make sure none o' the crew sees yah—and take this confounded animal with you."

Gail hid in her former room and soon heard the captain bawling orders to his crew. The ship swayed, starting the up and down rocking motion telling her they were under way.

Three hours later, the captain appeared at her door. "Well, we might'a got away with it," he sighed. "Nobody came lookin' fer ya, and I had one of the men steal a small fishin' boat and bring it aboard. Make 'em think this is how ya escaped. Gotta take your robe from ya, too. I'll throw it overboard—If'n they find it they'll figure you drown in the bargain. With any luck they'll be lookin fer ya body along the coast, but by then we'll be halfway to the colonies."

Herros gave her a wink. "Now yah said somethin' about payment? How much do yah have?"

Chapter Six

The *Evening Star* sailed to the Wild Lands, the trading colonies set up by the city-states of Bethand and Ambos. Gail handed over most of her saving to Herros to pay for the month's voyage.

She fell back into her old shipboard life she experienced the first time onboard the *Evening Star*. This time, however, she was surprised when Captain Herros still refused to permit her to walk on deck.

"But Captain," she protested when she tried to follow him out the door, and he push her back inside with an admonishment to stay put, "I'm a paying passenger, your crew wouldn't complain, would they?"

Herros scowled, checked to guarantee no one saw her, and slammed the door behind him. "You are a runaway slave," he rumbled shaking his finger at her. "The less me crew knows, the better fer both of us. They know I brought someone on board, couldn't hide the fact, but they don't know who, and I wanna keep it this way. Better fer you, better fer me."

Gail was so surprised at the vehemence of his statement she blurted out, "You don't think word would reach back to Zarbin, do you?" she said in alarm. "We're far away now…"

"Maybe not," he conceded with a grim smile, "but after I drop you off, I'll be stopping at other ports. Sea dogs get drunk in some bar and who knows what they'll spill to the rest of the patrons. I know those Priests of Moack," he nodded his head, squinted his eyes, thinking. "They have ways of learning things. Better ya stay in yer cabin out of sight until yer gone."

Gail bobbed her head up and down, slowly, thoughtfully, as she mulled over what the captain said. "I guess you're right," she sighed at last. She stretched out on the bunk and stared at the ceiling. "It won't be that long anyway. I'll live."

Gail passed the time wondering what would happen to her, how she would survive. She knew she possessed skills, but without the support of the temple and the priests could she make it on her own in a strange city? Captain Herros said this was the frontier, the Wild Lands, the people were sure to need healers.

A week into the voyage Herros stamped into her cabin. After their first meeting when he bought her, Gail took his wooden foot for granted. It was a part of him, as his arm or gruff voice. She had been thinking about healing. When she heard the thumping of his footsteps, she asked, "Captain, why didn't you ever have your foot fixed? They could in Zarbin. I'm sure in Bethand or Ambos the doctors are as good if not better."

"This?" He lifted the peg and issued a light chuckle. "Never thought about having my foot mended, I guess." He sat on the bunk beside her and stretched his leg out, looking at his foot as if seeing the wooden peg for the first time.

Gail said eagerly, "I know how. It would take about six months."

The captain's head snapped up, aghast. *"Six months?* Who's got time to be laid up fer half a year?" he exclaimed. He shoved his palm out in dismissal. "Didn't have time when I lost it, I sure don't have time now."

Gail reached out with a finger and touched the wood. "How did you lose it?" she wondered aloud.

"Anchor line wrapped around my ankle during a storm." Herros rubbed his beard, thinking back. "Windless gave way, almost dragged me overboard. Chain went *rip!* Foot popped right off." He chuckled. "Lucky for me or I would'a drown."

"That's horrible!"

Captain Herros lifted his leg up and let it plop onto

the floor again. "Yeah, well, ship's surgeon patched me up as best he knew how, kept me asleep and pain free most of the time—about all he was able do, being at sea and all. Two weeks later I was back climbing ropes."

Gail thought about Herros screaming in pain when it happened. "How old were you?"

The captain rubbed his chin again. "I guess I was about ten. Can't rightly remember, that's a long time ago. Kind'a lose track of the years out here." He slapped his hands on his legs and shoved himself erect. "Well, I gotta be runnin'—stopped by to see how you were making out."

As Gail watched him clomp back to the door, she hoped the men in the new world weren't as tough as the captain, otherwise she'd have no work as a healer.

Two days before they reached land, Captain Herros strolled into Gail's cabin. "Yah never told me which colony yah wanted me ta drop yah off at. I'll be stopping by both—makes no difference to me."

Gail shook her head. She hadn't thought this far ahead. "Is there a difference?"

Herros scratched his beard and shrugged. He withdrew a map from his back pocket, unrolled the parchment on her bunk, and pointed to the West Coast of Africa where two small dots were marked.

"Not really. New Bethand's bigger, more established. Might be harder ta find a job. Bionx's smaller, they need the labor, but she's subject to Ambos. I hear their haven' a civil war, yer buddy Duke Ledo's tryin' to take over control of the country. The war could spill over ter the colony."

"Duke Ledo? I don't know...."

Herros gazed at her, puzzled, and laughed. "Sure yah do. He's the noble those two knights was sellin' yah for, remember?"

Gail's mouth formed an O, and her eyes opened wide. She did remember—the big palace with the angry man on the throne. "It seems so long ago now."

Captain Herros smoothed out the map. "Yeah, well, all of this is in the past." He stabbed the map again with his finger. "Which will it be? New Bethand or Bionx?"

With a flash of apprehension, Gail realized this was the first real decision of her life. *School, captured, slavery. I'd better not mess this one up.*

"I don't want to wind up in a civil war," she said slowly, her mind turning over the choices. She enjoyed reading about battles in history, read all types of books about war, but didn't want to *be* in one. The mere thought sent shivers up her spine. "New Bethand," she said at last. "I'll find something to do."

"New Bethand it is," said Herros, slapping his hands together and rolling up his map. "We dock there day after tomorrow." He shot her a narrow glance. "Now, Gael, I want to hand you a word of advice if you don't mind…"

Gail snapped to attention. Anything he told her would come in handy trying to make it on her own. "Yes, I'll always need your advice," she said anxiously, waiting to hear what he would say.

"Well, it's like this. I've seen many young women move to these colonies, thinking they'll find a job. Some do, a lot of them don't. "If'n they can't find work, well…" He gazed at her speculatively, "They wind up on the street selling, well, you know."

Gail did know. She blushed, but replied, "You don't have to worry about me selling my body, if that's what you mean."

"I just thought you should know." He stared at his hands.

"I'll be fine," Gail assured him. She reached out and touched his shoulder. "I'm a survivor."

***

Two days later the ship sailed into a deep-water harbor. High up on a sandy bluff a stone fortress stood, protected by a stockade fence. Half-timbered buildings marched down the slope to a bustling dock and warehouses. Captain Herros made Gail stay hidden aboard the *Evening Star* while he unloaded crates of copper pots, iron farm tools, and bolts of cotton cloth.

"After I load up again, ya can leave," he told Gail. "Better fer me, better fer you. This way yah start fresh with no one askin' questions where ya came from. Here, put out yer hands." Herros reached into his pouch and poured a big handful of tiny white shells into Gail's palms. "Take these and hang onto them."

Gail studied the small casings curiously. "Shells?" She weighted the white circlets in her hands, baffled by what the captain was giving her. "Why?"

"Yep, cowrie shells. The natives and colonists use 'em for money."

"You're kidding." Gail dumped them into her pouch, but held one out to examine it.

"Sure, 'nuff." The captain wiped his hands on his robe. "Oh, they use gold and silver, too—but everything is translated into cowries by piece or pound. They're a goodbye present. Don't do me no good once I leave here."

"Th-thank you, Captain." Gail felt her throat contract.

"And thank you fer the seein' you gave me about zebra hides." He added with a smirk. "I'll remember ta sell 'em in Bethand instead of Ambos when I sail to Mu. If yah can't find a job, ya should go in the outback and pass yaself off as the Spirit Goddess," he joked.

"Who's that?"

Herros chucked. "Oh, the natives have this legend about a Goddess who created the world. Gave 'em all sorts of good stuff and left, but promised to return if they really need her again."

Gail put her hands out and laughed. "They'd have the wrong person, if they think I'm the one. Maybe I'll be the Goddess of 'help me out, what am I doing here.'"

The next morning Gail discovered herself on the deserted dock, bag in one hand, Amber's leash with a tugging cat attached in the other. Captain Herros told her directions to a tavern he thought well of, the Smokestack Inn, with general directions of how to walk there. Gail watched the sails of the *Evening Star* fade in the distance and faced the small city bustling with people. The salty smell of the sea she was leaving blew from the ocean, the odor of rotting garbage from the town wafted from the land. She gulped, braced her shoulders, and marched in.

The inn wasn't hard to locate. The tangy scent of roasting meat and wood smoke disclosed the inn's location a block before she saw the building. A few heads twisted her way as she pushed the doors open. Gail spotted a small table in the corner and hurried to it, making herself comfortable, while Amber squatted on his haunches and watched the people strolled about. A serving girl ran over.

"What can I get you?" The woman eyed Amber with an uncertain tilt to her head. "I don't think he's allowed in here." She took a quick glance around. "But as long as no one complains, I guess it'll be okay."

"He's fine," Gail assured the girl, scratching Amber behind his ear until the cat emitted a loud purr. The woman was younger then Gail, skinny, with short curly black hair. "Eggs and ham, how much?"

"Twenty cowries."

Gail counted out the small shells Herros gave her, and reflected her money wouldn't last long at this rate. She dreaded how much a room would cost. *Better find a job, quick, otherwise I'll be sleeping on the street.* Before the serving girl left, Gail added, "Oh—if you have any old bones in the kitchen—" she nodded to Amber, "—it would be appreciated." She smiled.

Her breakfast arrived accompanied by a knucklebone with strings of meat still clinging to the edges.

After eating, Gail issued a huge contented sigh, lounged back in her chair and folded her arms. *Might as well get started.* She surveyed the dining room. *Once a waitress....*

She beckoned to the serving girl. "Are they hiring here? Or anywhere?"

The girl nodded to a stout man with grey streaking his hair standing behind a counter in front of the kitchen serving as a bar. "You'd have to ask Nicos, my father. He's the owner." She grinned tentatively at Gail. "My name's Adiana. Good luck."

Gail wrapped Amber's leash around a chair. "Stay," she told him, and weaved her way through tables to the counter.

"Excuse me," she began, waving her hand to gain the man's attention, "Mister Nicos? Are you hiring?" Gail added, "I can do anything."

The tavern keeper strolled over, rubbed the stubble on his chin and surveyed her dubiously, after which he took her hands and examining her palms. "Not hiring," he grunted, "you no look like you use to hard work anyway. Maybe you go down the street to the *Moro.* They have work for girls your type." He swung on his heels as if to turn away.

Gail's eyes snapped wide and she blushed red. *He thinks I'm...* Her temper flared. She leaned on the counter and blurted out, *"I am a Priestess of Moack, trained in the art of seeing and healing."* She'd been pushed around long enough, and wasn't about to take implied insults any longer from this stranger or anyone else. Besides, she had nothing to lose. "You'd be lucky to have me work in this place."

Nicos swung back to her, bushy eyebrows raised. "I've heard of the priestesses," he replied looking at her in a new light. He slowly nodded while thinking. "Okay, you prove you know the future, and maybe we work something out." He shoved his hands on his hips and smirked. "Go ahead, prophesize something—you impress me."

Now? She hadn't expected this—but with grim determination she dropped on a stool and cleared her mind.

"I see three possible events about to occur," she intoned, using her best priestess voice. "In one, three men walk in here, order, and leave. In another, they order, argue about the bill, and you force them to go."

Gail's eyes flew open wide and fixed Nicos with a stare of apprehension. "In the third, they argue with each other and someone dies."

Nicos started to smile, and then his lips dropped down. "We will see," he said, and stalked to a sink to wash mugs. He kept his gaze fixed on the front door.

Three men entered. "Hey, tavern keep," the tallest yelled, a giant with sandy blond hair, "A flagon of your best wine—we 'ust sold a load'a ivory from the yips and we're celebratin'." The men all laughed and took seats. From their manner, Gail thought they'd been celebrating for a while.

Adiana hurried over with a huge flagon and three wooden cups. "That's fifty cowries," she said and waited.

"We'll pay, we'll pay," the spokesman guffawed and waved her away. "'ust keep 'em comin'."

The flagon emptied. One of the other men shouted, "Hey, lass! We've run dry! Bring us another!" He held the pitcher up and waved the container in the air. The third man's head was nodding onto his chest. "Quick, me friend's fallen asleep!"

Adiana brought another flagon to the table and shot a furtive glance to her father. "That's a hundred cowries now," she said and tapped her sandal impatiently.

"Yeah, yeah," the man muttered, reaching into his pouch. He withdrew a few shells and some sand. "Where'd me money go to?"

"Ya probably dropped it, fool!" roared the largest of the three. He withdrew two silver rounds from his purse and scattered the coins on the table. "Here, this'll cover it."

"Me money?" the second man mumbled. He stared bleary-eyed at the leader and wavered to his feet, drawing his short sword, "You took…"

One of the patrons at another table hastily stood and left.

Nicos was around the counter in a flash, a large club held in his hand. "It's time you go." He thrust the flagon into the second man's hands. "Here, you take, drink it on the way."

The two men stared at the club, shook their friend awake, and stumbled out of the door.

"Well?" said Gail with a smirk, as Nicos stomped back to his counter breathing heavily, "Good enough?"

Nicos stowed his club away behind the counter. "You make predictions to my customers," he huffed at last, "we split fifty-fifty."

"And board," Gail hurried to say. "I need a place to sleep, too."

Nicos shook his head and shoved a palm at her. "If you eat and sleep here, you serve tables, help out," he said emphatically. "We split seventy-thirty. I receive the seventy."

"Uh-uh." Nico's version of fair was almost as bad as working for the High Priestess Helena. She swung on her stool and waved a finger at the patrons in the half-empty common room eating. "Fifty-fifty. People stop here to see me, they'll buy a drink or food first. If they travel from the interior, they'll need a room to stay in for the night," she said. "You'll be getting rich."

He shook his head and grinned. "Sixty-forty. It'll be months before word goes around I have Seeress. You and your animal over there might eat me broke by that time."

Gail thought the proposition over, and wondered if she could squeeze anything else out of the deal, or what she'd forgotten. She shot a quick look at Nico's face and decided she'd better not push it too far. "Agreed, but I have one day off a week, and I don't serve for more than eight hours a day—" the tavern owner scowled "—unless you need me," she amended quickly.

***

Gail moved easily into her new life. It wasn't much different from working in the temple—except she kept more of her money, but Nicos was right. Most of the colonists emigrated from Bethand and knew little of the Priestesses of Moack, and few needed her services. Word of her presence was slow in spreading throughout the colony. Gail thought the situation over and took long walks with Amber, concentrating on the wealthier sections of the town where the residents might appreciate her talents.

Besides Nicos and Adiana, two half-breed natives worked in the inn—Umba and Tarob. They cooked in the kitchen and helped clean the rooms and dining hall.

When trading ships sailed in, or safaris arrived from the interior, the inn was busy—but these were rare events. Gail thought about saving her money and opening her own business, but the cash was slow in arriving, and Nicos kept grumbling about letting her go.

One morning Umba hurried in while Gail was wiping down tables. "Caravan comin' down the street, boss," he announced to Nicos, "Lotsa' men."

"Good. We need the business," grunted Nicos wiping his hands on his apron. "Jump back in the kitchen and start the fires going." He glanced around and shouted to Gail and Adiana, "You heard 'em, you two? Make sure this place is clean, we gonna be busy."

The door slammed open and four natives staggered in carrying a man on an improvised litter, another young dainty hovered beside the litter staring around in a panic. "We heard you have a healer here?" he exclaimed anxiously. "We need him—Lord Aaron's son has been hurt!" The speaker, sweating and terrified, gazed about the room helplessly.

87

Gail rushed around the tables to the stretcher. "I'm a healer. Bring him back here." She ordered and gestured to the sleeping rooms. "What happened to him?" Someone wrapped a dirty blood-soaked bandage around the young man's thigh and calf, from hip to ankle.

"Gored in the leg by a rhino," gasped the dainty, hurrying along beside the litter as the natives carried the wounded man to the rear of the inn. "We trekked in with the caravan—he has lost a lot of blood."

Gail nodded absently as the bearers paused in the hallway before a row of doors. "This one." She swung the entrance of an empty room open. The men brought the stretcher into the chamber and placed it on the floor.

The injured man's companion, a noble by his dress, fluttered around his friend. "Can you help him? Will he die?"

Gail ignored the dandy. "Put him on the cot," she directed the litter carriers. "The rest of you, clear out."

The natives lifted the injured man gently onto the bed and left, the dandy hovered over his friend; his knees sagged, he started to collapse with a moan.

Gail grabbed him before he hit the floor. "Umba, take this one— "she gestured to the young nobleman who was turning white "—out into the dining room and fetch him some wine. Then bring back salt, boiled water, and clean towels." Curious onlookers crowded the doorway. Gail shouted to spectators, "You heard me—*get out.*"

Gail unwrapped the filthy, red wrappings around the man's leg. *Muscles ripped and oozing, but arteries undamaged—bone fracture—nasty wound, but not fatal.*

Umba brought in a bubbling pot of water, coarse sea salt, and soft, white towels. Gail nodded without seeing him and started to work.

The man was unconscious. Good—this was going to hurt. She dissolved the salt in the water and soaked the towel in the sterile solution, and wiped away blood and dirt.

She cleared her mind and peered into the gash.

Germs and creeping bacteria she destroyed as best she could. She accelerated the healing properties of the body causing the bone to start knitting and the wound to close as she watched. Her worse fear was shock. His skin was cool and clammy, his breath shallow. She elevated his legs and increased the blood flow to his organs. Color returned to his face and he took a deep sigh. Nodding, Gail wrapped another sterile cloth around the gash and strapped the whole thing tight.

Gail brushed her hair back and noticed her clothes. Blood streaked down her tunic and skirt. "Umba," she said, "Tell the other one he may enter, if he's able."

The dainty reentered carrying a tankard of wine and looking relieved. He bent over the sleeping man and whispered to Gail, "How is he?"

Gail put a restraining hand out so the noble didn't come too close. "He'll live, but I don't want him moved for a day or two," Gail decided. "I don't know if I destroyed all the infection in the wound. Tell lord what's-his-face if he wants to see his son, he'll have to ride down here."

"Lord Aaron—the governor," the noble replied, still staring at his friend in trepidation. "I will tell him." The young man paused with a laugh and a shake of his head, and then flashed Gail a grateful smile. "My friend and I heard a rhino was ripping up a planter's fields, and thought we'd have some fun. Should have known better, I guess. My name is Ben-dor. Thank you. You saved his life and kept me from losing my job."

For the next few days, the inn was busier than ever, with well-wishers entering and leaving, drinking and ordering food, and gossiping while they waited to see the young lord.

Nico's face threatened to freeze in a permanent smile with the inn crowded from morning until late night. Gail decided her boss was happiest when he was screaming at his staff, perspiration dripping down his face, and his dirty bar towel clenched in his hand like a sword. When Lord Aaron rented all the available rooms, staffing each with servants for his son, Gail thought Nicos would die from joy.

Word leaked out to the well-heeled customers Gail was a Seeress also, and she found herself busier than ever. When she wasn't waiting tables, she was dragged into some back room to hand out prophecies concerning commodity markets and prices back in Bethand, future weather conditions and when to take in crops, or the political affairs in Ambos and their civil war.

Gar-el, the son of the governor, proved to be a handful as well. Even though his own servants staffed the inn, the young lord screamed for Gail to attend him for every little need, whining, "Where is the healer, only the healer can help me," every time he wanted a drink of water or his pillow fluffed.

"This is nuts," exclaimed Gail to Adiana, after reassuring Gar-el for the third time during the day his wound was mending, and his imaginary pains were just that—imaginary. Nicos waved to the girls and pointed to a tray with five tankards of ale, another was laden with plates of food. "I haven't even got paid yet."

"You've received nothing from Lord Aaron?" Adiana said, rushing with Gail to the counter and hoisting a tray onto her shoulder. "Father made sure he received his money up front for the rooms before he let the governor's servants move in."

"Good for him," Gail grunted. She and Adiana staggered to a table and passed out tankards to the waiting customers, "but how about me?" She pictured herself having to march up to the big white house, which was the governor's residence, and knocking on the door for her money. *No, demanding wouldn't work at all. They'd throw me in prison.* A wry smile spread across her lips as she loaded her tray with empty flagons. *But. I'd. Better. Get. Paid. For. This.*

From the day before the governor's son was to leave, until the morning of his departure, Gail worked a twenty-four hour shift with two small breaks.

On the morning Gar-el left, the governor himself arrived accompanied by a sedan chair, to escort his son to his villa, the young dandy, Ben-dor, by his side. The two held a whispered conversation by the entrance to the tavern and Ben-dor jabbed a finger in Gail's direction. The two strolled over to her.

"You are the one who saved my son's life, I believe," the governor said, awarding Gail a cursory inspection. He broke out into a faint smile. "I want to thank you." He held out his hand.

Gail didn't know whether to take it, curtsy, or both. She gripped his fingers lightly in a quick pump, and smiled back. "Governor Aaron, about my pay…" she began.

"Oh, yes, uh…" The governor's mild blue eyes widen in alarm and he glanced at Ben-dor, confused.

The young noble whispered, "Do not worry, sire, I will take care of it." He pursed his lips with a quick nod.

The governor caught sight of his servants carrying his son on a litter from the back room. "Well, I must be off." He leveled another smile at Gail. "I see they are bringing Gar-el." He hurried to his son's side.

Ben-dor stepped up to Gail, grasped her gently by the elbow, and flashed a grin. "Priestess Gael," he reached into his pouch, "this is for your services." He poured a large handful of silver rounds into her hands. "These—" he dropped three massive gold pieces into her palms also "— are from the governor and me, as a thank you." He checked around to assure himself no one else was listening and whispered, "I really do owe you a debt of gratitude. It would not have done at all if I lost the governor's son on a hunt." He shot her a grin.

Gail couldn't tell if he was kidding or not.

When everyone left, with more large tips spread all around to the inn's staff by a backslapping Ben-dor, Gail, and Adiana slumped in two chairs, slack haired and exhausted.

"I can't move," groaned Adiana. She slipped off her sandals and rubbed her feet.

Gail lifted her chin off her chest long enough to look around at the deserted dining room. "I don't think we have to. Everyone's gone."

Nicos strode over to them, wiping his hands on his apron. "Hey, you two, what you doing loafing around? Start cleaning up this place."

Dirty plates and mugs covered the tables—crumbs of food littered the floor.

"Noooo," the two girls moaned in unison. Adiana said, "Father, five minutes, please?"

Nicos chuckled. "I'm kidding. You both worked hard. I close the place for today, and me and the boys clean up. You two take the rest of the day off." With another laugh, he made a shooing motion toward the entrance and wandered back to the kitchen.

Gail exhaled a huge lungful of air and said to Adiana, "What do you think?"

Adiana echoed a deep sigh and stood. "Let's start wiping tables."

Gail groaned and pushed herself to her feet. "You wipe and I'll sweep. We'll finish up faster this way."

***

Nicos and Adiana found their pouches filled, Gail's also. She possessed three fat gold rounds in the way of a tip and meant to hoard every cowrie of it. Business remained brisk. The Smokestack Inn was "discovered," by merchants and the political elite of the colony who continued to meet, dine, and gossip in the common room. Nicos hired another girl and two more men in the kitchen.

Gail developed a growing list of clients for her seeing, and her savings continued to build. She determined to quit her job at the inn, run her business full time, and strike out on her own. First, however, she needed to find a place to live.

On her days off, she chased down rumors of houses for rent, or sale, but unearthed none within the colony walls. The recent Bethish-Caragon war brought a glut of refugees to the wild lands seeking refuge and housing was at a premium.

On a tip from Adiana, she located a small barn, which the owner claimed once housed lumber. As Gail tapped walls and inspected the inside of the roof, she concluded it also contained livestock—cattle and chickens she decided by the smell. The cow pucks and feathers were a dead giveaway. Amber enjoyed chasing the rats.

Nevertheless, Gail shelled over most of her savings and bought the place, bringing in carpenters, masons, and plasters, until she had a passable place to live.

She wandered around the building on the day the workmen left. *My own place.* The first night, Gail and Amber prowled through the small chambers investigating every nook. "This is *our* bed," she told the Oslo, touching her cot. She strolled into the combination kitchen-living room. "*Our* fireplace." Gail threw another log on the grate and giggled as the cat jumped back in alarm at the sparks. She drew up a chair close to the flames and opened a bottle of wine Nicos gave her. "Here's to us," she laughed, scratching the feline behind the ears as he climbed into her lap. She took a sip. "We're ballin'."

She hoped she was doing the right thing. On her last day of work, Nicos waved her over to the bar. "We gonna miss you, you're a good worker." He dried a tankard and put it away on a shelf.

Gail felt her throat tightening up. "I'm going to miss you too," she said, choking back tears. "You and Adiana have been like family to me. Thank you for all you've done for me."

Nicos wagged a finger at her nose. "You a business woman now, just remember to pay your taxes on time," he declared. "You don't want to make the governor mad at you, right?" He chuckled at his own joke.

"Taxes?" She uttered the word uncertainly. She'd never thought about taxes. "What taxes?"

Nicos saw the expression on her face. "You have a business, you got business tax. You own property? You have to pay property tax."

"I—er, I've never paid taxes before," Gail admitted with rising panic in her voice.

"Well, you pay now," Nicos replied. He nodded his head vigorously. "Better keep good records, the government checks."

A week after she moved into her new home, Adiana rode by to visit, accompanied by a basket totting Umba.

"Father sent you a home warming gift," Adiana announced when Gail opened the door, breezing through the entrance while Gail stood there with a foolish grin on her face. The girl snatched the basket from Umba and withdrew three bundles. "Wine, salt, and bread—the traditional Bethish house present." She laid the items on Gail's table. "He stuck other things in here, too—honey, flour, pepper—Oh." She grabbed another package and ripped off the wrapping. "Banana cake. I made it myself."

Gail stared at the victuals in amazement and at the crushed cake. "Yummy. I'll get some dishes." She hastened to a cupboard, hurrying back with a knife and three plates. She cut slices and passed them around.

"Umba, take that outside onto the porch," Adiana commanded to the half-breed. "I want to visit for a while."

Gail gave Adiana a tour of the house and then the two gossiped at the kitchen table. "Father is having so many problems with the new girl," Adiana informed Gail.

She nibbled at her cake. "The two yips he hired aren't too bad…"

Gail frowned. "You know I don't like people calling the natives yips, Adiana. Why can't people…"

The girl waved this off with a hand. "But they…"

Shouting at the front door interrupted the conversation. The two women stared at each other in surprise, and Gail rose and hurried to the door, throwing it wide to see what happened outside.

Umba was attempting to push a tall native with a black beard down the porch steps and out into the street. "No come in—Go away—Go away."

"Umba, *stop it,*" Gail demanded, glancing from one to the other. She said to the stranger, "What do you want?"

The native clutched tight to the railing, his jaws clenched, his face a mask of pain. "I heard a healer lives here," he grated between gritted teeth. "I need—healing."

"Umba, let him go. Quick, enter," ordered Gail. "Umba, help him to the bedroom."

The native winced, released the banister, and tried to stand erect, but with a low grunt of hurt, grabbed the railing again. Gail held one arm, while Umba seized the native by the other, and they walked him into the house. Adiana leaped back in fright as the two guided the native into the bedroom and sat the man on Gail's cot. The back of his shirt was bloody and ripped. She helped him ease the tattered remains off his body. The skin was a mass of lash marks. His hide reminded Gail of raw chopped meat.

The sheer brutality of what happened to the native shocked Gail into silence. She gazed at Umba, who shook his head, eyes wide, and started back at Gail. She exclaimed, "Good God, what'd you tangle with?"

The man grimaced. "Had a disagreement with a merchant over the price of my ivory," he grunted. "The merchant won."

"I guess. Lay down on your stomach." With a sigh

of relief, the native stretched out. Gail turned his head so she could stare deep into his eyes and a moment later, he snored. She rose to put a pot of water on to boil and noticed Adiana and Umba watching her. "I'm sorry, but you'd better go." She spread her hands wide with a nod to the sleeping man. "I'm going to be busy for the rest of the day."

"Not on your life," declared Adiana. In a lower voice she added, "You'll need help—and besides, I don't think it's safe to leave you alone with his kind. Umba—" she ordered the half-breed, "—tell Father I'm staying here tonight. Explain to him why."

The man's wounds were not life threatening in themselves, but the shock to his system was. Gail cleaned and bandaged the lashes and set his body to healing. By the time she finished, it was late in the afternoon.

Gail and Adiana settled back by the fireplace sipping wine with Amber curled at their feet. They waited for their patient to awake.

"How could they?" Gail fumed, "whipping that man like an animal—worse than an animal! I thought the Bethish were civilized!" She sat rigidly and glared at Adiana. "Aren't there laws about these sorts of things?"

Adiana took a sip of wine and squirmed uncomfortable before answering. "Well, we only heard his side of the story," she remarked. "These natives from the outback are rough when they want to be. Who knows what really happened?"

Gail paused, glass halfway to her mouth. *"Humph."* She sipped her wine in disgust and pointed a forefinger at her friend. "Oh, come on, you saw his back." Gail took another gulp of wine and this time scowled at the cup. "Even if he'd started a fight, he should have been turned over to the magistrate, not beaten and thrown into the street." She shook her head and muttered to herself, "I know there are laws, or should be."

Adiana said, vexed, "Yes, we have laws against things like this, and if he were Muian, it wouldn't have happened, but the others..." She shrugged.

Gail clenched her teeth. "You make it sound as if it's okay. Adiana, you know it's not right."

Adiana raised her cup to her mouth, swallowed wine, and focused her eyes on the fire. "We have the coastal tribes to travel inland and obtain whatever we need, and the half-breeds do the heavy labor—but the interior tribes?" She stifled a yawn with the back of her hand. "They're a ragged band of unwashed savages if you ask me. Most people say it's better to exterminate the whole bunch. As it is, they supply us with some trade goods to send back to Bethand, but they're like insects," she gestured to a sealed glazed jar on the kitchen table with the picture of a bee stamped on front, "we take the honey, and they make more."

"That's not right!" Gail slammed her glass down in indignation. "What happens when the inland tribes get angry, or fight back, or refuse to trade?"

Adiana gave a short laugh. "We have better weapons and horses. It doesn't matter what the yips think, or whether they *want* to trade or not. It's our right, to occupy this land as we see fit."

"I don't believe you believe what you said."

"They should be glad we're bringing civilization to this place," Adiana replied with an irritable shrug of her shoulders, "besides, it's business. If we don't colonize this country the Ambosian's will. You think we're bad, you should see how they treat the yips around their colony." Gail would hear this phrase over again when the colonists dealt with the natives. "It's business," justified anything.

Their conversation changed to other subjects, and drifted off into silence as they gazed at the flames in the fire. When Gail glanced up Adiana had fallen asleep. She rose and tip-toed into her bedroom to grab a blanket and found her patient awake and struggling to sit up.

"Hold on, lay back down," Gail commanded, pushing him flat on his stomach. "You're not ready to move around yet."

"I am fine," he replied, but remained prone on the cot. "My name is Pontus, and I thank you for your help."

The sincerity in his voice was genuine. Stretched out on the cot with his face relaxed from the pain he appeared years younger than she first thought when they brought him in. "Forget about it, this is what I do—healing and seeing."

"A Seeress, too?" He propped himself up on his elbows and raised his eyebrows while gazing at her. "I should have stopped here before I saw the merchant."

In spite of herself, Gail chuckled. "My name's Gail and next time you'll know better."

"Gaela?" he mangled the word in his mouth. "What a strange name for a woman."

It's an odd name for anyone. Why couldn't these people pronounce her name right? It wasn't this hard. She bent down and said, "Gail. G-A-I-L."

"Gaela," he mispronounced it again the same way, nodding. "How much do I owe you?"

She waved a hand in dismissal. "Forget about payment this time. The treatment was free, but spread the word to your friends here and in the interior, I need the business."

Pontus rolled on his side and supported his head with one hand. "I do not think you would want my kind visiting around here," he said seriously. "It would give you a bad reputation. The Muians would say you treat animals. Yips, if you understand me." He added softly, "I will be gone by the morning."

"Oh, no, you need another day of rest." She snatched out a sheet from the closet and covered him. "Those lash marks may have healed, but you're still weak from blood loss. Now go to sleep—I'll see you in the morning."

Sometime around midnight Gail woke and heard him rustling, and by the time she arose and dressed, he was gone. The next morning, when she stepped outside, two large ivory tusks leaned against her door.

Chapter Seven

After the incident of the native, Gail started taking notice of the darker side of colonial life. Before, she was too busy with her own life and surviving in a strange new world to pay any attention to how the natives were treated. She enjoyed walking to the market to shop, but one day, an incident changed her perception of how the colony treated the tribesmen.

Gail browsed in an open air shop searching for plates to add to her growing supply of utensils in the kitchen.

A loud crash and a gruff voice cursing loudly, issued from behind a canvas sheet set up in the rear of the store, screening excess merchandise from the sight of customers. "What's that noise?" Gail raised up on her toes trying to see past the counterman.

"I do not know, m'lady," replied the vendor, who was showing her dishes with different designs. He spun around and listened, a frown of worry passing over his face. "I will be right back."

The man vanished behind the canvas. Moments later Gail heard him yell, "Stupid Yip! Look what you have done to my stock!" A dull thud and a groan of pain rang through the small shop.

What in the world? Gail hurried around the table and tore the curtain aside to see what was happening.

A young half-breed lay curled on the ground holding his stomach—a wagon drawn up next to him. A broken crate spilled its wares on the earth. The driver and the vendor towered over the boy.

"C'mon, you, *quick.* Pick this stuff up. I ain't paying yah to sit around!" the driver yelled. He drove the toe of his boot into the side of the boy.

100

"And I am not paying for the broken pieces," snapped the vendor to the driver. He booted the native in the rear as the young man scrambled to repack the crate. "If you want to use brainless dolts like this one, you pay for his mistakes."

The merchant glanced up and saw a horrified Gail gaping at the scene. "Sorry m'lady," he apologized. "This yip dropped my merchandise while unloading. I will be back with you shortly after I assure myself I will not be charged for his clumsiness."

Gail studied the crate and the native. The box was the same size as the boy and weighted twice as much. Trembling in rage, and deathly white, she closed the curtain.

The vendor returned. "Have you decided which pattern you want, m'lady?" he said to Gail as if nothing unusual happened.

"Yeah." She threw a few silver coins on the table, grabbed a set of plates without looking, and left, mentally restraining herself from throwing the dishes at his face. After this, Gail tried to avoid the marketplace as much as possible. What she couldn't avoid, however, were the chain gangs of natives she saw on the streets, working to pay off fines for imagined crimes, while a colonial overseer lounged in the shade with a whip.

One of the few treats she allowed herself was attending the small amphitheater—what the colonists called a circus—and seeing the plays and poetry readings held during the afternoons. Once a week, however, at night, the owners unmasked darker, violent pleasures for the entertainment of the populace.

"But, Gael," Adiana exclaimed during one of her visits, "The games are *fun*. So exciting!" She lounged on the floor and folded her legs under her, careful to place her glass of wine where she would not knocked the cup over.

"They're horrible," retorted Gail with a shudder.

"Who wants to see some poor man ripped apart by a cave lion?"

"Those people are criminals or troublemakers like those yips we've been having so many problems with," scoffed Adiana. She scratched Amber behind the ears, "and the animals would'a died in the outback anyhow."

"What yips?" Gail asked, alert. "I haven't heard of any trouble with the natives."

"You don't know?" Adiana leaned forward in delight to recount news her friend hadn't heard about yet and whispered, "A group of them marched right into the colony and demanded to see the governor. Imagine the gall of those people?"

"Why? What happened? Were the natives conducted to see Aaron?" Gail focused on Adiana's face, trying to read the outcome of the march in her smiling eyes before she said a word.

"Are you kidding?" replied Adiana with a laugh. "The soldiers rounded the whole crowd up and arrested the arrogant savages on the spot. Imagine—what nerve."

"For asking to see the governor?" Gail said, incredulous. "Where are they now? Were they released?"

Adiana waved her hand in dismissal. "I'm sure I don't know." She settled back and savored the taste of her wine. "I overheard the story from a couple of merchants at the inn who stopped in last night. They didn't say."

"Well, I hope those people were released," Gail fumed, her outrage of the treatment of the natives flaming anew. "It doesn't sound as if they did anything wrong, and I doubt they'll go to the games." She ran her hands over Amber's spotted coat, thinking. "Killing them for peaceful protesting would be stupid. As for the colonials in jail, I don't think it's right either."

"Oh, don't be such an old woman," scoffed Adiana. "The whole lot deserves to be thrown to the lions. They're all murders and thieves."

"I don't care." Gail rose and sat in her chair, rubbing Amber with her foot. The Oslo rolled over and allowed her to rub under his chin. "They may have to be punished, but I don't have to visit the circus and watch."

"Besides," Adiana went on with a wicked grin, "all the good men attend the games. If I received as many invites as you, I'd go every week."

Gail laughed back at Adiana in spite of herself and covered her mouth to hide it. Being young, single, and with a growing business, she found herself with no end of invitations to the games, or gatherings, of the younger crowd in the colony who hoped to make alliances.

"In my land women have realized they don't need a man. We're liberated," Gail replied in a smug manner, "and I'm not searching for a boyfriend right now, anyway. I have too many other things happening in my life to become distracted."

Adiana nodded shrewdly and advised Gail, "Well, you should keep one or two in reserve, in case. They may all be second sons of second sons, but you can never tell, an uncle might die and one of those men will become rich."

"Adiana."

The more Gail thought about it, though, the more she realized Adiana was right in her own strange way. Not for a man, she thought. If the rich of the colony attended these games, it wouldn't hurt her business to be seen by the well-to-do, or to interact with a few on a social basis. She didn't *have* to watch, she reasoned. In fact, many people stayed outside of the circus and talked. It was a way of socializing; many of the rich planters journeyed into town once a month, and the circus was a focal point of the colony's activities. She might pick up clients, and if she must to go inside and watch, she would deal with the bloodshed for one night.

Ben-dor, the dandy who brought the governor's son to the Smokestack Inn, was a frequent visitor of Gail's after their first meeting, both professionally and socially. Besides being the secretary to the governor, he also controlled the scribal business for the colony, making the official documents and drawing up papers for the merchant community. He employed three junior scribes and talked about hiring a fourth.

Ben-dor also helped Gail set up a bookkeeping system, and organized the pile of parchment slips she collected from her business. Gail felt grateful to him and told him again and again how thankful she was for his assistance. As their friendship blossomed, however, he kept pushing for a relationship stronger than friendship, which Gail wasn't sure she was ready for yet.

A few days after her conversation with Adiana, he stopped by to learn about grain futures in Bethand for a client. When his business concluded, Gail invited him to stay for lunch and visit for a while. After they sat at her dining table and exchanged the usual small talk, the conversation turned to the recreations of the colony.

"But Priestess Gael," he told her in his half percussive, half joking voice, "You must attend the circus tonight. I know you do not enjoy the games, but you have never seen one. Everyone will be there, even the governor's son. You owe your time to him, checking up on your patients." He flashed Gail one of his winning smiles. "What do you say?"

"Well…" She felt sorry for Ben-dor. He was sweet, and always eager to send clients her way when he could. He made her laugh.

"All right, all right," she said at last, her mouth bending down in an indulgent frown. Gail rose and ladled out lunch, placing a bowl of stew on the table for him she threw together from leftovers, "but don't expect me to watch, and if I run out halfway through, put my queasiness down to my weak stomach."

"You will be fine," he replied, digging into his

lunch. He smacked his lips and exclaimed, "This is good." He reached across the table and took one of her hands. "Maybe I should stay and let you cook for me the rest of my life."

"Down boy," Gail replied, trying to appear stern and not succeeding. "I have Amber to feed. I don't need you. Where should we meet?"

"I will drive by tonight with my carriage and pick you up."

"Fine, I'll be ready."

"You know," he said with a serious face and now taking both of her hands in his, "one day I will be rich. There is plenty of opportunity here in New Bethand for a man of ambition. I was thinking of enlisting in colonial reserves—why I might become a general one day, maybe in the future be governor. Do you think…"

Gail gently pulled her hands away and placed one finger on his lips. "Don't run before you walk, my boy," she cautioned, feeling guilty without knowing why when she saw the expression on his face. "Tonight, carriage, circus."

That evening Gail dressed in her best robe and prayed she would make a good impression on the people she would meet during the night out. When Ben-dor arrived with his carriage, she was ready and determined to put on a good showing and try not to scream at the gory spots. The ride was short and the circus crowded. Ben-dor and she milled around the entrance, greeting people they knew, while Ben-dor pointed out people Gail should know.

"There is Merchant San-dal," Ben-dor waved to a fat man in a white robe. "He owns three trading ships running up and down the coast. And look—" He gestured to a tall man and woman clad in jewelry and gold chains entering the circus. "He is the younger brother of Senator Pot-mar of Bethand. He oversees his brother's estates here in the colony. They say he supervises over five thousand acres of good farmland and forest."

Ben-dor grabbed Gail's hand and drew her forward up the stairs into the main entrance. "Follow me. I will show you what is fighting tonight." The commoners and poor headed up long stairs to the upper galleries of the amphitheater, while the wealthier planters and merchants hurried to boxes lining the stadium walls where they would have a good view of the action. In the middle of these two groups sat the bulk of the colony's population: the butchers, bakers and carpenters, all out for a night of entertainment. Ben-dor by-passed the swirling mob and strolled toward a passage leading to the ground level of the arena.

"I don't think we're allowed down here," Gail said, as they walked along the dimly lit ramp. The foul smell of unwashed bodies and feces wafted up to her nose; the moans and low growls of predators filled her ears.

"Nonsense." Ben-dor kept walking until they stood on a low balcony above a series of cages. There were a dozen handlers wandering between the pens to keep control. "People stop by here all the time." He stepped to the edge of the walkway and pointed down to the prisons. "This is what fights tonight."

Giant aurochs bawled and butted their horns against the bars in anger—sabertoothed tigers prowled and screamed. Cave lions glared at the handlers. What drew Gail's attention were two cages directly below her.

One pen held two Muians, their faces streaked with fear, clothes and hair matted in filth. The other contained fifteen natives packed together so close they could hardly move.

"Why are they here?" whispered Gail.

Ben-jor replied in a loud firm voice, "Oh, those two were caught breaking into a storage building by the docks." He waved to the Muians and gave a slight laugh. "Not the first time it has happened. See—" Ben-dor gestured to one man who glared back in defiance, "he is missing his right hand. He has got caught before."

"And those?" Gail nodded to the natives. "Were they stealing, too?"

"No." Ben-dor rubbed his chin and thought for a moment. "Remember the ruckus in the market a few days ago? These are the ringleaders and a few of their fanatical supporters. I think they go to the lions."

One of the natives chose to glance up and waved when he saw Gail and Ben-jor watching. He was the native Pontus Gail healed. "Lady Gaela," he shouted gravely as if he were a bad boy, "I discovered myself on the wrong side of an argument again." He appeared calm about the situation he and his friends found themselves.

"You know him?" Ben-dor swung around to face Gail and eyed her in disbelief.

Gail's chest contracted. "I healed him once," she admitted. She dropped her voice, "I guess it was a waste of time."

"Let us leave." Ben-dor shook his head with a grimace and started back up the ramp. "It is time to locate our seats. I think they are ready to begin."

Ben-dor led her to a box reserved for colonial officials, and nodded to a few of his fellows who already sat there eagerly discussing the matches about to start.

"Best seats in the circus," he bragged, gesturing to the arena below. "You feel the roar of the crowd here from all sides, and the screams of the fighters." He gave Gail an amused look and teased, "Be careful or you may get splattered with blood on your new clothes."

"*Oh, yuck,*" exclaimed Gail in disgust. "If you keep saying those things, I'm leaving right now. I've met all the people I wish to meet."

The first match was an Aurochs bull against a sabertooth tiger. The tiger snarled and circled the larger animal. The bull kept the wall of the circus to its back, lowered its horns, and snorted.

Gail watched in fascination and clutched Ben-dor's arm as the bull charged and the tiger leaped aside. Before the cat escaped, the bull swung its horns and caught the tiger in the stomach, throwing the cat into the air. The tiger screamed with pain. In a whirl of hooves, the aurochs trampled the hapless animal.

Gail turned her face away at the last moment, the image of the mangled sabertooth burned in her mind. *Brutal—so brutal.*

The crowd roared in excitement. Ben-dor seized her arm tightly without looking at her and shook it. "Now it is the aurochs against the thieves," he murmured to Gail. He watched the gate intently for the Muians appearance onto the arena floor. "This should be a good one."

An iron gate lifted opened and the handlers forced the two Muians out into the arena by spear point. Knives were tossed to the stadium floor at their feet, and the men snatched the weapons up, glancing at the bull and then at the roaring crowd in fear.

The aurochs pawed the earth and eyed the two warily. In one swift motion, the bull charged and the men leaped apart to escape certain death.

"I can't watch anymore," Gail gasped, standing. "I'm going to take a walk and get some fresh air. I'll be back." Ben-dor nodded absently, his eyes riveted on the action in the arena.

Gail hurried down the stairs to flee the shouts of the bloodthirsty crowd. She reached the main level and stopped, taking deep breaths to calm her nerves.

The corridor was deserted. She took a few steps, first moving toward the exit, and then changing her mind and swinging to the ramp leading to the ground level.

The captive natives pressed up against the bars of their prison, watching the two Muians fight for their lives. Gail saw no sign of the handlers, who had left to watch the struggle from the first level.

"So Priestess, returning to see who you will place your bets on?" Pontus pushed through his mates, and stood smiling up at her through the bars of his cage.

"Aren't you afraid to die?" Gail asked in disbelief. She couldn't believe this man would stand there and joke when he and his friends were about to be ripped apart. "You know what's going to happen next, don't you?"

The native shrugged and looked serious. "Death searches for us all. I know few who died in their sleep. Of course I do not wish to depart life in this manner," he hooked his thumb in the direction of the arena, "but I do not have much choice, do I?"

Gail scanned the area for the guards. On impulse, she leaped down next to the prison. Seizing a bar used for moving the cages, she attacked the chain holding the pen shut. With a few quick jerks, the links snapped and the door swung open.

"There, you're free," panted Gail. "Escape and don't come back."

"Gael, what are you doing?" Ben-dor stood on the balcony, staring into the holding pen with surprise, his face a mask of disbelief. "You...."

With one leap, Pontus landed next to the startled man and wrapped a massive arm around Ben-dor's neck.

"Pontus, NO! Don't kill him!"

Ben-dor flopped like a fish on a hook, his eyes rolling, his hands going to his throat, and then he slumped forward, unconscious.

"Is he—dead?" Gail felt tears rising.

"No. I cut off the air to his head," denied the native, easing Ben-dor to the floor. "He will be fine." Pontus leaped down and seized Gail's wrist. "You are right, we must escape. Come." He tugged her toward an exit, his companions crowding around them in their haste to flee.

"I can't!" Gail pulled back. "I—"

"No time! We must go, and you must come with

us!" commanded Pontus. "When they find us gone, and your friend comes too, your life will be in certain danger."

Oh my God, he's right, Gail thought. *Damn, I should have left well enough alone.* Aloud she said, "We have to pass by my house so I can get my things."

Pontus nodded without replying and led her to a ramp. Outside, he said to his companions, "Go back to your tribes. We will meet again." In small groups, the natives darted away in different directions into the darkness. Gail and Pontus found themselves alone with two others. "Let us hurry, Priestess," he urged. "Pursuit will soon follow."

It was late at night and the streets were empty. Gail and the others hurried through the dark until they reached her house. Amber greeted her, buzzing and butting his head against her legs, but his purrs turned to growls when the others tumbled in behind her.

"Amber, stop that!" Gail attached a leash to his collar and pulled the cat into her bedroom ahead of her, where she began stuffing clothes into a bag.

When Gail hurried out, Pontus and the others were rifling through her pantry. Pontus paused long enough to scoop out a handful of kitchen knives from a drawer and pass them to his companions.

"Ready? The colonists will be out searching, and when they cannot find us, they will have the coastal tribes on our trail. We will not stop until we travel inland passed the Ubo River. If there is anything you want, take it now. We will not be back."

Gail looked around at her recently purchased home, and the possessions she had worked hard to earn. "No, I have everything I need." She glanced down at Amber and tugged on his leash. "Come on, let's go."

Chapter Eight

On the morning of the fourth day, they reached Pontus's tribe. On the first day, the colonists tracked them on horseback. They hid in thickets and Pontus whispered to Gail, "Do not worry. They could not find an elephant if he sat on them." When Gail looked at the native, puzzled, he added, "Forget it. They will not follow us into the bush unless they have a troop of coastal hunters to show them the way."

After the forests of the coast, the landscaped changed to endless miles of savannah sprinkled with woodlands. Herds of elephants, giraffes and antelopes grazed or drank from the numerous rivers they passed. At night, the sounds of predators filled the air and the red eyes of hyenas and lions ringed their camp. Amber went hoarse from growling.

Pontus's other companions was his cousin, Typhon and their friend Chron, the son of a powerful chief from the southern tribes. "We decided we had had enough," stated Pontus to Gail on their third night out. "I was not the first one beaten and robbed. It has always been so, but over the last few years, it has become worse. We located a few others that felt the same, and went to complain to the governor. We made it as far as the market before the soldiers moved in and arrested us. We will never try *that* again."

Gail listened to his story with her head in her hands, gazing into the fire. She was dirty, hungry and tired. Her hair smelled, and huge bug bites covered her body. "What are you going to do now?" she asked.

"Do?" He and the other men laughed. "What can we do?" In the light of the campfire, his face appeared more puzzled than angry. "I guess complain as much as possible,

111

when we are sure that no one is listening, but stay out of the way of the soldiers. What else?"

Gail wondered what she would do. *Where am I going? What will happen to me? Am I doomed to run forever? Could'a, would'a, should'a,* she thought with a bitter shake of her head. *I screwed up again. Now besides being wanted in Zarbin as a runaway slave, I'll be arrested by the New Bethand authorities for helping prisoners escape. Only place left for me is Ambos territory. I wonder if I can make it three strikes and out?*

A wild cackle echoing through the night shocked Gail out of her thoughts—an answering snarl and the protest of growls nearby. She moved closer to Pontus. "What was that?" It had sounded like the animals were right next to her.

The men had stopped along the way and chopped down long poles, sharpened them, and held the points in the fire until they were iron hard. The three young hunters laughed, unconcerned by the noise, but held their spears tighter. Chron threw another branch on the flames.

"Hyenas trying to take prey away from a lion," Pontus said. "Do not worry; they will play that game all night—first one lion and five hyenas, then two lions and ten hyenas. Whichever side weighs the most by the time it becomes light wins the prize."

On the last day, their party skirted a small woodland and weaved through hills strewn with boulders. With a sense of eagerness, the hunters hurried up a worn path. They came upon a thatched village, with a thorn palisade surrounding the perimeter, set by a river. Dogs and children ran out to greet the returning warriors, followed by men and women. By the time they reached the palisade, the whole village had assembled.

A group of hunters, who surrounded Chron and Typhon, asked excited questions of the two. Typhon held his hand up and pointed to a large hut.

Another party led by an older hunter and two smiling women sauntered over to Pontus and Gail. The grizzled warrior stepped forward and hugged the younger man.

Pontus returned the embrace and whispered into the old man's ear, casting glances at Gail. The two women, Cuco, Pontus's mother, and his younger sister, Maita, hugged him next. The older man, Jankus, Pontus's father, sauntered over to Gail.

"My son tells me you helped him escape from the colony," he said as the five walked into the village. He guided her to a large hut.

"I couldn't let him die," Gail admitted. "They were going to throw him to the tigers!"

"Well, I am glad that did not happen!" chimed in Maita. She hugged her brother's arm and added, "Things would be too quiet around here without him."

Jankus said to Maita, "Take our guest to our home, and make her comfortable. The council will want to hear from Pontus and the others. We will be back shortly."

Jankus, Pontus and the rest of the older hunters proceeded to a large hut to discuss the recent events.

Maita tugged Gail to a smaller dwelling set to one side of the other. "This is my parent's home," she said. "We'll stop here and relax, you must be exhausted."

They entered the hut and Maita flopped down on a pallet of Ibex skins. "Sit," she said to Gail. The girl patted a spot next to her. "In a few minutes, you can wash and we will get you some clean clothes," she surveyed Gail's ripped and dirty robe, "but right now rest, you must be tired. Are you hungry?"

"Yes!" The last of the cheese and bread taken from her pantry had run out yesterday. "Whatever you have."

"Wait right here." Maita sprang up and disappeared. She returned carrying a wooden bowl. Gail received a generous portion of rich stew, with hunks of fatty meat floating around in the broth. She ate, had seconds, and settled back with a contented sigh.

"Are you ready for that wash now?" Maita held up soft deerskins and clean clothing. "The men are all in council. You can have privacy." She led Gail down to a strip of gravel beach by the river. "The water runs swift here, so we aren't bothered by crocodiles."

At the word "crocodiles," Gail checked for herself before stripping and easing herself into the freezing water. She kept glancing around, waiting for a bite on her leg. She scrubbed quickly and got out.

While Gail fumbled getting dressed with the strange clothes, Malta said, "You must be brave to have helped my brother escape the colonists."

"Who, me?" Gail was turning the pants she had received over, trying to figure out which way they went. Malta rushed over and helped her. "Thanks. No, I wasn't being brave, but I couldn't let those men die. All they did was protest what the colonists were doing to them. You can't kill a person for that."

"Well, I am glad you were there," Malta retorted. "Ready?"

Gail finished dressing. The two women walked back to the hut, and met Pontus and Jankus coming from the council.

"You are looking better," Pontus said as Gail preceded him inside.

"Look better, feel better, smell better," Gail agreed sitting and hugging her knees.

"What are your plans now?" asked Jankus, squatting opposite her.

Gail had been thinking about that same question since she left the colony. "I don't know," she answered, perplexed. "I can't go back to New Bethand. Maybe try to make it north to the Ambosian colony, Bionx?" She had decided that was her best option. She started a business once; she would do it again, and no one knew her there. Gail asked Pontus, "If I could get someone to guide me that far?"

Pontus shook his head. "You cannot do that," he denied. "In matters as this, the two colonies cooperated. As soon as they discovered who you are the Ambosians would turn you over to New Bethand."

"Oh." A pang of despair stabbed her—Gail felt tired. "I don't know what I'm going to do."

"Pontus tells me you are a healer and seeress," Jankus started hesitantly. "Our medicine woman is dead, and our shaman is old, he will not see many more seasons. Could we convince you to stay here? You would have a home and place of honor."

"You can have the medicine woman's hut!" piped Malta. "No one has moved in yet."

"Gaela might prefer her own hut," admonished her mother. She nodded to Gail. "But we will build that too if you wish."

Stay here? Live like a savage in the outback? Gail surveyed the cramped hut made of clay, sticks, and reeds. Odd smells assaulted her nose, and strange voices came from outside. *I guess I have no choice—deal with it.* She took a deep breath.

"Th-thank you, all of you." She searched the strange faces around her. "I'll try to do a good job." She said to Cuco, "The medicine woman's hut will be fine, I'm sure. You don't have to go to all the trouble of making me a new one." She hoped no shrunken heads hung from the ceiling, though. What would she do if she found some, sneak out at night and bury the evidence? Gail gave a casual look around to see if anything hung from the rafters of this home.

Gail was surprised at how quickly she fell into the simple life of the inland tribe. Unless her healing duties called her away, or she was asked to predict the movement of herds, mornings were spent in chores of hauling water for her cooking fire, helping cultivate the patches of onions, carrots and grains the natives grew, or collecting nuts, fruit and berries from the nearby fields and woods. In the afternoons during the heat of the day, Gail spent the time with other women, gossiping in the shade while they prepared food for the evening meal.

Her greatest problem lay with Amber. The tribe kept dogs for food, fur, and as a warning system against prowlers in the night. To these half-wolves, the Oslo was an enemy who must be barked at and chased every chance they got. A truce developed between the two, but it took some time, and Gail was never easy when Amber sauntered out to investigate by himself.

The tribe consisted of one hundred and fifty-eight individuals, forty of whom were adult males of hunting age. Malta was constantly pointing out the eligible bachelors to Gail. She thought Pontus and Gail would make a good match.

"Please!" Gail was trying to make a waterproof pail with a handle. She had noticed none in camp, and carrying water in animal bladders caused her to make two trips to the river. A bucket would be easier, if she could figure out how.

"If it weren't for him, I'd be in my own home and bed," Gail replied, concentrating on what she was doing. She heard no answer, glanced up, and saw the expression on Malta's face. Gail hasten to explain, "Not that I dislike this village or anything—it's that I never expected to come here in the first place." To change the subject, she asked, "How about you? Do you have a man you've got your eye on?"

Malta looked serious. "I am the daughter of a king and will mate with the son of a chief or other high-born. I have not found any in the nearby tribes that interest me." She giggled. "Chron might be interesting. I do not know—

maybe—we will see."

Gail's duties as healer were easy, although strange to the natives, who were more used to traditional herbal remedies. She tried to combine the two and slowly the tribe accepted her methods.

After the bucket, Gail started working on a fishing net. One of the principal foods of the village were fish scooped out of the river by hand during heavy runs—or harpooned with a barbed spear, but when the fish were not running they could stand for hours without results. After one time crouched over, her back and neck aching, Gail decided to try a different way. Soon she had a half-dozen women weaving cordage out of plant fiber and knotting them into squares, with the young men watching with curious questions. Pontus's only comment was, "The net is strong enough to hold fish, but I do not see how you expect them to jump into it."

Gail giggled and shot a glance at Malta. "Why, it's simple." She grabbed his arm and squeezed his bicep. "I am going to tell the fish if they wish to see a strong warrior as Pontus, they must swim in and hold tight. The fish will leap at the chance."

The rest of the woman laughed. Pontus turned red and left. Gail resumed working.

She had noticed one thing. The goods the villagers traded for were far superior to the stone hand-held tools they made themselves. Gail taught them to make these goods themselves, and they learned quickly and well. There was less reason to trade as the village's self-reliance increased.

The net was a success. In one pull, the village had more fish than a week of doing it the old way. The majority were small, no bigger than Gail's hand. That was okay. Dried, ground into fishmeal, they lasted for months. But also scores of fat catfish, large river perch, along with eels, fell to her net—the village feasted for a few days.

Jankus and other tribal elders thanked her. "By this one act you have taught the village to feed itself for a lifetime," he said to Gail. "If for no other reason, this would make us glad you have come to stay with us."

"Why, thank you," Gail replied, surprised. Making the net was obvious at the time. "I wondered why you didn't think of it yourself." She gestured to the fields of cultivated foodstuff. "You copy the colonists in growing plants. They have nets—why didn't you make those also?"

Jankus nodded. "It was not many seasons ago that our ancestors journeyed to this land from the interior." He waved east. "Before then, we hunted and gathered our food as need be. We settled here, and met the Muians, and they taught us some of these things, but we have not learned everything, nor do we wish to follow all their ways."

***

Gail still basked in the glow of praise a few days later when runners from the other camps appeared at the village. She and Malta were busy going over the net, removing bits of seaweed and retying spots that had separated.

"Malta, what are they doing over there?" Gail asked. Another runner had appeared, going directly to Jankus's home and disappearing within. He reappeared accompanied by Pontus and escorted to the guest hut.

"Who knows." Malta watched the messenger and went back to cleaning the net. "The men are always conferring over where to hunt or hunting territory. If it is anything important we will find out—decision cannot be made without agreement from the whole tribe."

The next day, Jankus called the village together.

"A band of colonists and natives from the coast have crossed the Ubo River, and attacked one of our towns," he said in a sad voice. "My son, Pontus, wishes to band the tribes together and drive the invaders out. He asks for volunteers to join him. What say you?" he checked around. "Fight or flee?"

Pontus stood and moved to stand next to his father. A low buzz rose from the villagers as questions were whispered back and forth. The younger hunters stood and Chron, Pontus's friend, spoke for the group.

"We will go with Pontus and the other hunters to fight the devils! But the village should be prepared to flee if we fail." He glanced at the other men and nodded to Pontus. "But we shall not!"

Jankus waited for other comments. When none came, he said, "It is decided. Runners will go to all the nearby villages and our warriors will leave in the morning. I have spoken."

That night Jankus and his family invited Gail to share a meal. Pontus bragged about what they would do with the invaders once they tracked them down.

"It cannot be tolerated anymore!" he exclaimed, shoving a mouthful of catfish into his mouth and chewing. "They come and take. If they do not like the price, they take anyway. This is not the first village they have sacked because the people did not want to accept what was offered, but it will be the last!" He looked at his father, "We will meet the coastal natives and Muians in a great battle and put an end to this once and for all."

Gail scowled. She knew the arms of the colonists, giant machines called scorpions, which hurled a bolt six-hundred feet, and smaller crossbows, which the coastal natives were equipped with, that struck with deadly accuracy. She knew the weapons of the villagers.

"Are you sure it's wise to confront the colonists in open battle?" she asked Pontus. "After all, they have bows and bolt-throwers, horses and lances—swords. All you have are spears and hide shields."

Jankus surveyed her with new respect, and his eyes shifted to his son. Pontus waved her off and took another bite of fish.

"We outnumber them two to one," he said, licking his fingers. "Our hunters are brave and fight to defend their lands. What are a few arrows against that?"

"Have you ever fought in a battle before? Do you know how?"

"What is there to know?" scoffed Pontus. "The legends of our forefathers tell us. Our strongest warriors will meet and fight theirs. Whoever comes out the victor wins. It is as easy as that."

"I don't think—"

"You fret too much, Gaela," he said, nudging her with a smirk. "This is a man thing. Let the men worry about it."

Foreboding filled Gail. This was not going to work out well. He knew as much of warfare as a fish knew about flying. "But still," she cautioned, "Be careful. Shall I do a foreseeing for you?"

He waved his hand in dismissal. "Do not bother. The fate of the colonists was sealed when they crossed the river."

The next day he left at the head of fifteen other hunters to join parties from the other tribes.

The village packed and waited.

A week later, the warriors trickled back in. In small groups, they limped into the village, many barefoot, some with the wounds of fighting on their bodies, all with haunted looks on their faces. Pontus and Chron appeared last, each half-supporting each other. Two of the hunters were missing.

Pontus looked the worst. Slashes to his arms and back still leaked blood through the bandages he had used to stem the flow. His left hand was swathed in a dressing of leaves. Gail gasped in horror when she saw him.

"Quick—into my hut!" she directed Chron. Jankus, Cuco, and Malta hovered nearby. "How many others are in need of me?"

"None," said Jankus in relief. "A few minor cuts and bruises, and all are hungry; but nothing that threatens their lives."

Gail breathed a sigh of relief. "Good. Let's see what we can do with this one."

They laid Pontus on a pallet and Gail worked on cleaning his wounds. Once she cleared the blood and dirt away, the cuts did not look bad. She bound them with cool, healing leaves. When she unwrapped the dressing on his hand, however, she gasped.

His pinky and half his ring finger were missing.

"Pontus, what happened?!"

"Tried to stop a sword thrust with my hand," he said. "It did not work."

Gail surveyed his mangled fingers. Black, dried blood crusted over the edges. She cleaned the congealed mess and set the skin and bone to healing. "What about your shield?" she asked, as she worked on him.

"Dropped it," he admitted. "When we were forced to retreat, I let it go to run faster."

"Oh." Gail studied his hand in silence. "Don't worry. I'll grow you new fingers."

"Leave them," Pontus muttered. "It will remind me of what a fool I was."

Deep concern passed over Gail's face.

"Malta, go get some of that meat broth you mother used in her stew tonight," Gail ordered. "If there's none left bring the stew itself, and we'll strain the liquid out. I don't want to overload his stomach."

"I'm fine," insisted Pontus, struggling to stand.

"Let yourself be pampered," replied Cuco, pushing him back down.

"What happened?" asked Jankus, sitting beside his son. "Where are the others?"

Pontus gave a heavy sigh. "I do not know. Lost. Dead."

"Tell us all you remember," Cuco said. "Start from the beginning."

Pontus's expression sobered. "When we left here we met the other warriors. We numbered a hundred men."

"A big army." Jankus said with a nod.

"Yes, well, we marched until we found the colonists and lined up against them on the plains." He rolled over onto one elbow. "First we beat our spears on our shields, meaning to scare them away." He grimaced. "Some of our warriors marched out and challenged the coastal tribe's fighters. They laughed, but none came to meet us. Our men called them cowards hoping to provoke a fight.

"When that did not work, we charged."

Pontus shook his head, and gazed at the wall. "I should have listened, or at least asked for a seeing."

"You and your men are back," Gail replied, "that's all that matters."

Pontus did not hear her—his eyes watched the battle.

"First they shot their arrows and bolts, killing the warriors who ran fastest. Many men fell, but we did not stop; some threw their spears, but they fell short. The Muians charged on their horses with lances and swords and killed more of us. We broke—" Tears dripped down Cuco's face. Malta had her fist in her mouth as she listened.

Pontus rubbed his forehead. "We fell back and scattered in all direction; the colonists slashed any they found." He glanced at his hand. "That is where I lost my fingers. That night we located each other in the dark, and agreed to another attack. The next day we tried again, but this time we crept up on them through the tall grass in the morning before they broke camp."

"What happened after that, my son?" asked Jankus in a whisper.

Pontus took a deep breath and let it escape out of his lungs. He turned to his father as if seeing him for the first time.

"Maybe we did some good. At least we got close enough to throw our spears. After the second battle, they marched back across the river and left. Of course—" He glanced at all of them and narrowed his eyes "—they attacked and robbed another village before they did. But at least they are gone."

Pontus settled back and glared at the ceiling.

"It is time you go to sleep and get some rest," Gail murmured. She stared at him and he fell asleep.

"I want to check on the other men and make sure they're all right," Gail said to the others. "You can stay or leave, but Pontus will sleep for a while. I'll be back."

As Gail made her rounds, she picked up more details of the battles. After the second rout, Pontus singlehandedly led a running, rear guard fight through the savannah that allowed his tribe mates and others to escape. The majority of his wounds had come from that.

The village got back to normal. The hunters resumed their duties, leaving before dawn to stalk the herds of antelope or aurochs. The lone exception was Pontus. Long after his wounds healed, he sat outside the bachelor's hut staring into space. When asked to join the hunt, he would frown and wave the speaker away with his mutilated hand. He never spoke in anger, but he became withdrawn and no one knew what to do.

Gail determined to find a solution.

Chapter Nine

"Pontus, I need your help." Gail sat next to the young man who sunned himself outside his hut.

"Huh? Oh, Gaela!" He smiled and then grimaced, touching a shiny scar on his shoulder. "I am sorry, but my wound hurts. I cannot help you."

"That's okay," she said. "This won't take a minute. I don't need you to do anything." She held out a flattened stick and handed it to him. "What do you think?"

Pontus accepted the object and turned it end over end. His brow furrowed and he handed it back. "What is it?"

"A spear thrower. With it, you can throw a spear twice as far as by hand."

Frowning, Pontus took the stick back. "You are kidding!" He examined the hook at one end and the furrow running down the center with thongs at the other end. "How does it work?"

"Well, that's the problem," explained Gail. "I can't find a spear short enough to fit it." She slipped her fingers in the straps and rested the stick on her arm. "You place the spear in the groove with the butt against the rest," she pointed. "Then you cast it like this—" She made a throwing motion; the end of the stick flipped up. "I found some small practice spears for the children that almost fit. If you want, we'll go out to the field and try it."

Intrigued, Pontus nodded and stood. Gail ran to her hut and returned with three smaller versions of the spears the hunters used. They left the palisade and strolled to the fields beyond.

"Remember, I told you these spears are too big and clumsy to work right," Gail cautioned. She put one of the shafts into the slot, took a deep breath, and made her cast.

The missile flew out in a high, wobbly arc, traveled fifty feet, and burrowed into the soft earth. "That wasn't half bad!" she said to herself in surprise. She handed the spear thrower to Pontus. "Here, you try it."

He inserted a spear, hefted it, and made a few tentative throwing motions to get the weapon's feel. He took three short steps and heaved.

Pontus's trajectory was flatter than Gail's was. But the spear flew straight and true, more than two hundred feet. He nodded to himself, scratched his chin, and said, "You are right. Better use a smaller spear, maybe fletch it with feathers."

A few other villagers, who had been in the field, came over and made comments. Pontus passed the spear thrower around and said to Gail, "This will make hunting easier, and maybe, if we had had this, we would have stood a chance against the colonists."

"Well, maybe, maybe not," she hedged. "The colonists still have better weapons, and know how to use them, but I think your problem was more in the line of tactics."

"Huh?" Some of the other bystanders chuckled. Pontus's eyes shot up in puzzlement and he said, "So, besides a weapon maker, you are also a war chief?"

Gail smiled. "No, but I've read accounts of my own people in battle; how they won or lost wars. I have some thoughts." She said to the small group that had gathered, "If you're interested in hearing what I know, come to the council fire tonight. In any case," she shot Pontus another smile, "we've missed you. You haven't been there in a while." She turned and strolled back to the village.

The villagers made a habit of gathering at night in the center of the small hamlet, to gossip, trade information, or talk about the day's events. Gail and Malta wait by the fire in hopes of seeing Pontus who had not attended for many days.

"Do you see him?" asked Gail as Malta scanned the faces of the villagers coming and going.

"No, but it is still early. I told you he was busy all afternoon working on something. He may still be at it." She placed her hand on Gail. "My parents and I want to thank you for trying to break him out of his grief. This is the first time Pontus has been interested in anything since the battle."

"That was my idea," Gail admitted. "I'm trying to shake him out of the depression he's in. I figured something new to think about might do it. As the medicine woman, that's part of my job."

"I do not think anything will bring him back to his old self," replied Malta. "It was his idea to attack the colonists in the first place. He feels like a fool now, and all those people became dead because of him. He feels responsible."

"He shouldn't. The colonists attacked first, and the hunters who went with him were all volunteers. He—Oh!" Gail waved her arm. "There he is now, with Chron."

The two men sauntered over, Pontus clutching the spear thrower and a small, light spear.

"Here." He presented Gail with both. "I think this will do. I worked on it all afternoon—I still have to put some feathers on the tail, to give it balance, but I think this is what we were looking for—a little spear."

Gail hefted the shaft and nodded. It was longer than an arrow, but shorter than the spear they had used as a model. "Let's call them darts—that way we won't confuse them with children's toys." She handed it back.

"Chron wants you to make one of these—spear throwers? For him," said Pontus, "if you would."

Gail patted the ground next to her and the two men sat. "I think the correct name is atl-atl. And yes, I could make another, but I think Chron would be better off making

126

one for himself."

When Chron looked doubtful, Gail hurried to say, "Every man's arm is a different length. For the best fit, it must be made by the man using it." She laid her hand on Charon's shoulder and gave him a pat. "Don't worry, I'll help you, but this way you'll know how to make another if you ever lose this one."

"I have been thinking," Pontus stretched his legs out. "If you know how to make a spear thrower, you could make a bolt thrower like the colonists have, or bows?"

Gail had thought the same thing, but had discarded the idea. "The bow maybe, but the bolt thrower, no. It's too complicated and we need metal parts." She pointed to the spear thrower. "This is easy to construct, though, and makes your spears twice as effective; but I know what you're thinking."

Gail studied the two young men in the firelight. "I told you, it wasn't your weapons that caused you to lose that battle, it was your tactics."

"You said that before," rumbled Pontus. "What do you mean? We fought as our ancestors did."

"The one who wins the battle is the one who brings more speed and shock to the fight." Gail watched him to see if he understood.

Both Chron and Pontus said, "Huh?"

She took a deep breath and tried to remember what she had read in her history books. "You tried to stand up to someone who hit you faster and harder than you could strike back," Gail explained. "Speed and shock."

A few of the hunters strolled over to see the new dart Pontus held, and listened with interest as Gail explained what she was talking about. At the mention of fighting tactics, more heads turned in their direction. Three of the hunters who had fought with Pontus bent close to hear what Gail was saying.

"The colonists attacked you from afar with arrows

and bolts, and again with lances and swords. You never got into the fight. You should not have tried to fight the colonists fight."

"How else can warriors fight?" protested Chron. "If you do not battle man to man who will know which is the swiftest, strongest, or bravest?" He locked eyes on Pontus and said, "The colonists and tribes from the coast do not act like men."

How am I going to explain modern military tactics to these people when I don't half understand them myself? Gail remembered the time she had tried to show her grandmother how a computer worked, and shuddered.

"Look, when you hunt the antelope, do you announce your presence?" countered Gail. "Do you walk up to the Aurochs and say, "Here I am, bull, let us battle?"

The hunters laughed.

Gail chuckled too. "Right. When you hunt, you keep hidden, sneak around the herd until you're downwind, and when you're ready, spring out and attack." She raised her hands in the air. "Speed and shock."

"Men are not animals!" sputtered one of the warriors. "You cannot hunt them the same way."

"Men *are* animals," countered Gail. "Cunning animals, animals that stand on two legs, but animals nevertheless." She said to Chron, "Didn't you say they do not fight like men?"

She heard muttering from the other people gathering around her and said, "If you are to hunt them, you must use every advantage you find—stealth, concealment."

Gail checked how Pontus and Chron took this statement.

They looked uncomfortable.

Her attention swung back to the others. "If you fight the colonists again, which I don't advise, make a plan for an ambush. You understand the territory better than they do. You know the hidden places to lie in wait, to see but not have yourselves seen. Wait until they are in your trap and spring! *Speed and shock.*" She slammed her fist into her palm for emphasis.

Gail looked at the others and realized the whole tribe had clustered around her, listening to her every word. For the briefest of instances she felt embarrassed by her outburst, but realized what she had said was the truth.

The crowd was silent. Pontus scowled, rubbed his chin, and said in a whisper, "I understand what you mean, but the idea is foreign to us. We have never fought our battles that way, and all we know is what our legends tell us. It will take much talk to convince the other tribes to fight in the manner you suggest."

***

The rainy season started—long periods when the villagers huddled in their homes, or dashed between the torrid of raindrops to visit each other. Paths became streams and streams swelled into impassable rivers.

Pontus and Malta ran laughing through a curtain of rain to Gail's hut. "How are you holding up?" gasped Malta, wringing water out of her hair.

"Okay, I guess," replied Gail, peering out at the storm—a flash of lightning followed by a boom of thunder. She jumped and closed the door." I don't remember it being this bad at the colony."

"It is not," chuckled Pontus, sitting down and wiping moisture out of his eyes. "The farther you come inland, the wetter it gets." He rubbed his arms, gesturing east. "I hear stories of thick jungle and swamps if you travel that way, but here it is not bad. The river floods and brings good earth to our fields, and the grass grows green and lush for the herds to feed on."

"The shaman is coming to our hut tonight to tell stories," said Malta. "Are you going, too?"

"I don't think so." Gail pointed to an assortment of

leaves and flowers that lay on her cot, left in the hut from the dead medicine woman. "I have all these herbs to sort. I want to get them organized."

"You do not need those things," said Pontus. "The old healer used different magic. Your way is better."

"Oh, yeah?" Even with the bad weather, Gail had seen two strange hunters come into the village today and go straight to the bachelor hut where Pontus lived. She had a feeling she knew what the young men talked about huddled away from their elders.

A cold, wet breeze blew into the hut. Gail threw another log into her cooking fire. "Have you discussed my ideas about fighting with the rest of the hunters? That was a better way too."

Pontus chose his words carefully. "The warriors of this tribe agree the spear thrower is a good addition to hunting; and think you are right about how to beat the Muians, but they are uncomfortable about breaking with the old ways. The other tribes—" he smirked and looked doubtful "—are taking a wait-and-see attitude. They are still shaken by our defeat; fighting from concealment is strange to us, and uh…" He sounded embarrassed, "They are not used to hearing women give advice in military matters."

Gail's lips formed a hard line and she stared from Pontus to Malta. "Is this true?"

"It is not what you think!" Malta exclaimed. "Women have a say in every aspect of village life, we have a council of women—but in matters of hunting and warfare, well, those are—man things."

"The defense of this village isn't a 'man thing!'" snapped Gail, "It's the responsibility of every man, woman, and child here!" She was breathing hard. "As I said, I'm not urging you to fight, but if the colonists keep attacking and taking what they want, we will have too. You and the rest of the tribes had better realize that."

Pontus placed his hand on her shoulder in alarm. "Calm down, Gaela, Calm down. I am sure the other tribes will come around. We have to allow them time."

She shook his hand off and turned back to the herbs she'd been sorting. "Humph! Let's hope the colonists give them time!"

***

The rains slowed and stopped. The hunters went out tracking the herds, while practicing with their new spear throwers. The women dug up the fields and scattered seeds, trampling them into the ground. The whole village went out with Gail's fish net.

Not needed after one pull, Gail found herself in the way. With a wave of her hand to the other busy villagers, she walked down the beach. She had never investigated upstream before, and the hunters had cautioned her not to wander off by herself. Even this close to the village, scavengers were drawn to the refuge heaps of the small town. While not overly worried, she kept an eye out for anything unusual.

A flash of light caught her eye from a mound of gravel washed up high on the bank and left by the receding water. She dug at the mound with her foot and withdrew a small yellow nugget.

This is gold, she said to herself, turning the rock over. It looked, and felt, like the real thing. "I know it is!" She fell on her knees, shifting and straining pebbles through her fingers, and worked down the beach, pushing discarded stones aside as she went. Within an hour, she had a palm full of the precious metal.

"Hey! Are you all right?" Pontus ran up the beach looking for her, holding his spear thrower. "They said you had gone this way, but I did not see you anywhere. You know wandering off is not safe, unless you bring weapons." He stopped beside her out of breath. "What are you doing, making sand huts?" He nudged a mound of gravel she had left by the water. "Pretty silly for a grown woman."

"Pontus, look!" Gail held her hand out. "Gold!"

"Gold?" He screwed up his face in concentration. "I have only seen gold once, and that time it was in the shape of a coin. This is the raw metal?" He stirred the nuggets around in her palm with his forefinger. "They do not look like much. These sometimes wash up here after the rains. I did not think they were worth anything." His eyes widen. "Can these be turned in the rounds the colonists use for money?"

"Even this," Gail replied, holding up a nugget with worry in her voice, "may be traded for many cowries."

"Good," Pontus replied, the trader in him planning what he would do with the nuggets. "If they are that valuable, the colonists will trade whatever we want for these stones."

"Yes, that is true," Gail said, stirring the nuggets in her hand, "but—"

"Great." Pontus cut her off and nodded in satisfaction. "I would rather trade worthless stones we find on the beach, then our stores of ivory and hides we have to hunt for, anyway." He kicked a pile of gravel Gail had left and laughed. "A lot easier to stalk, also."

Gail's mind worked. "We can use them in trade, but I wouldn't let anyone know where they came from. It would be dangerous, and I don't know how we'll manage that."

"Really? Why?"

"Because the Muians would kill for this shiny metal; that's why." Gail gestured downstream to the village, fields, and land beyond. "If they knew where it came from, hundreds, maybe thousands, of prospectors would pour in here looking for this stuff. They wouldn't care if this was the village land or not. The raids you suffered would be nothing in comparison to what would happen. They would kill all of you off and not think anything about it."

Pontus looked down at the gold in her palm, and gently folded her fingers over it. "Maybe we should keep this our secret unless we find something we want to trade for."

They walked back up the beach. Gail dropped the nuggets into her pouch and asked, "Now that the rains have stopped, will traders be coming?"

"Independents, yes," agreed Pontus, skipping a rock across the water. "Those we do not mind. They travel in groups of threes and fours with pack mules, hauling in the things we need." He flashed a grin. "Or the things they *think* we need. They have come for years. They take ivory or hides as payment and everyone is happy."

"Are there many?"

"Traders? No. Each has his own territory." Pontus skipped another stone and watched it danced across the water. "Alak-an and his men have never tried to cheat us. It is the colonists, along with the costal tribes, that cause all the problems. They march in, take what they want, and if anyone complains, they burn the village." His voice took on a bitter tone. "I am sick of it. We are yips to them, dirty stinking yips. Well, this *yip* has had enough!"

"It would be a good idea to caution our hunters to stay away from the colonies for now," warned Gail. "We'll deal with the traders if we need anything that bad." She touched the white marks on Pontus's back, the scar on his shoulder, and glanced at his hand. "That should keep some of our people out of trouble, anyway." She winked at him and laughed.

"Only the smart ones," Pontus chuckled, following her gaze. He placed his half hand on her shoulder and gave it a small shake. "The rest of us are glad we have a good healer in the village."

"Hey, if you two are done taking strolls, why not help walk some of these fish back to the village!" Chron held up a large catfish by its gills.

Gail leaped back from Pontus. She hadn't realized the whole village was watching them walk down the beach touching and talking.

Malta is never going to let this go now, Gail thought. *She'll have us married with two kids by the time I walk back to my hut.*

Pontus laughed and called out, "I have seen catfish walk from pond to pond in the dry season, Chron. Jump on its back and ride him up to the village yourself!"

Pontus fell in beside Chron, began picking up fish, and tossing the finny prizes into a basket. Gail followed his example with one of her smaller handled containers and trailed the two men. Soon Malta walked next to Gail.

"Getting friendly with my brother?" she teased, tossing her hair, and giving Gail a sideways glance. "I thought you did not like him, but—" she added, "he is almost as handsome as Chron, is he not?"

"Hush. I was cautioning him to stay away from the colonies," insisted Gail in a whisper, turning a faint pink, "and to keep our hunters away, too. We don't need anyone else beaten."

Malta sobered. "True, we do not want to go looking for trouble."

Two days later, trouble came looking for them.

A panting runner came into the village as the sun was setting in the west.

"Colonists," he announced, "and natives from the coast! They travel this way in a long column—the other tribes have abandoned their villages and flee." The runner turned to Jankus who had been sitting at the council fire. "After I am done here, I will rejoin my tribe; they are already packed to leave."

"Your tribe is not staying to fight?" asked Pontus.

The runner scrubbed a hand across his face. "No, we are not." He accepted a bladder of water Pontus gave him and drank deep. One of the women hurried to an outdoor cooking fire and brought back a bowl of stew. "We are afraid of what happened last time. None will remain to battle."

"Sit, Kofu." Jankus waved to a seat next to him by the fire. "It is too late for you to leave now. Eat, rest—you may sleep in the guest hut for tonight, or with the bachelors, but until then tell us what you know, or what you have heard."

Kofu nodded and sat. After he finished his stew, he licked his fingers and said, "The colonists encircled that small village on this side of the Ubo River, you know the place? They demanded tribute."

"Tribute?" Jankus said. "Why?"

Kofu shrugged. "Who knows?—an excuse to take whatever they had, which was not much. The villagers gave them some ivory, along with the myrrh they collected for trade, but it is too soon after the rains to have much of anything to sell."

He turned to Pontus. "The colonists got angry and hung the headman as an object lesson."

"What!" The villagers muttered to each other in disbelief and fell silent again as Gail said, "What possible purpose could that serve? You said they turned all their trade goods over."

Kofu shook his head in dismay. "I do not know. Maybe their guides told the colonists the villagers were lying. All I know is that they left and headed north toward the border about a week ago. We found this out from refugees who had fled to our village. That is when my leader sent out runners to warn other tribes."

The silence around the fire turned into a murmur that grew into a babble of voices. Jankus put his hands up for quiet. "Has anyone else seen these colonists since?"

"No," Kofu denied. "I know the trails hereabouts. They mean to swing north of here, then circle around and head back west."

Jankus addressed the rest of the village. "We will begin packing tonight and leave in the morning, going east. Take whatever you do not want to lose."

"NO." It was Pontus. "The rest of you may flee like a frightened herd of antelope, but I will fight!" He picked out some of the other hunters by eye. "I will fight by myself if I have to, but I will never give up."

"Pontus," his mother Cuco said, her voice shaking in fear, "the other tribes are fleeing. What can you, and our hunters do, to stop the colonists by yourselves."

Jankus added, "My son, you tried that before with many more warriors than you are able to muster now. You know what happened, we must go."

Pontus hesitated, the muscles in his neck standing out as he bit back a reply to his father. Then he slumped, reached out his hands, and balled his fists in anger. "Yes, I know you are right. I will pack."

"Pontus!" It was Chron. "How—"

"No, my father is right. We lost last time, there are too many of them. We have no chance of winning. We must go."

Gail had watched this exchange with growing anger. What right had the Muians and their native allies to attack innocent people? Murder and rob what they wanted? She remembered the porter she'd seen kicked in the market place because he'd dropped some dishes and could contain herself no longer.

"NO!"

All the faces reflected in the firelight swung in her direction.

"No, Pontus," she repeated. "You were right the first time. We *should* fight. The colonists must learn that they cannot come in here and take what they want. You lost the first time, but even if you lose again, the Muians will understand that this isn't their playground to do as they please."

"Thank you." Pontus sat up. "But how do we fight without getting slaughtered again?"

"Remember what we talked about?"

Pontus looked straight ahead into the fire.

"Speed and shock?"

"And stealth," Gail replied. "Don't forget about that."

Pontus appeared baffled. He stared into the firelight as he tried to decide how he would handle these new tactics. Finally, he shook his head and looked at Gail.

She nodded. "I will come up with a plan."

Pontus told his father and the others, "Given a few hunters, and luck, I will defeat them, or at least turn the Muians back. I am sure of it."

***

"Remember what I said." Gail cautioned the hunters that night, after the others had gone to sleep. Twenty faces watched her from around the fire. "Find some place to set an ambush; keep concealed. It's the same as hunting a herd of elephants. When the colonists walk into your trap— attack! *Speed and shock.* Hit them and hit them hard."

Pontus grinned. Chron asked, "What happens if they fight back? They number more than we do, and their weapons are better."

Gail tried to think. This wasn't as easy as predicting the location of a lost son, or commodity prices, or the best place to sell hides. Too many small details existed, variables, to give a simple yes or no prediction—but she felt rightness in her answer.

"It depends. If they're disorganized and fight back in small groups, gang up on them and attack. The colonists will be confused and frightened—you won't. If they act in an organized group, look well prepared to defend themselves—run away."

"That's it, run away?" Chron said, annoyed by the

137

thought of giving up a fight they had spent hours preparing for. "You cannot mean that."

"Oh yes, I do," replied Gail, standing up and pacing around the fire, giving each warrior a stern look in the eye. "Remember, it's better to be alive to fight again, then be a dead hero. None of you has anything to gain by getting yourselves killed. Besides, you know the terrain. Hit and run. It shouldn't be hard to evade them."

Pontus stood. In one hand, he held his spear thrower, in the other, a handful of darts.

"It is a good plan." His face glistened in the shadows of the firelight. "With luck, and the good wishes of the spirits, it will work. He nodded to the group. "We leave in the morning."

Chapter Ten

E ight days later, the warriors returned. This time the village heard them long before they came into view. Twenty dirty, hungry, laughing men walked up the trail to the palisade, two leading tough little ponies the colonists used, while three others tugged on a string of pack mules loaded down with bundles. Pontus led this procession up to the gates, a bow slung over his shoulder.

"We did it!" he whooped to the startled villagers who poured out of the palisade to greet the returning warriors. Gail was in the lead, along with Jankus, Cuco, and Malta. Pontus ran to them, grabbed Gail by the shoulders, and whirled her around in a circle. "It worked!" he shouted. "Your plan worked, we did it! We defeated the colonists!"

"What happened?" gasped Gail, laughing as he placed her back on her feet.

"I will tell you in a minute," said Pontus with a wide grin. In a louder voice he said, "Everyone! To the council fire!"

Friends and relatives crowded around the hunters, escorting them into the village. After they had all gathered by the fire, Pontus began to speak.

"We traveled on the path leading north for four days until we met a group of villagers fleeing south. They told us the colonists followed two days' march behind their party, taking whatever they wanted from the villages they passed. We hunted along the trail until we came to a spot where it ran close to a cliff with steep drop-offs on both sides. We sent out scouts to warn us of the approaching Muians and waited."

***

The colonists rode down the trail. "When do we

arrive at the next village?" The leader of the safari paused and wiped sweat from his face. He swung his head in a wide circle in search of the town and then glared down at his Batu guide. "Well?"

The native studied the sun and pointed to a ragged gash between the hills. "That way, tomorrow afternoon if we are lucky," he replied in his singsong lilt.

"Good. I hope we get something better than these moth-eaten hides we've been picking up." He swatted at the gnats that swarmed around his face. "I hate the bush."

Pontus watched the line of horses and mules following behind the colonists. He waved across the gap of the gorge and shouted, "They come, be ready." Chron huddled next to him. Pontus asked, "Is everything prepared?"

"Yes," his friend replied. "The end of the canyon is blocked with boulders and logs we pushed down from the top. Typhon waits on the other ridge to prevent escape. Once they get in here, there is no way to get out."

"Good." Pontus wrapped his hand around a small bag hanging down from his neck and said a small prayer to the savannah spirits.

The head of the safari entered the gorge. Pontus waited until the last of the natives and mules were below him and yelled, "NOW!" He sprang up from the boulder he hid behind, and heaved a dart as hard as possible at a trailing Batu porter.

At the head of the column, four of the colonists had fallen; the rest spurred their horses up the trail. The coastal natives that followed milled about in confusion, tried to push on, but as missiles continued to rain down, changed their minds and retreated down the valley, pulling their mules with them.

"Chron, quick, they are escaping." Pontus and a few others picked off the natives one by one, as they scrambled back to the mouth of the gorge.

At the head of the valley, the colonists hit a blockage of rocks and fallen trees. They dismounted and banded together in a tight circle, bows returning fire uphill at the hunters, who hurled darts down in return.

Typhon gestured to three of the hunters near him. "Give me a hand," he grunted, putting his back to the boulder he was using for protection. Two other men joined them; the massive rock teetered, and started a slow descent down the valley side. It gained speed, pulling other rocks along in a small avalanche.

The boulders bounced and shattered into razor-sharp shrapnel, raised dust, as they cascaded down the slope, until they plowed into the knot of colonists.

The other hunters saw what Typhon had done and more boulders crashed down on the safari, clogging the bottom, sending the Muians scurrying back the way they had come while the villagers cheered in victory.

"They retreat—follow them!" Typhon and his men flitted from boulder to boulder, still hurling darts, and screaming death threats. With the trail blocked by falling stones, the colonists had no choice but to abandoned their horses and withdraw back to the entrance of the valley on foot, still shoot arrows at any targets they found.

The remains of the coastal natives had long since fled the gorge. The band of colonists stopped at the mouth of the valley, turned, fired one more volley of arrows, and followed their fleeing allies.

Pontus gestured to Typhon and they slid down the side of the gorge. "Should we continue to pursue?" gasped Typhon.

Pontus counted the rest of the hunters as they dashed along the valley floor to join the two. "Did we lose anyone?" he countered.

"I do not think so," replied Typhon. He repeated, "Should we follow the colonists?"

The adrenalin rush of excitement Pontus had felt

during the battle left him, and he felt exhausted. "Yes, but I ran out of darts," he said.

"Me too," replied Typhon. A few of the other warriors grunted agreement.

The rest of the hunters had come down the slopes waiting for his instruction. "Search the valley, and see what weapons you can discover," Pontus commanded. "Check where the colonists fell, we might be able to find bows there." He said to Chron. "Collect the horses and mules; strip the bodies of anything useable. When we are ready, we will trail what is left of the safari to the Ubo River."

***

Pontus concluded his story. "We killed a few more that had been wounded and fallen behind the others, the rest escaped us, abandoning what gear they carried and fleeing into the woods emptyhanded. Without weapons or shelter, they will not last long. We are safe, at least for a time."

The crowd dispersed, small groups clustering around each hunter as they told their individual tales. Gail walked with Jankus and Cuco to their hut along with Pontus and Malta. Cuco bustled around throwing together an impromptu dinner. Pontus looked at Gail and his face broke out in puzzlement.

"You look different, somehow," he said with his brow furrowed. His eyes opened wide and he exclaimed, "You have cut your hair. Why?"

Gail smiled. "Oh, it was too long and always getting twigs and leaves tangled in it, and my hair would *smell* if I didn't wash it good every day. I was afraid I'd get bugs." She patted her short curls. "Now it's easy to take care of. I think it looks kinda good, too. What do you think?"

"I, er—" Pontus glanced at his sister. Malta stared sternly back with her head tilted. "Yes, cute. It's nice."

"Thank you." Gail leaned forward and said eagerly, "Now tell us what happened, the details."

"There is not much else to tell. We counted twenty colonists, three times that many natives." He appeared confused, and then exclaimed, "We checked the packs on the mules afterward, and found not one item for trade. They were not even making a pretense of bartering!"

"Well, let us hope they now realize that they are not welcome in the outback if they are going to raid and murder people," said Jankus. He grumbled, "Sometimes I wish our ancestors never sought this land. The living is good, game plentiful, but this continual fighting in the last few years— He folded his arms, crossed his legs, and stopped speaking in disgust.

Pontus nodded. "We killed three quarters of their company. If they make it back to the coast, they will warn their friends not to come in here and attack us, or take what they want."

"If the packs didn't contain trade goods, what did they contain?" Gail asked.

"Nothing much, ivory and hides stolen from the villages they passed, but we scavenged ten bows, arrows, swords and knives off the dead. We will be well armed if they ever return and start attacking again."

Gail pushed aside the fear she felt at the thought of the colonists returning to fight and looked grim. She did not want Pontus and the others to get overconfident and start a war they could not win. "If they ever come back in strength, we'll need more than that, but let's hope they've learned their lesson and don't."

She quizzed every visitor who came into the village about word from the coast, or if they had seen anymore colonial parties trudging through the bush. She gathered little information though. Most of the travelers traveled from nearby villages to hear about the tribe's victory over the colonists, or to gossip about the region's affairs.

Pontus set up a bow range and kept the hunters busy practicing with their new weapons when they weren't hunting. Soon most of the arrows were lost or broken and the hunters resorted to spend long hours making more with flint tips.

One day, three traders wandered into the village leading a string of pack mules.

"Ho, Jankus! Do ya mind if we set up?" the tallest of the three called out to the headsman. Without waiting for a reply, all three began unloading the mules and spreading out blankets in front of the palisade gates.

Jankus nodded assent and tried to hold back a smile as the rest of the villagers crowded around watching. Copper and bronze pots appeared from the packs along with glass beads, a few bottles of Muian wine, hunting knives and bolts of cotton cloth.

The head trader, Alak-an, picked up a bracelet of red-colored beads and presented it to Cuco.

"Here ya go! This will look nice with the necklace ya bought last year. Take it—it's a present."

Cuco reached out and slipped it on her wrist. Jankus grinned at her and said to Alak-an, "I hope your gift does not cost me too much."

The trader laughed. "When we're done 'ere, I'm sur' everyone'll be 'appy."

Pontus and Gail drifted over to inspect the trade goods. Something about Alak-an was familiar. She had it—this was the same group of traders she had seen on her first day in New Bethand; the ones she had made the prophecy about in the Smokestack Inn to Nicos.

Gail's first impulse was to hang back and lose herself in the other villagers. She sidestepped behind Pontus. If the colonists discovered she was here in this village, they might come looking for her, but then she decided to take a gamble. In the previous months, she had lost weight, her fat turning into hard muscle. Her skin had darkened from the sun to a deep brown, and she had cut her long hair. No one would mistake her for a native, but she didn't look like a Muian either. She would act nonchalant, get close to the traders, and see what information she could pick up.

Gail nudged Pontus and they wandered closer to Jankus and Alak-an.

"... heard tell about some ruckus out here a few months ago," Alak-on said to Jankus.

"Colonial raiding party attacking villages," replied Jankus noncommittally.

"Yea. A few of those boys made it back to New Bethand. Serves 'em right!" The trader wiped his hands on his pants as if trying to rid himself of the colonists. "They make it bad fer everyone. Got the whole colony stirred up, though, I hope nothing comes of it, damn fools should know better than trying to come into the bush and steal from you people anyway. Pontus—" The trader reached out and clasped they young man on the back. "—haven't seen ya in a while. Done any trading in the colonies lately?"

Pontus shook his head. "No, I have not. Too dangerous. Besides, it is as easy to wait for you traders to come here, as to haul ivory and hides out to the coast." He eyed the trade goods strewn on the blankets. "But the choice might be better in the colony."

Alak-an chuckled and waved to his mules. "Just as well, I told ya, them boys are hoppin' mad. Tell me what you want and I'll bring er out, if I can haul it. Always willin' to oblige a customer."

Gail listened to the trader with growing concern. So, the colonists were not going to leave well enough alone. Why were they being stupid? She had to figure out a way for the village to protect themselves better, and this trader, Alak-an might be the way to do it, if he were greedy enough.

The bartering continued all day and well into the evening. The trader's stock of goods shrank, while the piles of ebony, hides, and ivory around them grew. When it came time for the evening meal, Jankus invited the traders to eat with them and stay overnight in the guest hut.

Gail waited until it was well after dark and then caught Pontus leaving the council fire.

"Let's go talk to the traders," she suggested.

"Why? Is there something you saw? They are all packet up for the night. We can get whatever you want in the morning before they go."

She tugged on his arm and said in an undertone, "It's not something they have—it's something we need."

The traders sat outside the guest hut, calculating their profits from the day's trading. They passed around a bottle of unsold Muian wine.

"Pontus!" Alak-an saw the two coming and waved. "Come on over and join us!" He looked at Gail. "And who's ya friend? I don't remember seeing ya around here 'afor?"

"My name is, uh, Gaela." Gail used the native pronunciation. "My mother and Cuco are cousins. We live in the far mountains of the sky." She waved toward the interior. "I have need of what you can sell me." She and Pontus sat next to Alak-an.

His lips formed a silent "O" and he said, "And what do ya want that you didn't see here today?" He watched Gail shrewdly. "Pretty cloths? Perfume? They don't come cheap."

"Bows, bolts, swords," she replied, ignoring his comment. "We have many dangerous animals in my country. My people need protection."

Alak-an's eyes narrowed even farther. "Whoa! Hold on." He gave Pontus a questioning look. "Ya know selling them things out here in the bush is forbidden. Not much trade in them anyhow. What game are ya two playin' at?"

"No game," replied Pontus, not sure what was going on. He pointed to Gail. "She is looking to buy. The question is, are you willing to sell?"

One of Alak-an's partners spoke up, "Why not? If they've got the money."

The trader scratched his chin, glanced at his partners, and said in a low voice, "If we got caught, do ya know what would happen?" He drew a finger across his throat. "It would be off with our heads!"

Gail fished around in her pouch and produced a large nugget of gold. She laid it in Alak-an's hand. "It would mean great riches also, for the traders who brought these things to me."

Alak-an gaped at the rock in surprise—his companions bent close and stared hungrily. One picked it up, weighted the nugget in his palm, and passed the metal to the other. "Where'd you get this?" he whispered.

"In my land we have many." Gail left that hanging and repeated to Alak-an, "Bows, bolts, swords."

The nugget passed back to Alak-an. He studied the gold in his hand. "I don't know where'd I get maybe more than one or two crossbows," he said cautiously. "The bolts fer 'em are no problem, but the rest? I told ya, they're not sold as trade items."

"Do not try to fool us," Pontus put in with a knowing smile. "You will buy a few here—'Oh, I lost my old one—Oh, I need a backup—Oh, this one is for my friend.' You will try that in the other colony, too, I bet."

Alak-an's face clouded up and he looked as if he'd bitten into a rotten piece of fruit.

"Well, and suppose'n I could get my hands on some. This—" he held his palm out with the lone nugget "—ain't enough ta cover the cost—or the risk."

Gail reached into her pouch again and this time withdrew a large handful of nuggets. She dropped a few more into Alak-an's waiting hand, and let him watch as she poured the rest back into her bag.

"If you get me what I want, we'll cover your cost, your risk, and more. But the question is, will you get me what I want?"

Alak-an's fingers closed around the gold. "I ain't makin' no promises." he snarled, "and it isn't gonna be quick. I'm gonna have to go to Bionx, and swing over to New Bethand, and come back this way again. That's a mighty long haul through the bush. It'll be a month or two before I make it here, but I'll see what I find."

Gail nodded and stood—so did Pontus. "That's okay, as long as you bring what I need," she said. "Tomorrow morning I return to my people. If I am not here when you come back, Pontus will act as my agent. Good night."

As they left the traders, Pontus whispered to Gail, "What are you up to? What was that all about?"

Gail glanced over her shoulder at Alak-an who was watching their receding backs. "Hush! I'll explain tomorrow after they've left. In the morning, I'm going to hide, tell them I've left tonight to go back to my own country. The less they know about me the better."

She planned to try to keep her association with the tribe of Jankus at a minimum. She already regretted telling Alak-an she was related to Cuco. If the authorities caught the trader, he would have no qualms about telling where the gold came from, or who had given it to him. The thing she feared—the colonists and the colonial army pouring in to this region—would come to pass. If the government back in Bethand found out the natives were trying to arm themselves, they would send troop here too.

In the morning, Gail stayed in her hut until the traders concluded their business and left. She leashed Amber. "Come on, lazybones, let's take a walk," and went in search of Pontus. She found him sitting outside the bachelor's hut with a few of the other hunters.

She gave a warm smile to his friends, and said to Pontus, "I'm bored. I want to take a walk by the beach, but I don't have anyone to go with me."

Pontus rose and said to the others. "I think we have finished talking about the hunt for tomorrow." He said to Gail, "I will walk with you, if you do not mind. I could use the exercise anyway."

Gail heard a few snickers and hushed talk as she strolled away toward the water. Pontus hurried to catch up. "Gaela! Now tell me what is going on. What was all of that about last night?"

She nodded to him, eyed the other hunters, and slowed long enough for him to catch up. She swung down the trail toward the river. "Come, I'll explain everything."

After they reached the water, Gail unleashed Amber and let him run free. She and Pontus strolled down the beach, Gail occasionally stooping to pick up a shiny nugget and place it in her pouch.

"We won the last battle with the colonists, but I'm convinced they'll be back," she said. "I know these people, *you* know them. Right now I bet they're talking about how to teach the 'Yips' their place. That trader, Alak-an, said as much."

"You do not think they would come back and attack us again, do you?"

Gail nodded. "That's exactly what I think. The colonists will learn from their mistakes and return. If we win *that* battle, they'll still come back, but stronger and better armed."

Shock and disbelief crossed his face, and then Pontus looked thoughtful. He stopped and scooped up a nugget, handing it to Gail. "I had not thought of that, but what can we do?"

Gail talked to herself as much as Pontus. "If we lose, they'll rape this country and kill us all. If our warriors keep winning, they'll come back stronger and stronger—so we must win, but to do that we'll need more weapons than we can salvage after battles. We'll need lots of weapons and lots of warriors."

Pontus gazed at her in awe. "You are having a vision?"

Gail shook her head. "Yes—no—maybe." She laughed and kicked a pile of gravel on the beach. "You forget, I'm the Seeress. It's my job to think of the future, but I don't need a foretelling to know what's going to happen here. That's pretty obvious."

She wasn't sure at all. She was venturing into unknown territory. The futures were too cloudy to read, and she had no experience in military matters. Her books didn't tell her what to do. She would have to fake it and pray for the best.

Pontus tore his gaze away from her and searched the beach again. "I guess you are right. I did not think that far ahead."

"And that's why I want to get more weapons. If this Alak-an will get them for us."

"He can."

"Let's hope he does, and let's pray no one finds out, and he doesn't get caught," Gail replied. She checked the tall grass for the Oslo. "Amber! Amber! Come back here, I told you, don't wander off!"

Amber came and brushed against her legs, spotted something in the bushes, and stalked off again. "Okay," Gail said, "we get weapons from the independent traders to keep on fighting. Where do we recruit the men? The other tribes have refused to fight—they're scared."

Gail looked for the Oslo. "Amber! Where'd you go? Don't run off again!" She picked up a stout branch from the bank and dug into the gravel.

Pontus shook his head.

"We'll get men," Gail said again to herself, shaking her head knowingly, lost in her own world. "As long as we keep winning, men will flock to us, the tribes will unite." She looked back at Pontus. "The problem is to keep on winning."

Pontus nodded enthusiastically. "We must keep our hunters training with the crossbows day and night."

Amber pranced back with a black snake twice as long as he was. The cat laid it at Gail's feet. *"Amber, get that thing out of here,"* Gail screamed, and swung at the reptile with her stick. With one quick motion, she caught the serpent in the middle and flipped it away.

The snake twisted in agony and slithered off with Amber in pursuit. Gail and Pontus ran back down the beach, laughing. After a moment, Amber stalked back looking sad and growling in short huffs.

"Bad cat!" Gail scolded. She put the leash back on Amber. "Practice while you're hunting," advised Gail to Pontus as they continued to the village. "Remember— stealth, speed, shock. I wouldn't nose it around to the others, though, that you're practicing for war," she amended, "especially to your father."

A group of women washed clothes at the river's edge. Pontus and Gail waved to them as they walked by.

"You do not have to tell me that. He has cautioned me over and again to stay out of trouble."

"Well, this time I think trouble has looked for us, and there's not a lot we can do about it," Gail replied. "Your father will come around, I think, but by that time it will be too late. Don't go telling the other hunters what we've been discussing here either. They'll get too eager and do something stupid, before we're ready."

The warriors practiced. They spent long hours on the practice range with spear-throwers and the new bows, longer hours on the hunt, tracking herds of antelope and elephants through the tall grass of the savannah.

Gail continued to wander up and down the beach, collecting gold nuggets wherever she found them, but they became harder to find.

Two months later the traders returned with Alak-an leading his string of mules loaded with wooden crates strapped to their backs. Gail faded into the background while Pontus and the other hunters helped unload the animals.

"That girl here?" Alak-an asked. The rest of the villagers crowded around, inspecting what the trader had brought.

"No," Pontus lied. "She trekked back to her village, but said she would be returning before the rains started."

Pontus pried one of the crates open and found it full of wooden stocks for crossbows. "What is this?" he demanded, glancing from the box to the trader. "Where is rest of the bows?"

Alak-an nodded to the other crates and wiped sweat off his face. "All there. Bows, triggers, strings, iron heads for bolts. I couldn't buy complete bows, didn't even try—there aren't that many for sale in New Bethand, and people'd get suspicious. I had to hustle to get this; bought some in new Bethand, some in Bionx. Got lucky and found a merchant ship brought some over from Bethand on spec. Tell that woman she'll have to assemble them herself when you see her. Sorry."

Pontus opened the other crates. In each, he found different parts of the bows. He shook his head in puzzlement.

Alak-an shrugged, and chuckled. He stuck out his hand. "You have money? I've gotta get back to the coast. Heard tell a ship's comin' in from Ambos, got war surplus stuff from the civil war there. Maybe I'll get luck again and find those swords ya wanted."

Pontus handed over a heavy leather bag of gold nuggets Gail had given to him without comment.

"Tell that girl we'll be back in about a month, give or take. Might be more take—" Alak-an rubbed his chin and his lips turned down. "Heard a rumor the colonists were gettin' a few expeditions together to raid in the bush. If'n they come this way, I'm waitin' 'til they're gone. I don't want any trouble. Where is her village anyway?"

"She told you—the mountains." Pontus gestured toward the east. "I have never been there. It is a long journey." He cocked his head and asked, "Expeditions, you say? Do you know where they are going?"

The two other traders had finished unloading the boxes with the help of the hunters. They waved at Alak-an to hurry. He nodded and said, "Nope. Only that they were goin' inta the bush. Make sure that girl gets these crates out of here if they show up. If the colonists find weapons, there'll be the spirit of the underworld to pay." He hefted the leather bag of gold and dropped it into his pouch. "I'm off," he announced. "Wish me luck."

The rest of the hunters began cracking open the boxes and examining the contents. Jankus walked out of the palisade and watched with a growing expression of disapproval on his face.

"What is this?" he asked Pontus, gesturing to the parts the men spread on the packed earth.

"Ah, er—crossbows, Father," Pontus confessed. "The few we have work so well in hunting game that I thought we could use some more."

"Hunting game, is it?" Jankus looked at his son. "You know it is prohibited for us to buy weapons from the colonists and illegal for them to sell."

"Yes, Father."

Jankus gazed at the crates again. "Make sure you use them well—and do not get caught." He spun on his heel and strode back into the palisade.

Gail had followed behind Jankus with a small crowd of women and children, and stood waiting until the old man had marched off. She hurried to Pontus and said, "I thought he was going to put a stop to what we're doing before we got started."

Pontus was watching the retreating back of his father. "Me too."

Gail put her finger to her mouth and asked, "Do you think he realizes what we're preparing to do?"

"I am sure of it," Pontus replied, looking sad. "What do we do with these things now?" The hunters had opened all the crates and taken out parts, trying to figure how they went together. They looked at Gail and Pontus in puzzlement.

Gail snatched up one of the stocks out of the crates, and took a crossbow from a hunter standing nearby and held both up. "We have weapons! I need a few volunteers to put them together. They can use the existing bows we have for examples." She raised her head and saw two young hunters whom she knew were good at making traps for animals and constructing their own spears. "You— You," she pointed at the men. "Are you willing?"

Both grinned and nodded.

Gail slapped her hands together. "Good. You've been elected. Some of you gather up these pieces and bring the crates into the village. I'll leave you two in charge of assembling the weapons," she said to the two young men. "If you have any questions, ask."

A few of the men leaped to the crates, the majority stood hesitant and glanced from Gail to Pontus. With a frown, he gestured to the boxes and they led the procession into the village, the two new mechanics whispering to each other with shrugs and shakes of their heads.

As the hunters got down to business of sorting parts, Gail took Pontus aside to a log in the shade of the palisade.

"I did not think what we planned would be obvious to my father," Pontus said. "I hope we do not have to use these weapons."

Gail swatted at a fly and remarked, "You heard what Alak-an said—more expeditions. I've been chased out of so many places since I've come to this land—I'm tired of having people push me around." She swatted at more flies and surveyed the village. "This is Gaela's last stand," she joked.

Pontus studied her eyes, which had gone bleak. "I know it was my fault that you had to come here—"

"Nonsense!" Gail replied with a laugh. "It was my choice to free you—anyway, it had to be done. What the colonists were doing was wrong." She looked around to make sure no one else was near. "Now let's get down to business. We've got crossbows for everyone and extras," she said, ticking off points on her hand, "and heads for bolts as well. Alak-an said he's going to bring back swords; we have weapons covered. Men will come when we win more battles, but we still need one more thing."

Pontus watched her, intrigued by the inner workings of her mind. "Go on," he urged. "What else?"

"A spy."

"A spy?" Pontus shook his head. "Why a spy?"

"For information. All the great generals had spy systems, Washington for one."

"Who is this Washin—?"

"Father of my country," Gail said, remembering her high school history classes. "We need at least one," said Gail, studying the hunters. "Alak-an is too unreliable as a source of what's going on in the colony. We need someone who is familiar with New Bethand. We can get the information out by sending in a hunter claiming to look for work, but this way we'll be prepared when the Muians make their move. The question is, who will be our spy." She glanced at the men again. "Do you have any suggestions?"

Pontus stood and surveyed the warriors. "Chron has gone with me a few times to trade. He knows the market section." He paused and said, "We cannot have him go there and stand around, watching. People would become suspicious and questions asked. He would be arrested."

"Hmm... you're right." Gail caught Chron's eye and waved him over. "Does he know how to cook?"

Chapter Eleven

"**B**e careful!" Gail admonished Pontus.

Pontus gazed out over the warriors assembled behind him. "I will. I wish a few more warriors from the other tribes decided to join with us," he groused. "If I had additional men, I would try to stop those colonists raiding in the South, too."

"One battle at a time," Gail said, checking his newly constructed crossbow for the fourth time, and handing it back to him. "Let's stop the raids closest to *our* village first."

Gail counted noses—eighteen warriors from their tribe and another ten from the surrounding villages. Not much, she admitted to herself—not much to go up against three scores of colonists and natives.

"Remember," Gail said for the tenth time, "if you don't think you'll win, don't fight. There's always time to regroup and attack later. Understand me?"

"Right," Pontus agreed. "Will you wish me luck?"

"Luck!" She remembered a phrase from reading. "With your shield or on it, soldier."

Gail watched the warriors leave with mixed feelings. The tribesmen had better arms than they had before, but the colonist would be anticipating an ambush. The few who survived the first battle had forewarned them, and this was a punitive raid as much as one for booty. The Muians would be ready to fight and they outnumbered the villagers. This wouldn't be the easy victory Gail and Pontus hoped for.

As the days dragged by and turned into a week, Gail became increasingly nervous. She took long walks with Amber, sometimes accompanied by Malta, sometimes not. On one walk Malta remarked, "It is so quiet around here with all the men gone. When they are in the village, they are noisy and bothersome, but when they are gone..." She sighed. "Has Chron sent word yet? It will be nice when he returns—I miss him making me laugh."

"Too soon," commented Gail. "Amber! Stop chasing that squirrel—you're not hungry." The cat gave Gail a reproachful look and returned to stalking its prey. With a leap, he pounced and the squirrel scampered up a tree, chattering as it climbed. The squirrel stopped out of Amber's reach and twitched its tail.

Malta picked up a stout stick and used it to swat at the bushes as they watched Amber and his prey. "I do not understand why you need a spy in New Bethand anyway, if you know the future." She leaned on the stick and brushed hair off her forehead. "What use can he be?"

Gail sat cross-legged in the shade. "Amber, forget it—you'll never catch him." The squirrel had leaped from the branch, scampered across the ground, and raced up another tree, Amber in hot pursuit.

"When I search for the after times, I don't see one future, I see a range of possible maybes," Gail said with a chuckle as she watched the Oslo. "Some are probable, others possible, and some are improbable and farther in the background."

Malta leaned on her stick and stared at Gail, speechless. She started to speak and Gail held her hand up.

"The problem is, these futures aren't static. They shift and change according to how events in the real world change, understand? And that's what a good spy system does; it tells me the *now*, what's happening so I know which possibilities to look at."

Malta still looked confused and dropped down beside Gail. "I do not understand," she confessed. "I suppose I am dumb."

"No, you're not. It took me almost a year to learn, and some people never do."

"You are right—I guess it's because I miss Chron," confessed Malta. "I was hoping you would send someone else, but I still do not see why you had to send anyone."

Gail laughed as Amber pounced on the spot where the squirrel had run through the knee-high grass. The squirrel darted out between Amber's legs and raced back up the tree. "Let me explain it a different way.

"I see a future. In one, the Governor does nothing in response to our defense of our lands. In another, he sends out a small force of troops as a show of force, in still another, he sends a large force that ravages our land and burns our villages."

"Is that going to happen?" Malta was round-eyed in terror. "You saw that?"

"Those are some of the possible futures I saw, yes," said Gail. "A spy lets me know different things, though. Are the colonists talking about attacks while sitting in the bars and taverns? Are the plantation owners bringing their families into the colony for protection? Maybe, are ships docking with large groups of new colonists? All these little things let me know *which* of the possible futures might become real. They—"

Gail froze. The squirrel Amber was chasing chittered and disappeared up into the canopy of leaves. Down the trial slinking toward the two women was a wolf.

This was not a dire wolf as Gail had seen when she first arrived in Mu. This animal was smaller, rangy, and appeared half-starved. Its ribs showed through its mangy hide. At the sight of the two, the wolf halted, snarled, and then approached with its hair bristling.

Gail and Malta rose to their feet. Malta picked up the stick she had dropped. Gail snatched a rock.

"Gaela, back up. I do not think he will bother us, lone wolves do not attack people."

"Whatever you say," said Gail in a whisper, keeping her eye on the beast.

The wolf did not run off, however, as Malta expected. Instead, it bared its teeth and crept forward.

"Gaela, what are we going to do?"

"I don't *know*." Gail flung the stone at the wolf. "Go away you, go away!"

Instead of retreating, the wolf leaped.

A snarling streak of yellow and black fury hit the wolf in mid-air. It was Amber. Both animals sprawled to the earth and sprang up glaring at each other. Amber hissed and swatted at the wolf; the beast responded by snapping back.

"Oh, no you don't." Gail snatched up two more rocks and advanced on the fighting animals. "You go away now—oh, shoo!" She hurled a rock at the wolf.

Malta followed Gail, brandishing her stick. "You heard her—scat."

The wolf growled at the two women and backed up. Amber leaped again, swatting with both paws. With a yelp, the beast twisted and sprang away.

"Amber, no." Gail threw herself on the cat and restrained him from trying to follow. "Good kitty, good Amber," she cooed, scratching between the cat's ears and patting him. "You saved us."

Amber made a chirping sound and purred. The hair that was sticking straight up relaxed and he nuzzled Gail's hand, putting his head under her arm.

"Let's get out of here." Gail leashed the cat. "We'd better get back to the village and warn the others there's a crazy wolf on the loose."

"I wonder why he acted that way," Malta mused as they walked back along the trail, casting glances behind them to make sure the wolf didn't return. "Wolves do not attack when they are alone. They do not."

"Maybe he was starving," suggested Gail. "He looked as if he was having a bad time—I could see his ribs."

"Might have got kicked out of his pack. Sometimes that happens. The pack leader gets run off by a younger male."

"Anyway," Gail said, "we have to tell the rest. The children won't be safe as long as he's around."

When they got closer to the village, they heard a commotion. Gail and Malta broke out in a run. "Oh, no," Malta began, "that wolf did not—"

"No, Malta, look." Gail gestured. "The hunters have returned—there's Pontus— Pontus! Pontus!" She waved.

The hunters had entered the palisade. At the sound of his name, Pontus looked around, recognized the two women, and waved back. He strode toward them.

Malta hit her big brother with a flying bear hug that sent him staggering backward. "Oh, we missed you! Are you okay? How did it go?"

"Whoa—I'm fine, but do not kill me, the colonist already tried." Pontus untangled her arms from around his neck. Gail took the opportunity to give him a quick hug. Pontus appeared tired, but happy.

"So you found the colonists?" she asked.

Pontus's grin faded and he said, "Yes. Come back to the village and I will tell you as we go."

"Oh, we have to tell the rest of the village about the wolf," Gail said, alarmed, falling in step with Pontus and Malta.

"Wolf?"

"Yes," replied Gail, "We saw a wolf back there. He attacked us."

Pontus narrowed his eyes searching in the direction she pointed. "I will gather hunters together, and we will go looking for the wolf," Pontus assured her.

"Good." Gail felt relieved. "Tell us about the colonists."

"We trailed their safari for two days," said Pontus, "but found no place to set up an ambush." He licked his lips, remembering. "They have become wiser. Every time they came to a suspicious place, they sent out flankers and scouts. We kept hidden and bid our time.

"The colonists came to Kartum village. The villagers had fled to the hills around the town at the approach of the Muians, leaving behind four elderly people who refused to abandon their homes—three men and one woman. When the colonists realized the village was deserted they became angry, hauled the people out, and hung all four, then set fire to the huts."

Pontus shook his head. "We were hiding in the grass, watching. I had to restrain our men from attacking right there."

Malta looked horrified. "I can't blame your hunters," said Gail in disgust.

"The trail out of the village led through a forest. Scouts or not, we determined to set an ambush there and punish the murderers for what they had done. We lined up along either side of the trail and hid ourselves."

Pontus's wolfish smile came back. "I guess they thought they were safe because no one had tried to stop them when they torched the village. The colonists did not bother to put out scouts. When they walked into our ambush, we attacked."

A glow shone into his eyes as he said in a hushed voice, "They did not know what to do. First, they tried forcing their way up the trail. When that did not work, they retreated. Half of them were already dead."

Pontus took on an ominous tone. "Once they fell back we stopped attacking and shadowed them through the woods. The colonists emerged into the fields of the village and things got ugly. The hunters from Kartum village had seen the smoke from the burning huts, and came to investigate, knowing they had left old ones behind and fearing the worse. When they saw the hanging bodies and the colonists emerging from the woods, they charged.

"The colonists and their allies fired their bows at hunters, and many of the villagers dropped, the rest scattered; but the Muians had forgotten about us, or perhaps, thought the Kartum hunters and we were one and the same who had circled around. In any case, they did not watch behind as we approached. When they realized we were there, it was too late. It felt like scooping fish up during a run.

"The Kartum hunters took our arrival as a signal to charge again. They swarmed over the colonists while we rushed from the rear. When we finished, not one colonist or their servants remained."

"Wow!" whispered Gail. "How many men did we lose?"

They reached the entrance to the village. Everyone else was inside. Pontus replied with a note of pride, "The Kartum hunters lost ten men. We lost none. We left the weapons of the colonists with the villagers so their warriors could defend themselves if the Muians returned. The headman thanked me and pledged he would ally his people with us next time our territory was invaded."

The rest of the warriors had clustered around the council fire surrounded by a crowd, as Pontus strode up children and barking dogs ran to greet him.

Pontus raised his hands. "I need hunters to go with me into the woods and find a wolf who attacked these women," he shouted. "Who will join me?"

Men hurried to him, crossbows and spears in hand, shields over their arms. "Gail—Malta, show us where the wolf attacked you."

The girls led the hunters up the trail until they came to the spot where they had last seen the wolf. "Here," Gail said, gesturing to the crushed bushes, "we were sitting under that tree when the wolf came stalking us."

Pontus squatted and surveyed the scene. "Okay, you girls go back to the village. We will take it from here."

"Can we come and watch?" Gail asked. "I've never seen you hunt for anything before."

"Well, all right," Pontus replied. "But you will have to be quiet," he cautioned, "no talking, and stay behind us. Do not be disappointed if we do not catch this wolf. Most hunts are unsuccessful. That animal could be miles away from here by now."

Gail and Malta gave him solemn nods.

Pontus pointed to the trampled grass. "First we must find his trail; pray to the forest Gods we are lucky." He bowed his head and touched the small pouch around his neck.

The hunters circled until they picked up the tracks of the wolf running off into the woods, then fanned out in a long line.

Gail and Malta walked behind Pontus. Gail was amazed at the stealth of the hunters, as they faded into their surroundings like wraiths to reappear fifty feet away. After an hour's search, Pontus raised his hand and the hunters froze. Gail strained to see and spotted the wolf crouched in a thicket of bushes, half-hidden in the shadows.

Pontus motioned and the hunters circled the copse. When they finished the formation, they began hurling darts and firing bolts.

The wolf leaped away and tried to escape. At the top of one bound a crossbow bolt hit the predator behind the shoulder and it crashed into a bush. The hunters closed in with Gail and Malta following.

"That was exciting," Gail said to Malta.

"That was nothing," snorted Pontus, toeing the dead animal. "On a real hunt, we might trail a herd for a week. This was easy."

"Look at his hide, he is all mangy," another hunter commented. "It is not even worth skinning."

"You are right," comment Pontus dragging the carcass of the animal out where all could see. "The thing is all skin and bones. No wonder he was willing to attack people." He turned away. "Come, let us go."

"Malta said the wolf was driven from his pack," Gail said to Pontus as they trudged back to the village. "That's why he was starving."

"Maybe. Wolves are good hunters, but separate one from their pack and they do not do well."

"Strength in numbers," agreed Gail. "United we stand, divided we fall."

Pontus appraised her critically. "Something like that, I guess, but a wolf pack will separate out one animal from a herd and tire it out. Sometimes it is easier to dig a pit and chase the herd. One animal falls in and you have him. Wolves cannot do that so they have to use numbers."

Gail gave a thoughtful nod. "Yea, traps are useful, I remember that now." She paused. "Hmm... That wolf attacked because it was hungry, right? In a way, hunger is a trap, too. The wolf had no other choice but to do something it didn't want to do."

Pontus studied her with concern. "Yes, that is true, but I do not think wolves feel that way. After all, man or animal, we all have to eat. Is there something on your mind?"

Gail shook her head. "No, not yet anyway. I'm trying to get something straightened out in my thoughts—things I remember from school in my old life. Maybe tonight, at the council fire, I'll have a better idea of what I'm thinking." She laughed. "Don't you know by now it's dangerous to put ideas in my head?"

Pontus chuckled. "Your ideas have all worked out, so far. We never would have come this far without you."

As they neared the village, Pontus added, "After the battle of Kartum village one of their hunters asked us if the forest Goddess had guided our feet to their huts. When I asked him which Goddess he was talking about he replied, 'The first one, the Goddess of all, Gaela'."

"You've got to be kidding!"

"Really," Pontus replied. "You are starting to get a reputation here in the outback."

Gail smiled, but said nothing. When she returned to her hut, she went over the things she had seen and heard that day.

A starving wolf, hunger, traps, divide and conquer. How did they all fit into their problem with the colonists? The hunters had stalked, almost like shadows, what did that mean? How did they all come together?

Gail reclined on her pallet of grass and peered into the possible futures, searching for the changes, which had occurred from the most recent battle. When she was done, she sat, chilled.

By the time people gathered at the fire, Gail had a list of ideas in her head of what must happen to survive. She ate and leashed Amber.

"Come on, you old pussycat. Let's see what trouble we can raise."

She felt a knot in the pit of her stomach. *What if they don't listen to me, don't believe? What if I'm wrong?* Gail hesitated at her doorway and almost turned back. She pushed down her fear and stepped outside.

They ambled to the fire and Pontus and Malta made room for her on a log. Amber curled up at Gail's feet and watched with interest as sparks drifted up into the evening sky.

"Did you straighten out all those ideas chasing around in that little head of yours?" Pontus joked. He leaned over and peeked into her ear. "I do not see anything leaking out."

"Oh, Pontus, leave her alone," Malta giggled. "You are such a tease."

Gail shook her hair. "That's okay, Malta, let him make fun if he wants to," she chided, giving Pontus a stare that told him he was in trouble, and would pay for his

165

remark at some future date. "When he hears what I've thought up, he won't be laughing anymore."

Pontus smirk disappeared. "Why? What ideas have you come up with now?"

"A plan. A plan to win this war."

Chapter Twelve

"What!"

At the word 'war', a few heads went up and the hunters moved closer to hear what was happening.

"What are you talking about?" Pontus repeated, sobering. Malta stopped laughing and looked serious.

"At least, the beginnings of a plan," corrected Gail. "First off, we've been going about this fighting business all wrong."

"What do you mean? We have been following your orders."

"I know," Gail said, "Sometimes I can make mistakes, too. The futures are confusing, but I have it straight now."

Pontus watched her, sensing something important was happening.

Malta exclaimed, "I don't understand. The hunters have been defending the villages and defeating the colonists. What's wrong with that?"

"Nothing," admitted Gail, speaking to Malta, with her gaze fixed on Pontus, "but that is the exact problem. They've been *reacting* to the colonists, not acting. We have to attack."

"Are you out of your mind?" gasped Pontus in horror. "The colony is well defended—they have soldiers with better weapons, and outnumber us. To attack would be suicide."

Gail went on, nonplussed. "But we aren't just fighting the colonists. We're fighting the coastal tribes too."

"But if we attack them, it is almost as bad as attacking the colony," put in Typhon.

167

"We won't attack them directly," said Gail. "We'll attack the things they hold dear. We'll burn their crops, their outbuildings, wagons—if we get lucky enough, their huts and storage buildings."

"What good will that do?" protested Pontus. "That will antagonize them more. Then they will get mad and try to do the same to us."

"Not if they're afraid to come into the interior," countered Gail. "We'll build traps along the trails, stage small ambushes. Besides, if you were the chief of a village and it was attacked, what would you do first?"

Pontus said nothing. Typhon spoke up, saying, "The first thing I would do is keep my hunters close and prepare in case someone else tried another raid, put out guards at night, maybe set traps."

"Exactly. Prepare for an attack, rebuild, and repair what you could. Meanwhile, I'd discover who had attacked me, if I didn't know already."

"Then they will attack," injected Malta. "So what good did we do?"

"If we start now," said Gail, excited, "and booby-trap the trails, it'll take a month. Meanwhile the coastal tribe's crops will be ripe and ready for harvest. We hit their villages, and burn everything we find, and maybe hit them one more time before the rainy season starts. They'll be facing starvation and unable to replant until after the rains stop and the floods subside."

Pontus began to see her plan and nodded encouragement. "I see. It will be four or five months before they even think of attacking us, and if they have fallen into ambushes they might think twice about attacking at all, or helping the colonists raid."

Malta's eyes darted between Gail and Pontus. A few of the hunters looked doubtful. One said, "They will attack us again. We can be sure of that. They will come in a large force seeking revenge."

Gail looked up. They had drawn a large crowd around them, listening. "And if they do try, and lose another battle—" she left the sentence unfinished.

"If we are going to do this, though, it must be quick. In two months, the rains start," put in Typhon.

One of the hunters who had come over to listen asked, "There are five costal tribes. Should we attack all of them? After one or two, the others will be prepared and waiting for us. We would never succeed."

Gail said to Pontus, "What do you think? Is it necessary to attack all five?"

"Whenever we have been raided, it has always been the Hausa who accompany the colonists—Hausa and Batu." He turned to Typhon for conformation.

"Hausa and Batu," he said, "every once and a while you will see a Xena with them, but not often. The rest of the tribes are too far north. They are more aligned with Bionx."

"Hausa and Batu, it is," Gail agreed. "We should make these small raids, ten men each, on the same night. We hit their main village and get out—quick." She checked with Pontus in the gleaming firelight for approval. "Agreed?"

"It is one thing to protect our village and the lives of our people," Pontus replied, "But to start a war that may kill us all—" He sighed. "I know the colonists will attack again, it is only a matter of time." He searched the faces of the others. "But it would be better than sitting waiting for their next raid." He slapped his hands together. "It will not cause any more problems than we already have. Why not— it cannot hurt."

"One last thing," Gail said. "The extra weapons we have—they must be hidden in case our village is searched by the colonists. We can't let them know we are behind these raids."

"I know of a cave, two days' march from here, that

is the perfect place to put our weapons," replied Pontus. "It is hidden—none know of it."

"Good. We'll leave in the morning. We have lots of things we must accomplish if we are to do this."

In the morning, Gail and Pontus left.

"How come no one else knows about this cave?" Gail asked. Three of Pontus's friends led mules packed with heavy crates as they tramped across the grasslands. "Is this your secret hiding place where you go when you want to be alone?"

"No. I found the cave when I was out hunting by myself," Pontus replied, scanning ahead and behind. "It is in a small valley, concealed. Be careful—" he pointed, "and keep a bolt handy, I see a pride of lions up ahead."

Gail clutched her crossbow closer. In the near distance, a few trees spread their branches. The big cats lounged in the shade watching them as they approached. Pontus and his party swung wide to avoid the pride.

"I'm glad you convinced me to practice with this thing," Gail said, making sure the arrow was still in place and had not fallen out. She watched the cats as they passed, the animals watched back. "I've never shot a weapon before. Do you think they'll attack?"

"No, they have eaten well this morning." A mass of flies rose from a half-eaten carcass. "Too hot, too lazy now."

"Good." A large beetle landed on Gail's bow. She flicked it off with her thumb and forefinger in disdain. "Now if we could get rid of these bugs, I'd be all set. They love me."

A group of low hills rose on the horizon. Pontus gestured, "That is where we are going. We will be there before sunset."

When they arrived, Gail saw a game trail seeming to disappear into rock.

"Where's the cave?"

Pontus laughed. "Behind those bushes. Here, follow me." They scrambled up the path, Pontus pushed bushes aside and made a turn, and a small vale with a narrow opening came into view, nestled in between two mounds.

They followed the game trail, entered into a large, flat area spreading for an acre, with a dark entrance to a cave burrowed into the side of the hill. A small waterfall tricked down the rock forming a shallow pool.

"What made you come in here?" Gail asked, as they trudged up to the cave mouth. "It doesn't look that big from the outside."

"I was searching for a place to sleep for the night. Saw the trail, and decided to see where it went."

The cave was high and dry. They stored their weapons and settled down for the night. Gail remarked, "You know, this would be a good place for the people to hide in case anything happened in the village."

The following morning, they packed and left as soon as the sun rose. When they reached the plains Gail remarked, "Are we going to ride the mules back, or walk?" Her feet were still recovering from the previous day's march. She hoped Pontus would say ride, but she didn't want to be the only one mounted.

"Ride?" Pontus and the others gave the mules a dubious look. "Ah… we do not know how to ride," Pontus blurted out at last.

Gail's mouth dropped open in disbelief. "You've never rode on a horse before? Never?"

"Horses and mules are expensive," explained Pontus. "Those are for the colonists and coastal natives who can afford them. Sometimes—" he closed his eyes, thinking. "—a few of us have worked on the plantations, and learned to ride, or at least, been around, horses." He studied his friends. "Do any of you know how?"

Pontus received a bunch of mumbled, "Nos."

"It's easy," Gail exclaimed. "Here, help me up."

She strolled over to one of the mules, patted him, and said, "Give me a boost."

Pontus seized one of her feet and lifted. Gail scrambled onto the back of the animal. She gave a small wiggle to seat herself and locked her knees and legs around the mule's sides. "See, not hard at all. Hand me his rope."

She took the leather throng, gave it a light snap, and shouted, "Giddy up!"

The mule moved a few feet and stopped.

"See," Gail said, flashing Pontus and the others a smile. "Easy."

The men laughed.

"What's the matter?" Gail asked.

"You look silly, sitting on that animal," Pontus said. "I know people do it, I have seen it done, but close up—" He eyed Gail again. "You ride, we will walk. I do not think we would learn that fast, anyway."

"Have it your way," Gail replied with a frown. "Pass me up my bow." Pontus hand her the weapon. Gail cradled it in one hand and waved it over her head. "Onward!" she quipped.

By noon, they had traveled halfway back to the village. Pontus called out, "Let us be careful." He waved to the trees. "This is where those lions rested." Their party moved to the right.

Gail nudged her mule to hurry. As they drew even with the trees, the male lion rose, and let out a roar.

The mules reared and kicked. Gail's animal bolted across the savannah.

"Hey, stop! Stop—*stop!*"

Gail was tugging on the rope with all her might. The frightened mule paid her no mind as Pontus and the others disappeared behind her in the tall grass.

Gail found herself slipping. She dropped her crossbow, and clung to the mule's neck in desperation as she closed her eyes.

I'm gonna die, I'm gonna die, she kept repeating. *Stupid mule, stop.*

The mule slowed to a walk, halted, and began cropping grass. Gail slipped off his back, still trembling, and caught her breath.

It would be a long walk back. She stood on her toes and make out the tops of the trees. If she didn't run across Pontus and the others, a lonely trek back to the village. She grabbed the mule's rope and jerked. "Dumb mule."

Once she calmed herself, she started planning. Her weapon was gone; she kept looking in the trampled grass as they walked along the trail of broken grass, hoping to find the bow. When she did, she breathed easier. Now it was a matter of finding Pontus—and not running into a lion.

"PONTUS!" she yelled, and waited. When she heard no answer, she cupped her hands and called again.

"GAELA!"

She heard a response, and a moment later Pontus and his friends came into view, running toward her through the grass.

"Pontus." She ran to him and threw her arms around the native in a bear hug. "What happened? Did the lion attack you?"

"No. Are you okay?" he gasped, holding her shoulders and surveying her. He looked at the mule who had trailed behind. "When that animal ran off, we thought we had lost you."

"I'm fine," she responded. "Just shaken." A small smile touched her lips. The other hunters and mules were all present. "What happened when I, er—left?"

"Nothing," replied Pontus. They collared the wayward mule and walked back the way they had come. "That lion did not attack. He was warning us they were around and did not want us too close. That is all. Once we got the animals under control again, we turned around and you were gone."

One of the hunters added, "Now you know why we do not ride."

"Yea, I guess so."

"Do you want help getting back on?" Pontus asked.

"No, that wouldn't be a good idea," Gail replied with a laugh. "I think it will be a while before I decide to ride again, too."

***

The next few weeks were busy, especially for Gail. She insisted the hunters scout and map the two villages they were going to raid—that way each warrior knew where and what they would burn. On the morning the two parties left, Gail summoned the men together and repeated, "Now remember if the wind blows toward the village, burn the fields last. You can retreat into them afterward and fire the crops behind you. The villagers will be hesitant to run into the blaze."

Pontus lead the party against the Hausa, Typhon took charge of the other to raid the Batu. With the bulk of the men gone, the others hustled around hunting, reaping, and fishing, preparing for the rains. To be on the safe side, Gail had the villagers store their surplus food in the cave where they had put their weapons, "Just in case," she told Jankus. With Pontus gone, Gail led a second and then a third trip until the village had an ample supply of food in the event of a reprisal attack by the coastal natives.

The frenzied activity slowed one day with the arrival of Alak-an leading his mules. Pontus was still out on his raid. Gail went to greet him.

"Alak-an, how fortunate I'm here today." Gail smiled and surveyed the boxes that his men were unloading. In a lower voice she asked, "Did you bring what I asked?"

He glanced at the milling villagers and nodded toward four large crates. "As I promised," he said in an equally low voice. "Long and short swords, and the heads for bolts, pikes and battle axes."

"Good." As if it were an afterthought she asked, "What do you hear from the colony? Anything interesting?"

"Hmm... nothin' much. Was a lot of talk when an expedition didn' come back from hereabouts, but that died down when the other safari came in." He glanced at her shrewdly. "You folks didn't hear anything about that first expedition, did ya?"

"No," Gail lied, crossing her fingers behind her back. "You're the first visitors we've had since you came here last time."

"Say, that reminds me," Alak-an said, checking over the villagers that crowded around the merchandize his men unloaded. "Where's Pontus? And the rest of the hunters? This place is deserted."

Gail almost uncrossed her fingers, and then decided against it. "Out hunting. It's getting close to the rainy season. We have to put up stores—nothing else new?"

The trader nodded in understanding. "Nope." He scratched his beard. "Pretty quiet, but I've been out in the bush here fer a couple of weeks. Who knows what's been happening back there."

Gail withdrew a heavy leather bag out of her pouch and handed it over.

Alak-an hefted the sack. "I won't be comin' back this way till after the rains," he commented, slipping the bag into a large leather purse slung over his shoulder without checking inside. "Any other, er, *special* orders?"

"More of the same." Gail hooked her thumb over her shoulder toward the mountains beyond. "I told you, we have lots of wild animals where I come from. My people need protection." She joked, "I almost got eaten by a lion traveling here."

"Ah, yea, well, I guess that happens. Had a run in with a pride myself a while back. About those weapons, I ain't makin' no promises, but I'll see what's out there."

The next day as Alak-an left the village, Pontus and his warriors strode in.

"Ho, Pontus," Alak-an hailed him. "How was the hunting?"

"Hunting? Ah—good. Yes, it was a good hunt."

Alak-an surveyed the line of men. "Don't see no carcasses," he commented.

"Oh," Pontus looked around, chagrined. "Another party is carrying those in. We ran ahead to surprise the village."

"Uh-huh." Alak-an rubbed the black stubble on his chin. "Think it's safe fer me to go back to the colony? You didn't see any, uh, dangerous animals, did you?"

Pontus's eyes widened slightly. "No. No dangerous animals. A herd of mammoths, that is all."

"Well, see ya, Pontus," the trader waved. "Good luck and stay out of trouble."

"The same to you, Alak-an. May the spirits of the forest be with you."

When Pontus got back to the village, he said to Gail, "I think Alak-an suspects what we are up to."

"I know he does," Gail confirmed. She took him by the hand and led him to her hut, where she had had the villagers hide the weapons.

"This is what he brought this time." She showed him the crates the traders had fetched, "but as long as he has our gold in his pouch, he won't say anything to anyone. It would mean his head now if he did, and he knows it. Besides, he's getting rich. He doesn't want to disclose the source of his new wealth."

Pontus broke open a box of Ambosian short swords. He took out a gleaming blade and held it up. "Marvelous," he breathed, swinging it back and forth. He tested the edge with his thumb.

"How did the raids go?" Gail asked, picking up a

similar long knife and examining the point.

"Exactly as you planned." Pontus put the sword down and sat on the crate. "We stirred up a termites' nest. The flames rose to the sky."

"You got their outbuilding?" Gail asked.

"Yes," he replied with glee. "It was so dry, and the Hausas came out of their palisade yelling and screaming in surprise. They ran in every direction like ants. I do not know if their village caught on fire, we did not stay to see, but the wind was blowing in the right direction when we fired their fields, and I saw embers landing on the thorn bushes they use for their stockades."

"The other raiding party hasn't come in yet," Gail said. "I hope they have as much success as you did." She gave her short sword an experimental thrust and sat next to Pontus, handing him the knife.

"Keep that one." He pushed the blade back to her. "You paid for the weapon—it is yours now." Pontus flashed a smile when he saw the expression on her face. "Maybe I will make you a scabbard to wear."

The sword was as long as her arm. Gail thought about her forays in the kitchen when she would flavor meals with her own blood trying to chop vegetables with a small kitchen knife.

"You have to be kidding. I'd kill myself if I tried to use this."

"Nonsense," Pontus scoffed. "Besides, you do not have to use it, but a general needs a sword."

"A general? *Me?*" said Gail, shocked. "What would make you say a thing like that?" She was about as much a general as Malta was. *Maybe a general pain in the butt.*

"Well, you have been finding us weapons, planning battles, and thinking up strategy. Is that not what generals do?"

"Generals lead," Gail said with a smirk. "That's you." She tapped him on the chest. "I'm your, ah, aide-decamp."

"What is that?"

"Ummm… I bring you a drink of water when you want one."

They both laughed.

"But seriously," Gail continued, changing the subject, "I wonder when that other party will get back. Once they do, I want to send a runner to Chron and find out what their reaction was. Then we should plan another raid."

"They should be back any time. In fact—" he cocked his head, listening to a commotion of cheers outside her hut, "I think I heard them coming now." He stood and peered out the door. "Yes, that is Typhon and the others. Let us see how they did." They ran out of the palisade with the rest of the village.

Pontus met a jubilant Typhon leading a group of hunters at the head of the trail. "Success!" he shouted, raising his crossbow.

Gail was ecstatic. She ran up to him and exclaimed, "We have to hurry now. First, we need to get word from the colony, make a second raid, and hit them again before the rains set in." The beginning of her plan was coming together, and she saw no way of turning back.

Startled by her outburst, Typhon and Pontus found themselves speechless. Gail did not notice. She rushed on, "We'll have to be quick." She restrained her excitement and asked Typhon, "Are you up to another trip?"

He put his hand to his head and groaned. "Yes, if you need me to."

"Good." Gail took a deep breath, "Go to the Smokestack Inn, find out what Chron has heard, and get back here as soon as possible."

"Can I wait until the morning?" he groused, with a pitiful moan. "I have not eaten yet."

Gail realized she had been pushing too hard. They couldn't do it all at once. Time was on their side right now.

This war might go on for years. She must think this out, not go running off without planning.

Gail ruffled Typhon's hair. "Of course. Don't dawdle in the colony, though, it's probably not safe to do so anyway."

The next day Typhon left with instructions of what to ask Chron and look for. The rest of the hunters got busy bringing in more meat, drying it, and smoking what they could for future use.

Meanwhile Gail and Pontus debated what they should raid next.

Long after the rest of the village had gone to sleep, Gail and Pontus sat in her hut, along with Malta, arguing.

Pontus insisted they make multiple raids on the other, smaller villages of the Hausa and Batu.

"No—No—*No*." Gail paced up and down before him. "Two raiding parties, two villages, one night. We should hit the main villages again."

"We already attacked those," protested Pontus in exasperation. "There is not much left to burn. Now, if we hit three or four of their minor towns—"

"The small villages hold nothing," countered Gail, stopping and swinging her arms wide. "Most of the food and weapons are in the main towns. If our men stay out for more than one night, there's too much chance of being tracked and discovered. We don't want any fighting that far from our camp at this point."

"But—"

"Do you want to get everyone killed?" Gail glared at him.

Pontus said in a hushed voice, "Have you had a sighting?"

"No. I don't need to see the future for this. It's an unnecessary risk."

Pontus sat in motionless silence while he thought. "Well… how about this: two raiding parties, one night, but we hit their *second* biggest towns."

Gail calmed down and considered what he had said. "Hmm, we never planned a second raid in the first place, that's why I want to hit their main villages again. These other towns, we would need to scout them first. I don't think we'll have enough time."

"Already done," said Pontus with a hint of pride in his voice. "We did it when we investigated the main villages the first time. They were on the way."

Malta had been a silent witness to this argument. She said, "I hate all this talk about fighting and war. I wish we could go back to the way things were."

Gail replied, "Remember, things weren't that good before. You can't let yourselves be pushed around. I was, I was a slave, and that's what the colonists will make you, if you let them."

"But is there not some way we can have peace?" Malta protested. "Maybe if we talked to them?"

"We tried, Malta," Pontus said. "First it got me whipped. The next time I was condemned to death."

Gail reached down and stroked Amber. The cat purred and nuzzled closer to her. She was worried. Even though she had looked into the future, she was venturing into territory where she had no real idea of what she was doing. *I hope I get this right,* she thought. *What if I mess up?* "We still have to wait and see what Typhon has learned."

A dirty, hungry, tired Typhon limped into the village three days later. As Gail and Pontus made him comfortable in Gail's hut, he said, "Chron is not happy with you." He grimaced at Gail as he rubbed his sore feet.

Pontus gasped, "Is he all right?"

"Oh, he is fine," replied Typhon. He pointed at Gail.

"Me? What did I do?"

"On your recommendation, the owner of the inn

180

gave him a job, but not as a cook." Typhon's frown broadened out into a grin. He winked at Pontus and said, "They have him cleaning tables, scrubbing the floor, and doing the dishes."

Malta had entered and sat. She said, "I cannot picture Chron with a brush and a bucket. He must not be happy with his job."

"Oh, yes," replied Typhon, "but he says those are the good jobs. He especially hates emptying the chamber pots."

"The news," urged Gail, ignoring the chuckles from Malta and Pontus, "What has he heard from the colonists? Was anything said about our raids?"

"Yes. One of his jobs is to take the patron's dirty clothes and sheets to the laundry. The two washmen who work in the shop are half-breeds and told him the villages suffered great damage, and both the Hausa and Batu voice revenge. They are not sure, however, who to take out their anger on. They have fortified their villages, built guard towers, and keep a twenty-four hour guard."

"Well, that puts an end to the idea of attacking those villages again," put in Pontus, giving Gail a sideways glance.

Typhon crossed his arms and stretched out his legs. "To confuse things more, Chron suggested to them that it was the forest spirits taking out their vengeance on the villages for leading the colonists into the outback. The half-breeds laughed—they do not believe in the old ways anymore—but before he left, Chron said he saw both whispering to each other."

"What else did he say?" urged Gail, returning Pontus's look with a frown of her own.

"Well—"

"It is not a good idea that you four should plan war without the rest of the tribe." Jankus stood framed at the doorway, disapproval on his face. "I know you are trying to do good, but sometimes many minds think better than one."

Pontus looked guilty. Gail rose from her pallet and said to Typhon and Malta, "Come, he is right. We will finish this at the council fire. It's about time to gather anyway." Without looking back, she grabbed Amber's leash and walked outside.

The sun was setting behind the village as Gail stalked to the fire. In small groups, the villagers wandered toward the center of the compound. Pontus, Typhon, and Malta followed Gail while Jankus came after them. Once they settled down Jankus said to the people, "Typhon has returned from New Bethand with news we should all hear. My son and Gaela will discuss a second raid on the Batu and Hausa." He sat, face impassive, his arms folded over his chest as he watched his people.

Gail asked Typhon in a loud voice so all could hear, "Now, did Chron say whether the colonists had any opinion on what had happened?" demanded Gail. "Were they talking of revenge attacks?"

The circle of people hushed, waiting for Typhon's reply.

Typhon shook his head. "I asked. Chron did not know much, but he said the general opinion of the Inn's patron was that the fire had started from lightening, or carless blazes set by the villagers and not put out right."

One of the women sitting near Jankus said, "They could believe it is true. It happens during the dry season. I remember a whole town of the Hausa going up in flames and burning down that way."

Someone else added, "In the dry season, the land crabs come out of the mangrove swamps by the thousands. They flood the roads and fields so thick you cannot walk without stepping on one. The coastal natives collect as many as they can, and cook and feast using fires and big iron pots. They drink *emu*, palm wine, until they cannot stand. The colonists know this."

"It may well be," Gail replied, "that the Muians think that way. All the better for us, they won't interfere, but the Hausa and Batu will know better, and right now, it is them we are worried about."

Typhon inhaled and said, "Whatever we do, it must be done quickly. When I crossed the Ubo, it was rising. The rains have started in the mountains. Soon they will start here."

The villagers muttered to themselves. When their voices rose to a growl, Gail stood and raised her hands for silence. All eyes turned to her.

"You have heard what Typhon has said." She looked at each hunter and then at the rest of the villagers. "Should we conduct another attack on the coastal tribes, or leave them alone and see what they do after the rainy season?" She said to Jankus, "No matter what we do now, they are certain to attack us after the rains have ceased."

Pontus rose. "The Hausa and Batu must learn they cannot come and attack our villages, or any village. I will lead another attack before the rains start. This way the coastal tribes will learn we will not stand by while they kill at their pleasure. Who will follow me?"

All the younger hunters stood and clustered around Pontus, followed by the older warriors, and some of the women.

"The village has spoken," Jankus said. His expression gave no indication of how he felt.

Gail lifted her chin, her eyes shining. "Two raiding parties, one night," she said. "We'll attack their second largest villages."

The people went quiet. A small group around Jankus scowled at the decision; the rest of the hunters roared their approval. Pontus shouted, "Great, we will go in the morning. Typhon," he said to his cousin, "you'll lead the second party?"

Typhon rolled his eyes. "Sometimes I wish I had

stayed in New Bethand with Chron cleaning chamber pots."

Chapter Thirteen

Pontus watched the sentry walk around the outer edge of the Batu village. When the man reached the corner of the palisade and disappeared, he waved his men forward; they crept like silent shadows until they hid a hundred yards away from the thorn fence encircling the enemy camp.

"Quick, blow the fire into life and light the torches," he whispered to the hunter next to him. After all the brands caught, he breathed, *"Now!"* and ran, hurrying his men along with him.

As the sentry came back around the southern edge of the palisade, Pontus and his men retreated into the fields, lighting fires as they went to the screams of the Batu hunter who ran into the village. From within, answering cries came back; men, women, and children poured out trying to smother the blazes. A group of hunters broke away and raced into the crops chasing Pontus and his men, but by that time, he and his raiders had fled a mile away, grins on their faces, as they saw smoke and light from the burning village rising in the night.

***

All the attacks happened as planned. The raiders returned to the village before the rains started and made reprisal impossible; but even though the trails disappeared, and the rivers became torrents of impassable water as they overflowed their banks, communication in the backcountry still managed to go on.

Word of Pontus's exploits against the colonials and coastal natives traveled north, south, east and west. Whispered from mouth to mouth, his victories spread among the other tribes, and runners drifted into the village to offer support.

Pontus dodged raindrops from his father's hut and pushed the door open to Gail's. He shook himself like a shaggy dog.

Gail and Malta were busy preparing vegetables for a stew they were making. As Gail and Malta grew closer, Gail had invited Malta to move into her hut, as much for the company as the feeling of security of having someone there at night.

Amber hissed and sprang to his feet as Pontus sprayed him with water, and then the cat purred and nibbled at the man's legs in play.

"Hey, cut it out, Amber." Pontus nudged the Oslo away. "Why does that cat always go for my feet?" he asked Gail.

"He likes you," Gail said, putting down her cutting knife and moving over so he could sit. "He wants your attention. It's his way of getting you to scratch him."

"Who was that runner from?" asked Malta, brushing her long hair out of her face.

"Kartum village," Pontus said. "They came to reaffirm their pledge to give us men to fight the costal tribes and colonists after the rains stop." He held up his fingers. "That makes five villages, at least eighty extra men."

"Still not enough," commented Gail, picking her knife up again and chopping. "Before this is done, we'll need hundreds." She shrugged her shoulders, "but at least it's a start."

"Hundreds?" Malta dropped her bundle of wild carrots. "That many?"

"We're going to have to show a united front and look so ferocious that on one will dare attack us," Gail said. "Remember what Chron said? Ships arrive every day from Mu, bringing people escaping from the wars there. Half can't find work—the governor has a ready-made army if he wants and can bring thousands. If they do, we'll need as many hunters as possible."

"That reminds me," Pontus said to Gail, "what are we going to do with the extra weapons we have hoarded? I thought we would pass them out to the other hunters."

"We will," agreed Gail, "but make sure you save enough for our own warriors—and the first ones to join us get the weapons before anyone else." She checked her stew. "Maybe that will help some of the tribes that aren't decided to make up their minds and join our side. But also play up the idea that when the coastal tribes are defeated, there will be plenty of weapons to go around."

"Will there be?" asked Pontus sniffing the food.

"Plenty of tribes uniting with us?"

"Yes. The way you talk, I do not think there are enough warriors in this area to get the army you need, unless the northern tribes and the southern fight with us."

Gail shrugged. "I don't know, but maybe our allies will tell their allies. In one future, I see us with a big army so someone will get the idea, and bring in their friends. I told you, we'll need all the warriors we can get." She speared one of the carrots to see how tender it was. "Pontus, do you want to stay for dinner?"

"You do not have to ask me twice." Pontus put his hands by the fire. "This time of the year I can never get warm or eat enough." He asked, "You do not think the Hausa and Batu will back off? They will go through with their revenge attack?"

"I hope not. I hope they've figured out it's not to their advantage to raid us—but the futures are unclear on that point." Gail's eyes narrowed and she shook her head. "We'll have to see."

Malta's head twisted between the two. "What is going to happen if they *do* attack?"

Pontus asked Gail, "Well? Do you have a plan?"

Gail ladled stew into bowls, looking nervous. "Maybe. We'll have to see what happens, and when it happens. Supper's ready." She passed over the bowls to Pontus and Malta.

"Are you saying we are back on the defensive?" Pontus blew on a hunk of meat, chewed, and swallowed. "I thought we were supposed to be acting, not reacting?"

Gail sighed. Every day it became harder, more complicated. The pressure never stopped, wouldn't even let up for a minute to let her gather her thoughts. Was she making the right decisions? Every time she acted, the futures changed, sometime for the better—sometimes for the worse. Events were forcing her to guess, with no clear outcome in sight.

"We are," said Gail, "but sometimes it's wiser to wait and see how things develop, rather than running out blindly and fighting when it is unnecessary."

Something about Gail's tone made Pontus look hard at her. She appeared old. "Gaela? Do you ever regret saving me and coming to live here with us?"

"*What*?"

"I know you did not plan any of this. I was wondering if you are happy."

Gail thought about it. If she were back in her own time she would be in college right now, maybe graduated, job hunting, on her own. Well, she was certainly on her own, and she had a profession and a job, sort of. How old was she? This was her second rainy season here, one, one and a half years as a priestess. She had to be twenty-two or twenty-three by now. She wondered what her parents and friends were doing at home.

Gail looked at Pontus and Malta. They were her friends and loved her. They were her family now. "Yes," she said at last, "Yes, I think I am happy."

The rains slowed, stopped, the waters of the rivers receded. Gail sent Typhon out to find Chron, while Pontus directed the hunters to scout the trails leading from the coast.

The runners reported nothing. Typhon returned with important information, and found Pontus, Gail, and the rest of the village out surveying their fields for the spring planting.

"The tribes are stirred up," Typhon said, calling Pontus and Gail aside. "Even with the grains they bought; still they felt hunger in the villages. They have figured out it was one of the tribes here that attacked them and have vowed revenge."

"But when?" asked Gail. "Did Chron say when?"

"All he has heard is 'After the planting,' but," Typhon lounged back and sharpened his sword with a stone, "I can tell you this, I passed a Hausa village coming back and they were planting already. The whole village was out. The earth was as muddy as it is here. They could not turn the soil over properly, but still they tried. It will not be long."

"How about the colonists?" asked Pontus. "Are they going to help the villagers?"

Typhon laughed. "The official story is the colony does not want to take sides in intertribal warfare." He rubbed his nose with his forefinger. "But the colonists themselves are saying, 'Let the yips fight it out among themselves. The coastal tribes will do our dirty work.' I heard that myself when I was in the market. Chron did say though that the governor offered the tribes as many horses as needed if they want to make an expedition."

None of the other villagers had noticed the arrival of Typhon. Pontus peeked around and whispered, "Let us go back to Gaela's hut. We have made a map of the area that should be studied now that we know the time is near."

They hurried back to the village. It was deserted. Gail returned to her hut and withdrew a folded bundle from under her pallet of grass.

"Well, that is it," Pontus said. He unrolled the crude map made out of antelope hide. The coast, woods, and savannah were marked in charcoal. "We are here," he stabbed a finger at a circle, "and they are there." His finger moved to the coast. "What next?"

"Did you hear if the Hausa and Batu were going to attack together?" asked Gail.

"I did not hear anything directly," replied Typhon. "Neither did Chron, but the impression is they are going to band together and sweep the country—hundred men or more."

Gail rose and studied the map over Pontus's shoulder. "Good—the more the better—the sooner we do this, the quicker it is finished."

"What?"

"You heard me," Gail replied with a sour smirk. "Keep sending out scouts. We'll have to know when their ready to move. Let the other tribes know we'll need their hunters on a moment's notice."

"Anything else?"

"As a matter-of-fact, yes." Her finger traced faint secondary lines on the map. "These trails. I want to booby-trap them."

"Bo—booby-trap? What is a bo—booby-trap?"

"You said you dig pits to catch large animals? Elephants, rhinos?"

Pontus nodded.

Gail spread her hands about two foot apart. "Same thing, except on a smaller scale, big enough for a man to put his leg in."

"His leg? How will that hurt people?"

Gail let out a bitter laugh. "We will place sharpened stakes in the bottom, wedge two spindles with more stakes inserted along the edges. Cover them. When a man steps in one, the stakes will drive into his foot, the spindles will spin and more barbs will drive into his leg."

Both faces of Typhon and Pontus mirrored horror. "I see what you plan, but that would not kill a man," exclaimed Pontus at last. "What good would it do?"

"No, they won't kill," replied Gail, "but they're quick and easy to build, and it will take a man out of action so he can't fight." She added thoughtfully, "They would work on a horse, too."

"It seems like a lot of work," Typhon said, "but as long as we are at it, why not do all the trails?"

"No, these smaller ones," Gail denied. "I want to make sure they follow the main path. That way we know where to place our ambush, and they won't be tempted to outflank us." She kept jabbing at the map to make her point. "If they do send warriors that way, it will slow them down long enough to react." Gail repeated the phrase to herself, "Outflank us." Maybe she *was* becoming a general.

Information kept trickling in. The Hausa and Batu were massing, horses brought in, and wagons loaded, scouts reported they had left. On the morning Gail was to put her plan into operation, the whole tribe assembled to go over details. Pontus had sketched a large map on the hard earth by the council fire so everyone could see. Jankus stood next to Pontus, pointing out details and asking questions of his son in whispers.

"Gaela, My father wants to know why we do not attack the Hausa and Batu on the west side of the Ubo River?" asked Pontus, pointing at the squiggles on his map. He gave her a questioning look. "I was wondering that too."

"It depends on whether your warriors stay ahead of their horsemen," replied Gail. "You said they could—can they?"

"Oh yes." Pontus made slash marks on the west side of the map. "The ground is still wet. The closer they get to the river, the softer it will be, the thicker the trees and bushes will become." He said to the rest of the hunters, "We could stop them right there, right?"

A loud rumble of assent issued. Pontus went on to

Gail, "The horses will get bogged down in the mud. If we attack on the west side of the Ubo and are defeated, we can always regroup. If we let them cross the river and something goes wrong with our plan on this side, our whole territory will be open."

Gail stood and went next to Pontus, but looked at Jankus. "True, but on the west side of the Ubo the Hausa and Batu will be all strung out as they approach. Once they hit the river, they'll bunch up—that's exactly as we want them. Besides, if there's fighting and we have to retreat, I don't want our backs to the river—I want the enemy's back to it."

Jankus's dark eyes narrowed. He folded his arms, and nodded.

Gail said to Pontus, "Make sure your men keep baiting the riders and not get caught, if not, cut and run."

"Do not worry," Pontus boasted, "I will make sure of it. I am not going to let anyone get caught."

"How do you think—" Gail shook her head and glared at him in disbelief. She blurted out, "You're not planning on leading them, are you? You can't! We need you at the ambush site to direct the battle."

Pontus gestured to the warriors surrounding him. "Sorry. My hunters, my responsibility."

Gail placed her hands on her hips, and kicked dirt on his feet in frustration. "It's too late to get anyone else. If you're not going to be there, who will we get?"

The rest of the warriors were looking at her. Pontus was grinning. "Your plan."

"Who, me?" she squeaked. "Oh, no! Oh, no!" Gail backed away from the map, her palm out in horror. "No-no-no. I'm not a soldier—I wouldn't know what to—"

Jankus came forward and took her hands. The other elders stood behind him. "This has been your idea from the first, your plan. It is *your* responsibility."

Gail felt her heart pumping inside her. She took a

deep breath. *He's right*, she thought. She had been bossing everyone else around, issuing commands, and hadn't done as much as a spear cast. If she was going to keep this fighting going until peace was reached, she'd have to put herself in harm's way sooner or later. She had studied the futures and knew it would happen, but she didn't realize it was sooner.

"Oh, all right." The panic subsided. "There's not going to be much to do besides say, 'Attack' anyway."

***

Pontus leaped out from behind a bush, his body streaked with dried mud in long lines. He waved his spear-thrower at the approaching riders, and yelled, "Yip—Yip—Yip!" in defiance and disappeared again. Warriors behind him did the same.

One of the Batu horseman spurred his mount forward, slashing at the shrub with his sword. He gave a puzzled look when he realized his prey had vanished, cursed, and waved his companions forward when the hunter appear from behind a tree farther on. His horse snorted, picked gingerly through the sodden ground and ferns, and sank hoof deep into the muck. Ahead, the tribesman heard the rush of the Ubo River and urged his mount on through the muddy ground.

***

The dry creek bed on the other side of the river had spider web like cracks spreading in every direction. On either side of the grotto, bushes and trees marched down until they ended in a jumble of boulders and logs washed down from the recent rains.

Gail, Amber, and Jankus stood at the crest of the grotto and waited for Pontus to lead the coastal hunters into their trap. Gail glanced down at herself and grimaced. At Pontus's urging, she had donned a captured chain-mailed shirt that came down to her knees, her short sword hung at her side.

I look like Joan of Arc, she though, and then she remembered Joan of Arc had been burned at the stake. "Better make that Wonder Woman," she muttered. "She always wins in the end. Now all I need is an invisible plane."

For three days, Gail and the others had waited and watched for Pontus and his hunters to lead the invaders to this spot, creating frustration by staying out of the reach of the coastal hunters until they crossed the Ubo River.

True to Gail's prediction, the natives tried to circle around Pontus's small band of fighters. They hit the mantraps and halted their advance, drew their troops back, and concentrated their assault up the main trail as Gail hoped. The villagers kept teasing. The Hausa and Batu warriors had grown mad with rage and chased on the heels of Pontus and his men.

A sweating hunter, out of breath, came sprinting along the trail from the river. He scrambled up the hillside and gasped to Gail, "They come."

The first hunters appeared yelling as they trotted down the creek bed; behind them came other screaming warriors shouting insults to their pursuers.

"... *Hausa fight women—go back and beat your wives.*"

"*—Batus eat horse dung—that is why they smell.*"

Another group followed the first, Pontus bringing up the rear. A grim smile played on his lips. He said nothing, but loaded a bolt into his crossbow and shot it. The warriors retreated up the creek bed and vanished into the mouth of the grotto as the first of the invaders appeared.

Pontus stood and thumbed his nose at the oncoming warriors, turned, and waved his butt in their direction.

Mounted Batu and Hausa warriors, carrying crossbows, massed at the valley's mouth. Pontus screamed a last insult, shot one more bolt, and disappeared into the boulders.

The warriors charged.

Scores of the enemy stormed up the watercourse, more milled behind, as the leaders picked their way through the debris on the creek bottom. When the valley filled with riders, Gail issued her command:

"FIRE!"

A warrior standing next to her lit a bolt with grass wrapped tightly around the head and soaked with boar's fat. The shaft flew into the air, flaming and trailing smoke, and the valley erupted into a mass of flying darts and arrows.

Horses screamed and reared as their riders clutched bolts and fell from their saddles. Some of the warriors tried riding up the sides of the valley to attack the villagers, but fire from above cut the natives down before they had traveled more than a few feet.

Others turned to escape, only to ride full tilt into their fellows trying to push their way up the valley. All died in the hail of missiles.

"Stop it, Amber, not now." The cat tugged on his leash, while Gail tried to watch the fight and decide whether to engage her reserves. The cat hissed and leaped. "What the—?"

At the head of the valley one of the villagers was down—Pontus with a crossbow bolt protruding from his thigh. He dragged himself up the hillside, trying to find protection among the boulders. An unhorsed Batu warrior stalked him with a sword.

"NO."

Amber broke his leash and bounded down the hill. Gail raced behind, not sure what she would do when she reached Pontus, but determined to do something. She fumbled at her side for her sword.

Amber leaped as the warrior lifted his sword for a killing stroke. The cat hit the Batu in the back and both tumbled down the slope. Gail tripped, her arms flung wide, and she stumbled over the Oslo. She pitched forward, her sword plunging deep into the Batu warrior's chest. Gail gasped for breath and cried at the same time, scrambling away from the dead body beneath her. For the moment, the roar of battle faded from her hearing.

"Gaela—Gaela, are you all right?"

Pontus crawled down the slope to lie beside her. He shook her shoulder. "It is okay, Gaela, everything is okay."

She struggled up and threw herself on him, laughing and crying at the same time. Amber bumped against his back, purring.

"Gaela, they retreat. What should we do?"

Typhon stood there, agitation plain on his face.

"Ah—gather the hunters and pursue them, but stop at the Ubo River. I don't want our men scattered all over the place."

Typhon let out a yell and waved his crossbow over his head. Hunters streamed down the hillsides, following him as he sprinted back down the creek bed. Gail turned back to Pontus and asked, "Can you make it up to the camp? All my healing supplies are there."

Pontus grimaced. "I will make it."

Together they scrambled back to the top, Pontus dragging his wounded leg, while Gail supported him with her shoulder jammed under his arm. As they reached the small command post, Jankus rushed over as Pontus sank to the earth with a groan.

"Jankus, let's get a pallet under him and start water boiling. I have to get that bolt out."

Pontus's face locked in pain; his breath came in short gasps. Gail concentrated and his features relaxed as he fell into a deep sleep.

When the water was ready, Gail sponged the blood and dirt away with a soft rabbit skin, fresh blood oozed out of the wound. She grasped the bolt gently and prayed.

Concentrating on the channel the arrow had cut, she guided the head backward, feeling with her mind the twists and turns of the flesh. When the bolt was free, she concentrated again, closing off the flow of blood until it was no more than a trickle. She finished by bandaging it with clean cotton cloth and sat back on her haunches with a sigh.

Gail's clothes were soaked in blood. Two other healers from other tribes moved about in the camp, bringing the wounded from the battle to the command post for treatment.

"Gaela! Gaela!"

A young hunter, just out of boyhood, stood in front of her trying to get Gail's attention. His face had gone white.

"What's the matter? What's wrong?"

"It was terrible," the boy said, his voice shaking in fear. "A massacre."

Dread flooded through Gail, something had gone wrong, the worse of the futures had happened; the Hausa and Batu had turned on the villagers and destroyed them all. She asked in a small voice, "What's the matter?"

"The Hausa and Batu warriors retreated to the river, but their wagons were trying to cross at the same time— they got all tangled up. The drivers tried to turn their mules in midstream, and that made things worse. Some became stuck, some went into deeper water and turned over—one floated away—the riders floundered, the horses drowned. We kept shooting volleys of bolts and flinging darts at the trapped men. Soon we ran out of targets."

The boy's voice trembled. "The water was pink."

"My God," breathed Gail.

"Typhon wants to know what you want him to do." The hunter's voice was steadier.

"Ah, tell him to send out two parties of ten men each," Gail said, "to make sure the Hausa and Batu keep retreating. Deal with smaller groups as they please; larger parties leave alone, unless they try to reform and attack again. In that case, let us know so we can decide what to do. Uh—"

Gail brushed her hair back and tried to think if she'd forgotten anything. Everything had happened too fast. No, she was right—keep her people together, stay organized.

"Have the rest of the men salvage whatever they find: arms, supplies, and wagons," she ordered. "Then tell Typhon and his warriors to come back here."

"Yes, Gaela." The hunter bowed his head. "As you say."

Chapter Fourteen

W ord of their victory spread farther than Gail realized. Delegations poured in from the south, the realm of Chron's father—and from the far north, the domain of Bionx, pleas for help flooded Pontus. Theirs was the same problem, constant raids by the Muians and their coastal allies had left the northern tribes raped, their villages in ruin. The hunters looked to Pontus for guidance on how to drive the colonists from their land.

"What can I teach them?" Pontus complained. "We have already called for a boycott of the colonies. There is not much else to do." His leg had healed except for a slight limp, which Gail assured him would disappear once he was able to use it more.

Most of the village had gone out fishing. On Gail's urging, she and Pontus walked along the river to exercise his muscles, occasionally picking up nuggets of gold as they found them, and debating what he should do.

"It's up to you if you want to travel north." Gail picked up a stone, examined it, and tossed it into the river, "But you know more than you think." She walked a few paces, kicked aside rocks, and picked up another stone. This time she nodded to herself and tucked it into her pouch.

"What do I know?" Pontus waved his hands in exasperation. "We followed my plans and the tribes lost. We followed yours and we won. You should go."

"Nonsense," she scoffed, with a twist of her head. "They don't know me, and I don't know those people. But you can give the villagers the spear thrower, teach their warriors how to use it. Tell the northern tribes about unity in numbers, how to set an ambush, and most important, make them understand about stealth, speed and shock."

"But those are the things that you taught me." Pontus picked up a flattish stone and tried to skip it on the river with a savage thrust of his wrist.

The rock took one bounce and disappeared in a wave. Gail laughed, and placed her hand on his arm before he threw another. "Yes, I taught you, and now you know how to teach the northern tribes. Once they've learned this, and fought a battle or two, your work is done. They wouldn't need you anymore." When he didn't answer, she added, "You said I was a general. Would it be easier if I gave you an order?"

Pontus quit even the pretext of searching for nuggets. He stopped, shook his head, and sat on the bank, stretching out his leg and massaging it. "What if the Hausa, or Batu, or the colonists come back? What then?"

Gail wished he would see how important this was. *He needs more urging, that's all.* She laughed and sat next to him. "You heard Chron's last message. The natives are afraid to come back here anymore. It's bad ju-ju. The forest spirits are angry." She hid her face in her hand and giggled. "The survivors even talked about the angry First Goddess who attacked them with a roaring lion. I wonder what Amber thinks about that!" She sobered and said, "As for the colonists, they haven't been hurt. Why would they bother us?"

Pontus sighed glumly. "Are you going to miss me?"

Gail realized she would. "Yes, of course." She took his hand in hers and squeezed it. She wanted to say more, but instead sprang to her feet. "Let's hurry and get back to the others. They must have the net in by now, and need a hand hauling fish up to the village."

The next day Pontus left with a few of his hunters, traveling north. Without him, the village felt deserted to Gail and she found it difficult to concentrate. She spent the time working with the women, or healing cuts and scrapes from daily life.

The few times she searched the futures they showed a kaleidoscope of changes and dangers. This confused her, because she saw no events in reality to match them against what she saw around her. So it was a relief one day when Alak-an, and his helpers led their string of pack mules up the trail to trade.

"Alak-an." She ran out to greet him with real pleasure. "I'm glad to see you."

"Oh, it's you," the trader grumbled as he unloaded crates. "Yer here again? Every time I see ya there's a war or battle about ta happenin'."

"Well, I hope that's in the past," replied Gail. "I hear the costal tribes lost a fight. I don't think they'll be raiding anymore."

Alak-an gave her a sideways look, wiped sweat from his face, and sat on a crate. "Don't be too sure of that. The colony's gonna do something; they're in an uproar."

"*What?* Why?"

"Prices going up, that's why," he replied, nodding to himself. "The coastal tribes don't raid 'cause they're afraid to come back here—they don't bring back cheap stuff to sell to the merchants. Right now, hardly anything's coming out from the interior, none of yer people going into the colony to trade either. Less stuff means the merchants back in Mu raise their prices—right? And who gets the blame?"

"Us?" Gail said.

"No, not directly, anyway," said Alak-an with a knowing wink. "They blame the Governor. He's the one who's supposed to keep the peace and the ivory, spices, and incense flowing."

"Oh."

"Yea, oh." Alak-an glanced back down the trail. "He's got the merchants and the settlers here bitchin' at him on one side, the merchants and the Bethish senate at home complaining on the other."

Alak-an slapped his knee at the thought. He continued more seriously, "Heard tell the Governor's gonna send troops back here, a show of force, ta get 'the yips' to start trading again, and hauling out the stuff the coastal natives use ta bring."

"But how—"

"By bow point if necessary. Oh, they might be nice about it at first, but ifn' that doesn't work—"

"Oh, dear." Gail had seen this as a possible future, but hadn't realized it would happen so soon after the battle. Things had taken a turn for the worse.

"Look," Alak-an waved a finger at her and went on in a lower voice, "I know them weapons I sold ya went straight to this village, and ya used them against the Batu and Hausa. None of my business. In fact, I think ya were right in defending yourselves. All I'm sayin' is when those soldiers come through here, better be on ya best behavior if ya don't want trouble. Understand?"

"Yes." A hundred questions raced through Gail's mind. Things she didn't understood before now made sense. She had to get some place quiet to see how the futures were changing. "I understand." She dug around in her pouch and withdrew a small sack. "Here."

Alak-an reached out and took the bag, but looked confused. "What's this fer?" I didn't bring any weapons this time. They're clamping down hard, can't move as much as a kitchen knife."

"Sometimes knowledge is as much a weapon as a crossbow can be," replied Gail.

"Hmm… In that case I'll give ya one more piece of information." Alak-an replied, slipping the bag into his pouch.

"What's that?"

"The plantation owners are up in arms too. With all the men the tribes lost, they can't manage their own fields, let alone rent themselves out to the farmers for the

202

harvesting."

"But what does that have to do with us?" Gail protested. "I know the colony's been flooded with refugees. There must be—"

Alak-an rose and went to help one of his men spread out their trade goods. He surveyed the merchandize with a quick nod and returned to Gail.

"Remember, them farmers are mostly lackeys fer their big brothers and uncles, they don't own those fields. They gotta show a profit or they're out. Yea, they've have plenty of workers, all of them newcomers, none of 'em know the first thing about farming. They don't work as hard as the natives do and they want more money. The planters are complaining that if something isn't done they'll lose their whole harvest."

"Oh dear." Thing had gone from bad to terrible.

After Alak-an left Gail hurried to Jankus. "We must take the horses and mules to the hills, and hide our weapons in Pontus's cave. Alak-an tells me the colonists are sending an army here."

"Are you sure of this?"

"Yes, I was told by Alak-an." Dread filled Gail. "He might be wrong, but he was not mistaken."

Jankus paused for a long time. "Pontus is gone. No one knows the location of this cave but you."

"Oh, darn, you're right." The few others who knew where the cave was had gone north with Pontus. She had made a few trips by herself, but always accompanied by some of Pontus's friends that had gone with them before. "I'll lead the party," Gail decided.

She spied Typhon sitting with a group of hunters in the shade of a tree. Gail waved them over.

"Yes?"

"I need some men," Gail explained to Typhon. "We have to gather together whatever we won from that battle with the Hausa and Batu and bring it up to the cave. Alak-an says the colonists are coming, I don't want anything in the village that showed we were a part of the fight. I'm leading the party myself—I'll be gone for a day or two."

Typhon glanced around and gestured to a few more of the hunters. They hurried to him. "Gaela has orders for you," he explained as they walked back to the shade of the tree, "Here is what she needs…"

"Jankus," Gail said, "send runners to the other villages; they must know what's happening. I hope I'm back by the time the Muians get here."

"Yes, Gaela, as you command," replied Jankus in a slight mocking voice. "Anything else?"

"No, I don't think so," Gail fretted, turning over all the possible threats that might occur while she was away. "If I think of anything, I'll let you know."

Jankus gazed out over the village and fields beyond. "Would not it be better for you to stay hidden too?"

Gail startled. She had forgotten the colonial authorities still wanted her. "Do you think I have to?" She dreaded the thought of sitting in the hills all by herself, and she had to know what was going on. "I've changed so much. I'll stay in the background, but I need hear what the soldiers have to say."

The leader issued a short laugh, folded his arms, and looked her up and down. "Yes, Gaela, you have changed. You should stay in the background if you wish."

Word came into the bush that a large military force of colonial troops was marching through the savannah, stopping at each town, making a wide circle. When they arrived at the village of Jankus, the inhabitants came out to greet the soldiers.

Foremost in the troop rode a colonial officer sitting on the back of an elephant. A canopy protected his head from the sun while two-foot high walls of bronze surrounded him a four sides to defend him from attack. Red and silver trappings covered the animal along with leather armor for the head and trunk.

Following behind rode ranks of cavalry in mailed armor, carrying swords and lances. Bringing up the rear, oversized crossbows mounted on carriages, which could throw a bolt six hundred feet, filled wagons and bristled in every direction.

This procession marched up outside the palisade of the village and stopped. The muttering from the villagers, who had run out to watch their approach, died away as the elephant stopped and knelt before them. A squad of cavalrymen rode up beside the animal and helped their leader dismount.

"Who is the headsman of this village?" The officer surveyed the assembled natives with hands on hips, a stern look of disapproval on his face.

Jankus stepped forward. "I am Jankus. This is my village—I am headman here."

Their eyes locked. The Muian took a few steps forward until he towered over the smaller tribesman. "I see. There has been much trouble back here in the bush, natives fighting natives, attacks on peaceful trading expeditions. You wouldn't know anything about this, would you?"

Jankus bowed his head and looked at his feet. "No, Your Highness," he said with a straight face.

"I'm sure." The officer sniffed. "I am the governor's son, Gar-el. My father and I have been empowered by the Bethish Senate to maintain peace in this territory. There will be no raids or disruption of commerce, no more fighting. Any native engaged in subversive activity shall turn himself over to the authorities in New Bethand. Do I make myself clear?" He shouted the last words.

"Yes, You Highness."

Gar-el nodded. "Good. That's what I wanted to hear—none of this unrest nonsense. Now, what is it that this village trades?"

Jankus thought for a moment. "Ivory, ebony, hides, myrrh, and sometimes amber when we find it."

"Very good," said Gar-el. He turned to a soldier standing next to him. "Mark that down—village Jankus." He said to the headman, "We expect you to bring these things to the colony for trade. Make sure the merchant you see knows from which village you came from and tallies what you brought. Understand?"

One of the bolder hunters in the front ranks of villagers spoke up. "Will we be given a fair price for the things we bring in?"

Gar-el sniffed again and glared at the man in distain. "Of course, but I must inform you, the price of these items have fallen in the last few months, both here and overseas. You won't receive what you did before." He waited for a retort. When he heard none, he nodded and said, "One other thing, the farmers have asked me to pass the word; they are hiring field workers to help bring in their crops. If anyone is looking for extra cowries, they'll hire you."

A low muttering rose from the villagers. Gar-el ignored this. He said to Jankus, "Any questions?"

Jankus ground his teeth as he replied, "No, Your Highness."

Gar-el addressed the soldiers standing by. "Search the village to make sure they have no illegal weapons, and then we can leave."

The men entered the palisade, going hut by hut, ripping up sleeping pallets, and kicking down bared doors, to the muttering of the villagers. When they were finished the leader reported to Gar-el, "No weapons, sir, but we saw plenty of ivory stored."

The Muian surveyed the village one last time with disgust. "Filthy Yips. Okay, I think we are finished here," he said to the soldier taking notes. "Mark that down too. Village Jankus, ivory stored. Finish up and let's go." He remounted his elephant, gave his troops a sweeping wave, and the procession moved on.

Gail was sandwiched in the middle of the villagers. Typhon and Malta pushed their way over to her. "I wish I could catch that man alone on the savannah one day," said Typhon as he stared at the receding column. "I would teach him about 'filthy Yips'."

"I healed him once," replied Gail, anger at what he had said and done to the village mounting inside her. "I should have poisoned him instead."

"Do you believe what he said about demand for our ivory?" asked Typhon.

"Alak-an told me prices were up," replied Gail. "This one," she gestured to the retreating soldiers, "says demand is down. I *think* they are still trying to steal from us, only in a different way, this time through intimidation."

"What are we going to do?" asked Malta. "Still not trade?"

"No. Typhon—" Gail hooked her thumb back toward the village "—the hunters have brought in ivory and Gar-el knows it now. Ask Jankus if you may bring it to the colony for trade. Don't argue with the merchants about price, take whatever they offer. Keep your eyes open, but don't linger, not even to see Chron. Come right back here, okay?" She snapped her fingers and exclaimed, "Oh, and we'd better send word to Pontus and tell him what's going on."

When Typhon returned, he brought ominous news.

"It is worse than we feared," he announced to Gail. "I think everyone should hear this."

Gail shouted to the others who were in the fields working and gestured to the middle of the village. When everyone assembled she said, "Now, tell us what happened. Did they take the ivory and not pay for it?"

Typhon gave a bitter chuckle. "Oh, they paid." He tapped his pouch, which rattled with a few cowries. "Not much, but they paid."

"What's the problem, then?" Gail asked. "We knew they weren't going to give us a fair price."

"It is what happening during and after." Typhon sat, but talked loudly enough for all to hear. "If you dicker with the merchants or stay around afterward, they arrest you."

Gail startled. "What? You're kidding me."

***

Typhon and his men carried their ivory down to the docks, but this time, instead of a few soldiers standing around as usual, squads of armed guards lined the streets. He thought it was odd, but moved on anyway. He went to the factor's warehouse and noticed four sentries standing by. Inside, two more groups of natives stood ahead of him in line.

The buyer glanced up from a tally sheet, as the leader of the first band of tribesmen had his men lay their tusks on the floor in front of his weighing scales.

"Here." The merchant reached into a bag of cowries and poured a handful of shells on the table. "Put your ivory over there." He gestured to a pile of tusks.

"B-but, you have not weighed them," sputtered the startled native. "How can you know how much they are worth?" He stared at the shells scattered on the table, his mouth working as he calculated what was there. "This is not nearly enough."

The Muian leaned back in his chair and drummed his fingers.

When the native heard no reply, he turned to his friends. "Let us leave, this is not worth it." They picked up their ivory and stepped out of line. The next group of natives watched and they too turned to go.

"You giving me a hard time, yips?" The factor waved to the guards who gestured to the squad of soldiers outside. "These yips are causing a problem," the Muian told the sergeant as he walked up to the table. "Don't want to sell their ivory at a fair price, trying to jack me up."

"Yea?" The soldier eyed all the natives in the warehouse. "All of 'em?"

"Just these two bunches." The factor gave Typhon and his men a critical look and pointed to them. "This group is okay, so far."

The soldiers rounded up the other natives. Typhon watched in horror as they were marched away at sword point, their ivory forgotten on the building floor.

"NEXT!"

Typhon and his men hurried up to the table. "Where do you want this, boss?" Typhon asked, bowing his head and looking at his feet.

"Over there with the others." The hunters scurried over to the pile and unloaded their ivory on top of the rest. Typhon put out his hands and received a palmful of shells. His eyes shifted to the entrance of the warehouse and he asked the Muian, "What is going to happen to them?"

The factor gave a gruff laugh. "Those yips? Fines and the labor gangs. One cowrie a day until it's paid, probably on the plantations." He kept his eyes on Typhon and said, "You're a smart boy. Let me hand you a word of advice. When you leave here, head straight for the outback, otherwise you'll wind up on those gangs, too. The governor don't want none of your kind hanging around on the streets. Understand me?"

Typhon looked at his fellow hunters. "Yes, boss. Thank you. I understand."

"Good. Give the name of your village to the guard when you go."

***

Gail's face was white. "Why, that's slavery," she said. "They can't do that!"

"They *are* doing that." Typhon raised his hands in helplessness.

"Then we won't," Gail replied.

209

"Won't what?"

"We won't deal with them, that's what. We'll stay out of the colony and not trade." Gail asked Jankus, "There's nothing we need that we can't make ourselves, is there?"

The headman exploded in a booming laugh. "Not really. Some metal tools for farming, hoes, and shovels. We used to make them out of bone, but if need be, we could do so again."

"What do you think the colonists will say?" Malta sounded upset and looked from Typhon to Gail.

"Probably send the army in here and force us to sell them what they want," grumbled Typhon, "Gar-el said as much when he passed through, but we do not have much choice in the matter, do we?" He spread his hands wide. "They are keeping tabs on which villages are trading, and which are not. If we stop, they will know."

"I don't believe the colonists are so stupid." Gail pressed her lips into a thin line. "What else do they expect? That we would let ourselves be enslaved?"

Gail leaped to her feet and paced about the council fire, muttering to herself. Finally, she stopped and said to Jankus, "If Pontus was here I know what he would say—fight—but this is not his decision, or mine. The whole village must decide, and the other villages as well. If they follow our lead, it means war with New Bethand."

Shadows hid Jankus's face, but Gail heard his voice fill with sorrow. "Your words hold truth, Gaela. I will send runners to the other villages tomorrow. We will sit in council and decided that to do."

As the villagers disbanded for the night, Gail caught Typhon's eye. "Follow me to my hut," she murmured in a low voice. She and Malta sauntered off with Typhon trailing.

Amber greeted them with purrs and low growls as the three entered. Gail scratched behind his ears and said to

Typhon, "we must get word to Pontus. He's had enough time to organize the northern tribes, and we need him here. He can always go back again next year. We must look to the horses we've captured. The hunters need to practice as they did with the spear throwers—if we fight the colonists, we'll need cavalry." She asked Typhon, "Does anyone here know how to ride?"

He gave her a sheepish grin. "When Chron was young he worked on one of the plantations. He learned to ride delivering messages between the planters. I guess he know as much as anyone in the village."

Gail sat on her pallet. Amber crawled up in her lap and made himself comfortable. "That means Chron knows more about horses than anyone else. He's in charge."

Typhon nodded. "As you command, Gaela."

Included in the runners that left the next day, one hunter traveled north to find Pontus. In the meantime, Typhon took over the training of the hunters. Gail decided she needed some training herself. The incident with the Batu warrior at the battle of the valley had left her shaken.

She had toyed with the idea of learning how to defend herself after that incident, and forgotten about it. After her run-in with the lion on the savannah, she had determined to practice with her bow, but events had been so hectic she never found the time. While she had to wait on Pontus and the other villagers to assemble, this gave her the perfect opportunity to become better acquainted with the weapons they used, especially if she found herself forced to fight for her life.

One morning, clutching her spear thrower and a handful of darts, she found Malta down by the river washing clothes.

"Come on, I need your help," Gail said to the other woman.

Malta wrung out her laundry and put it in a basket. She looked at the weapons Gail held and asked, "What have you got there?"

Gail smirked at her friend. "What do you think, silly? Weapons."

Malta pointed to a group of hunters trotting off into the savannah. "Did someone forget to take theirs?"

"No. I need to practice with these." Gail held the spear thrower up. "I want you to go with me. I'm nervous going alone," she admitted.

"Oh," Malta said, bewildered. She glanced at her basket of clothes, shrugged, and pushed it higher up on the bank so it would not wash away with a wave. "Okay, let's go."

"Pontus showed me how to use a crossbow, and I've practiced," Gail said, as they walked passed other people out toward an uncultivated part of the planting fields. "I've hacked and thrust with that big knife he gave me until my arm aches, but this is the first time with an atlatl. I don't want to look like a fool by myself."

They wandered off into the field. Once they were out of view of the other villagers, Gail fitted a dart into her spear thrower. "Well, here it goes." She gave Malta a small smile and hurled the dart.

The missile wobbled a short distance and landed in the grass. "Not bad," Malta said with a grin, "for a first try." She walked over, plucked the dart from the grass, and flipped it back to Gail. "I think this is going to be a long day."

Gail smirked and replied, "A long *couple* of days, yeah."

It took her more than a few days, but Gail practiced in the mornings, sometimes with Malta, sometimes bringing Amber with her. She did not realize how good she had become until one day the cat brought her a present.

Gail and Malta were out in the field. Amber tagged along, chasing whatever he scared up in the long grass. Gail made a few casts, hitting her target, a ball of weeds that

Malta rolled in front of her, every time. By now, Gail had even progressed to hitting her target nine out of ten times when thrown in the air.

"Great!" Malta ran and retrieved the spears. "You are better than most of the hunters," she remarked, handing the darts back to Gail.

"As long as they don't ask me to go out stalking game with them I'll be fine," replied Gail, "I couldn't imagine myself chasing down a herd of antelope. Amber, what do you have?"

The cat trotted up to her, something long and light green twisting in his mouth. He placed it at Gail's feet.

"*Snake!*" Gail and Malta danced out of the way, as the reptile wiggled toward their feet, trying to escape the Oslo. Before she knew it, Gail had loaded one of the darts in her spear thrower and hurled it. The missile pinned the serpent to the earth where it writhed and fell still.

"Amber," Gail yelled at the cat, "don't you ever do that again, you hear me?" The Oslo gave her a puzzled look and rubbed against her legs, then went to sniff the serpent. Gail and Malta crowded around the cat to examine Gail's marksmanship.

"You *are* getting good," exclaimed Malta in admiration, pointing. "Look, that snake is not much bigger than the dart point. You split it right in the middle."

"Yeah, well," stammered Gail, blushing, "I guess when you gotta do something, you gotta do it right."

***

It didn't take the surrounding tribes long to decide to continue their boycott of the colonies. Released prisoners from the plantations had arrived at their home villages, and told horror stories of being beaten and half-starved as they worked off their fines. The natives were outraged and many demanded an immediate attack on the colony. Most had acquired weapons from the recent battle with the coastal natives, or had adopted the use of the spear thrower from

Pontus. They were eager to take out their revenge again. In a joint meeting of all the tribes, Gail urged caution.

"It is late in the season—the rains will soon be upon us." Gail paced among the elders ticking off points, not certain if they would agree with her or not. Outraged, the chiefs and councilors demanded immediate action, but to attack now without proper preparations would mean defeat. She had to convince them to wait and do things right.

"We must have supplies, stockpiles of bolts and darts, and most of all, we must train our fighters together so they can act as a unified force."

A few thoughtful nods came from the chiefs. Gail went on with more confidence.

"The colonists will not attack until after the rains. We'll use this time to prepare. And who knows," she smiled, "maybe the colonists will return to their senses and agree to a resolution to our problems."

The arrival of Chron and Pontus interrupted the council. Malta sprang up from the listeners and ran to the two men as they strolled into the circle, embracing both.

"Charon—Pontus! I'm so glad you are back." Tears of joy streamed down her face as she hooked her arm in Chron's.

"What are you doing here?" Gail asked Chron. "Did something happen in the colony?"

Pontus said, "I fetched him. When the runner told me what was happening, I left the north and came back, but went to New Bethand to see for myself. The soldiers almost arrested me for loitering, but I escaped and went to the Smokestack Inn where Chron hid me in his room. We decided it was becoming too dangerous for him to remain in the colony, and we both snuck out during the night."

"I am glad you have returned," Jankus said. "We are discussing whether to attack the colony or wait and see what happens. Do either of you have any thoughts?"

"It does not matter," Chron said, "now or later. The

Bethish Senate has recalled the Governor and appointed his son to replace him. Gar-el promised to increase the trade goods coming out of the interior and keep the 'yips' in line. It is rumored the senate is dispatching troops to help him." He fixed the elders by eye. "War is coming, mark my words, no matter what."

Chapter Fifteen

I n the beginning of the dry season, the northern tribes call Pontus away to help them wage war against the colonists of Bionx. Before he left, Gail urged, "See how many of their men are willing to join us. We must unite the tribes. Remember, divided we can't hope to defeat New Bethand and Bionx at the same time. Our sole chance is to hold one at bay while we defeat the other. Even a handful of warriors would be useful right now."

With misgivings, Gail watched Pontus trot down the trail. She was stripping herself of the people who gave her confidence, those who backed up her plans. As Pontus left, Gail turned to her other two lieutenants, Typhon and Chron. "Chron, I need you to travel south and rally the tribes. They are your people. I've searched the futures and things are merging together. We need them. Tell your father now is the time, to call his villages together and have his people gather their weapons. I will need him at a moment's notice."

Chron nodded and went to the bachelor's hut to gather his traveling gear.

She addressed Typhon. It would be him and her. He would be enough. "You and I, my friend, are going to have the hardest part. There's a strong possibility Gar-el will send troops in here to force us to trade. We must prepare."

Confusion passed over Typhon's face. "We have prepared all rainy season. What else is there to do?"

Gail let out a hoarse laugh. "We have been preparing for a war, yes, but if the colonists come back, we must be ready for a battle. I do not intend let Gar-el and an army come near this village again. We have to find a place for that fighting to take place."

Typhon appeared more confused than ever. "How

will we select the place where the fighting is to take place? Gar-el will go where he wants. We cannot tell him what to do."

"Oh, yes, we can," Gail replied, "the same way we made the Hausa and Batu come to us." She paused. "I need you to find me that spot. Here is what I'm looking for, and this is what I want to do." She explained what she planned.

After Gail had outlined her idea, the native whispered, "If it works, we will have a great victory, but if not—" his jaws tightened as he thought of the consequences. "—everything we have fought for will end in nothing. Our hunters will be killed and so will you be."

"I know," Gail replied. "You had better discover a good place."

When the attack came, Gail hoped she was ready. She had taken a handful of men and scouted a small range of hills Typhon had told her about, and located the perfect spot to lure the Muians into a trap, if she could provoke Gar-el.

"Typhon, you know the plan. Have one of our men captured, and tell the Muians the native forces have massed by these hills." She gestured the low mountains behind her. "They're looking for a fight. Gar-el wants a quick victory to prove himself; with any luck, they'll come straight here. But to be on the safe side, we'll send out men to harass the colonials and retreat back this way. Are our men prepared? They know what they have to do?"

"Are you sure of this?" countered Typhon. "You look—strange. I know the plan, but I think it would be better if you stay at the village. I will lead the men."

Gail was wearing a mailed coat again, along with her short sword. Amber tugged on his leash, but her eyes were focused on the futures, and the one she walked into.

She gestured to the fifty men behind her. "No, I won't tell these guys to do something that I wouldn't do myself. This is too dangerous, and if something goes wrong, we might have to change our plans on a moment's notice. Now let's get moving."

Gail marched her men to the base of a small butte. "This is it. Let's make camp and wait."

Scouts kept a running tab on the whereabouts of the colonial army, bringing back reports of their progress. Small groups of warriors made predawn raids on the Muians, showing themselves as the sun rose and fading back into the savannah in Gail's direction. Her one fear was that Gar-el would not take her bait, but sweep through the villages destroying everything they came across.

Everyday Gail made it a point to climb the butte she had chosen for the battle and gaze out across the plain, Amber by her side.

Here I am, come to mama.

Three days later, Typhon reported to her, "They come, Gaela. An army of two hundred men plus wagons loaded with the giant crossbows they call scorpions and their operators."

"You're sure? Is Gar-el with them?"

"Yes, and no. As soon as they 'captured' our runner, the army turned south, coming straight in this direction."

"Good."

"Gar-el was with the troops. Our man stayed for a day and then managed to escape. He overheard the officer in charge tell Gar-el it was better if he went back to New Bethand, because if for some reason they lost the battle, it would not be Gar-el who had lost, but his general. If they won, however, Gar-el had won because it was his plan and army."

"You mean he's not with the soldiers now?" The futures hadn't shown that, or had she missed something? Everything was confused, too many changes. She sighed. "Go on."

Typhon shuffled his feet, studying Gael's face.

"The governor must have agreed, because yesterday our scouts tell me they saw a small party leaving, an elephant in front."

"Damn!" Gail kicked the earth, scattering dirt and rocks. Amber hissed.

Typhon's jaw dropped. "What is the matter?"

"If I'd known he was by himself, we could'a captured him and this whole business would be over." The futures had shown that, if only she had followed the right one. What else had she missed?

"I did not—"

"Never mind." Gail took a deep breath. "No use crying over spilled palm wine, as we say."

The following morning the colonial army came into view. Gail watched their progress from her mountain retreat and then rushed down to her warriors.

"They see us," announced Gail to the fifty tense men clustered around her. She gazed over the plain as horses and wagons loaded with scorpions raced toward their position. "Up we go."

Her men climbed the slope of the butte.

"Gaela, hurry, they will soon be here." Typhon tugged on her arm.

She shook his hand off. "In a minute. I want that general to get a good look, let that Muian know he's trapped the Spirit Goddess, or whatever they are calling me now."

When they army was close enough, Gail began the climb up the slope of the butte. Three sides of the stone monolith rose in vertical cliffs a hundred feet into the air. The fourth side that Gail ascended was almost as precarious, with boulders and small bushes blocking the way. When she reached the top, Gail's body was drenched in sweat, and covered with dirt. She looked back down the way she had climbed.

Okay, you have us trapped. What are you going to

do now?

The army reached the base of the mountain and stopped at the bottom of the slope. A troop of cavalry broke from the main group, and made a slow circle around the rest of the butte, looking for trails down. Finding none, they returned, reported.

Gail perched on a boulder, watching the enemy below. Typhon came next to her and asked, "What do you think they are going to do, attack?"

"Don't know," mumbled Gail. She checked the time; the sun was past its zenith. "Have a couple of the men start gathering firewood for tonight. The rest can stand by."

The colonists dismounted and set up their giant bolt throwers. A slow, ponderous, covering fire started as the soldiers began an assault.

"Here they come," yelled Gail. Typhon ordered the men up to the edge of the mountainside. "Should we return their fire?"

The arrows from the scorpions were proving ineffective shooting uphill. Most passed over the heads of the natives. Some even fell back on the advancing colonists.

"Don't waste your bolts," advised Gail. She gestured to the stones and boulders. "We have plenty of ammunition right here." She picked up a rock and hurled it downhill as far as she could throw it. The missile bounced, shattered and sprayed the soldiers below with chips.

The warriors got the idea and a hail of breaking boulders rained down on the Muians. The colonists made a slow retreat, with curses and threats.

"I don't think they'll try that again," commented Gail to Typhon. She yawned. "Post a guard here in case they change their minds. The rest of us will get some sleep. We're going to have a busy time later."

After midnight, Gail made the rounds and woke any of the warriors who still slept.

"Part one down, now for part two," Gail told the hunters. "Get the ropes and let's get out of here."

The natives drew cords from their packs. With long practice, they knotted the fibers together, tied the braids off on boulders, and threw them over the far edge of the butte.

Gail surveyed her men. "Everyone got their weapons strapped to their backs?" she asked. "Nothing loose that will make noise?" She heard a murmur of agreement.

Apprehension showed plain on the faces before her. With more bravura than she felt, she said, "If any of you fall, fall silently, will ya?" Soft chuckles answered her, and some of the tension she saw disappeared.

"Okay," she said. Let's do this." The villagers slipped over the rim of the butte, and made their descent through the darkness to the base of the mountain far below.

Gail, Typhon and Amber were the last to attempt the drop.

"Gaela, do you need my help?" asked Typhon.

"No, I'll be fine." Gail scratched behind Amber's ears. "You, honey, are going to have to stay here for a while. Mama will be back."

Typhon slipped over the edge. Gail waited a few minutes and followed suit. Amber paced back and forth with low whines, and disappeared, searching for a way down for himself.

Gail felt her heart hammering in her chest, her gasps sounding too loud in her ears, as she inched herself downward into the Stygian darkness.

I hope this works. So dark, can't see how far down it is. Damn it, the skin's ripping off my hands—I hope this works.

Gail's arms bunched, her shoulders and neck ached, and the muscles felt like they were going to tear from her bones. She kept lowering herself, hand-over-hand, teeth gritted, her palms growing slippery with her own blood.

She could go no farther. She would let go and hope for the best; she closed her eyes, held her breath, and tensed her legs.

Rough hands grabbed her. "Here, Gaela, let me help you." Typhon held her waist, supported her as she fell the last two feet to the earth.

"I think you're going to have to lead the men," Gail said. Her hands burned, and even without being able to see her flesh, she knew they bled and the skin was gone. "I don't think I can hold my sword."

"You have done your part," he replied. "Will you be all right here?"

"Yes, I want to get my breath. I'll follow you in a minute."

Typhon scrambled down to the base of the butte where the other warriors waited. They faded away into the darkness like silent wraiths.

Gail took a few deep breaths to steady her nerves and picked her way through the night around the mountain. When the light of the colonial encampment came into view, the cries of battle had already faded away.

The campfires of the colonists burnt low. Reflected in the ruddy light, Gail saw the bodies of men still wrapped in their sleeping blankets.

She stopped dead. She saw Typhon standing over a corpse, a bloody sword in his hand. "Typhon, are there any prisoners?" Her hunters wandered about the campsite, but no live Muians.

Typhon strolled among the bodies to her. "I do not think so," he replied, wiping the blood off his sword. "When we attacked they were all asleep. We killed most before they knew what was happening." He gestured toward the plain where a false dawn broke. "A few ran in that direction—I sent men to find them."

"Oh, okay."

A yellow streak hit her feet, claws dug into her

222

mailed shirt.

"Amber!" She petted the Oslo's head. "Where did you come from?"

"Came running down the hill as we attacked," said Typhon with a faint chuckle. "Guess he was looking for you."

Gail bent down and hugged the cat to her. "Dummy, I told you I was coming back. You could have got yourself killed."

"I think that is the commander over there." Typhon pointed to a tent. A body slumped half-in, half-out of the entrance.

Gail leashed Amber and walked over.

The dead man was Ben-dor.

"Yes, that's probably him."

A nameless emotion swelled up inside her.

"What are your orders next, Gaela?"

She gazed across the savannah where the sun had risen.

"I wish I didn't know."

***

The season was growing late. The rains would soon be starting. When Gail and her men returned from the battle at the butte, a thousand questions bombarded Gail and Typhon from the anxious villagers. More came from runners who had waited and wanted to report to their tribes. Gail left Typhon to deal with the questions and retreated to her hut. A frantic Malta greeted her.

"Pontus has not arrived from the north, and we have had no word from Chron," she said, giving Gail a savage hug. "And I was so worried. I am glad at least you are back."

Gail returned Malta's hug with a hard squeeze of her own and sat on her pallet. She was glad to have the young woman's company. Gail felt alone, desolate, all this planning of battles and war. She knew what had to happen, but the details!—the blood. The visions never showed the blood. She was in over her head. Gail closed her eyes and calmed herself. *Push on.*

"Don't worry Malta, I've searched the futures and in none of them have I seen Pontus or Chron killed." She smiled bravely at the young woman. "Now I don't guarantee they won't lose a body part or two, but nothing of importance that might bother you, I'm sure."

"Gaela!"

Malta blushed red under her dark tan. To hide her embarrassment, she grabbed an old piece of deer hide, shredded at one end, which was one of Amber's toys. "I missed you, too, you old pussycat," she cooed to the Oslo as she wiggled it across his vision. The cat responded by pouncing. Malta jerked it out of his reach.

"I haven't been away long," Gail said, smiling at the cat's antics as it chased the toy, "but has anything happened here? What's been going on?"

Malta lost interest in the deer hide, and after a good chewing Amber did too. "Nothing. With Pontus away, and Chron, too, I have only Mother and the other old women to talk to, and they only want to discuss what to cook for dinner." She laughed.

Gail laughed along with her. It was good to talk to Malta and take her mind off everything. "Go on, what else?"

Malta gave a deep sigh. "Well, that is about it, I guess. I told you, the village is about deserted. All the rest of the men are out hunting, preparing for the rainy season—they are not around most of the time. It is still a couple of weeks before we start harvesting the crops, so there is nothing to do there either." She groaned, "And I am bored."

The crops. She knew she'd forgotten something. Malta's words snapped her back to the problems at hand. *On with the war.*

"Malta, I've got to go find Typhon," Gail said, rising. "I'll return in a bit, okay, unless you want to take a walk with me?"

"Sure, why not? Better than sitting here by myself." She stood. "Amber, you stay. Take a nap."

The two girls left the hut. They located Typhon sitting with a group of elders and children recounting the recent battle.

"…and I took my sword and went like *this!* And a soldier died." The old people nodded, the youngsters' eyes were wide and they gasped each time Typhon slashed with his hand. "Another ran at me and I went like *that!* And he dropped. Two sprinted at me at once and I—"

"Typhon, we have to talk," Gail broke in.

Malta added, "And I think you are scaring the children, too. Their mothers will never be able to get them to sleep tonight after listening to your tales."

Typhon gave the group a sheepish grin and rose. "I will be back," he promised the elders, "after you," he pointed to the boys and girls, "have gone to sleep."

With a few moans and protests from the children, Typhon walked with Gail and Malta to a secluded section of the compound where they could talk in private.

"Yes, Gaela, what is the matter?"

"We must burn the fields," Gail said.

Startled, Typhon turned toward their crops. "What? Who's—ours?"

"The planters," Gail stated with conviction. "We must send out small parties of two or three men to each plantation and burn their fields before they start taking in their harvests."

For a moment, Typhon's mouth hung open as he tried to fathom what Gail contemplated. Finally, he blurted out, "Why? I understand destroying the coastal tribe's fields, but we are not at war with the planters."

"Even after the way they've treated our people?"

Gail shot back.

A troubled expression passed over Typhon's face. "I understand what you mean. Some of the planters are cruel, yes, but I have talked to our people, the ones arrested and beaten, and most of the abuse came from the colonial soldiers, or the overseers appointed by the colony authorities, not the planters themselves. The merchants and governor have been giving us all the trouble. Once they have been taken care of everything will go back to the way it was."

"Things will never be the same," declared Gail. "They shouldn't be, and the planters *are* part of the problem. If nothing else, they should have told the overseers to stop. They didn't. Why? Because they feel the same way as the rest of the colonists. It doesn't matter how you treat a yip." Gail took a deep breath.

"If we burn their fields, New Bethand will have less food. There will be hunger. They ship some of their crops back to Bethand—there will be shortages. I want to make things as difficult as possible for the Muians."

"But the colonists won't starve," Typhon protested, taken aback by the savagery of Gail's words. "The town is on the bay—plenty of fish, clams, and crabs."

"Some will go hungry," Gail plowed on. "The poor, all those new immigrants that have come in will be on short rations. They will complain. The merchants will whine, the Bethish Senate will grumble. More, the planters will bring their families into town and add to the situation. Anything to cause Jar-el more problems."

Typhon still appeared dubious, but he said, "As you wish, Gaela."

Malta exclaimed, "Gaela, how can you be so cruel? That town has women and children in it who have never harmed us. You know that."

"I know. That's what makes it all the harder."

Chapter Sixteen

"You're sure the colonists from Bionx won't try to reinforce New Bethand?" Gail asked Pontus. Jankus and the other leaders stood by, listening intently as Gail laid out the battle plan. She bent over the deerskin map they studied, discussing their next attack and asking questions. She glanced up when Pontus chuckled.

"They would be foolish to try," he replied, pointing to the black dots he had drawn. "The northern tribes have been having great success. If Bionx sends troops south to reinforce New Bethand, they will leave themselves open to attack."

Gail drew her attention back to the map. "The Ambosians don't realize many of the warriors from the north have come south to join us?" Pontus had returned with hundreds of hunters, all pledged to the cause in the south and to Gail. They came out of gratitude for what he had showed their people, and what he had done.

"No," Pontus denied. "The first thing the Muians did when they lost a few battles was to pull their troops back to guard their plantations and town. Our spies tell us word came from overseas. They were denied troops from Ambos—too many soldiers were lost in their civil war." He gave Gail his wolfish grin.

Gail looked up. "No one told me that. Any word if troops have left from Bethand to reinforce New Bethand?"

"No, we have heard nothing yet, but when Bionx found out no help was coming, they rode out under a flag of truce and signed a temporary truce. Basically they are on their own."

"Good."

Pontus looked across the field where his men had

set up small hide shelters. "That is why I was able to recruit so many—at least for the time being, there will be no fighting in the north. Hate for the Muians consumes these men. Friends and loved ones have been hurt or killed. If they cannot destroy the Bionx colonists, then they wish to fight the ones in New Bethand."

Other tribes had gathered to join Gail, some from the far interior, some from the south. Gail had foreseen this and the futures had slowly drawn together for her. Gail still saw great danger and many things would go wrong, but one fact stood out: the battle they were planning now must happen. They had to win, and Gail thought she knew how.

She drew two lines opposite each other and split each into three with quick strokes of charcoal.

"These are the colonists," Gail said, pointing to one line, "and this is us." She gestured to the other. "First the soldiers will try a cavalry charge against the center of our line."

"Why not sit back and pick us off with their scorpions?" asked Jankus, gesturing to the enemy position. "It would be easy and keep their soldiers out of danger."

"They might fire a few," conceded Gail. "Chron, Typhon, what do you think? Would Gar-el be happy sitting back firing bolts at us?"

The muscles in Chron's jaw worked and he said, "Not on your life. He is out to make a name for himself. He wants to crush us and do it in style." He stabbed a finger at Gail. "Before I left the colony I heard him bragging in the Smokestack. He said if he were in charge, he would send cavalry at us, and right behind them the infantry. He is the governor now—his soldiers have suffered defeats. He will be in no mood to shoot arrows."

"What was he doing at the Smokestack?" Gail asked, curious.

Chron gave a gruff laugh. "I think it had something to do with Adiana, or one of the other servers, I am not sure which one. He talked to them all, but he and his cronies meet there two or three times a week, before he was made governor, to drink and boast what they would do when they ruled."

"He is right," confirmed Typhon. "We all saw him when he came through here. Arrogant—letting us know he was ready to teach the yips a lesson if they got out of line."

"I thought as much," said Gail with a sour expression. She poked the map again. "I want to equip our center line with long poles; sharpened and hardened in fire at one end, a counterweight at the other—something like long spears." She glanced at Pontus. "These will be your men—this can be done?"

"Yes, but—"

"It's to stop his cavalry. I'll tell you in a moment. After we've destroyed their riders, we'll start forming our valley."

All three of the leaders looked puzzled.

"Gaela," Pontus started to say, "There is no valley. It is all open—"

Gail put two fingers to his mouth. "Hush. I'll tell you that later, too." She placed her palm on the marks showing their flanks, rubbed them out, and drew two more lines until she had a U. "Now this is what I want to happen—"

***

The following morning was cool and dry. A light breeze flowed from the sea to the land making the colonial pendants flutter as they advanced across the plain. Trumpets blew, and at the head of all this, Gar-el rode on his war elephant.

In contrast to the colonial pageantry, the natives emerged from the tall grass in silence, stretching into a long, thin line opposite the Muians. The hunters began a rhythmic chant, beating their swords against their shields:

Ya-hu-yah!

Ya-hu-yah!

Ya-hu-yah! Over and over. Occasionally one of the hunters would dash out and hold his arms high, screaming defiance.

Besides the hundreds of warriors Pontus had brought, Chron and his father had gather a thousand. Chron led them north, all sworn to fight for Gail. A chosen few Chron was using with his cavalry, the rest under their generals would be the left flank of the native army.

Typhon was in charge of the right flank. His were the warriors from the central plains, the tribes of Jankus, and those from the interior. All had kinship ties with Typhon. All swore allegiance to the "Spirit Goddess—Gaela."

Gail, Pontus and Typhon paced down their line, inspecting the men, and making comments to the leaders of each individual unit.

Gail noticed warriors scrambling out of line and picking up dirt and stones from the ground as she passed. Each man placed the earth in the small bags around their necks. After this happened a dozen times, she asked Pontus, "What are those men doing?" She patted her side. "Do I have a hole in my pouch?"

"No, Gaela. They pick up the ground you have walked on for good luck."

"What?"

"You are the Spirit Goddess to some," replied Pontus.

"That's nuts! Who would possibly think that?"

"They feel you are invincible in battle. They want some of that luck to stay with them." His next words hit her like a hammer. "They worship you."

"Tell me this is a joke!" She turned to Chron. "Don't tell me your men believe that too?"

Chron looked straight ahead. "When I went south, men spoke you name in whispers, 'Gaela, the Goddess of the Savannah.' I saw no reason to tell them otherwise."

This can't be happening, she told herself. She closed her eyes and counted to ten. *These people are talking crazy. I've been winging this for months. Who would spread—*

"It was *you*," Gail said, giving Pontus an accusing look.

Pontus replied, deadpanned, "On my second trip north they were already speaking about you." His eyes shifted to the colonial line. "Although, on my first visit, I did mention that all battle wisdom came from your lips."

They had reached the end of the line. Gail said, "We will talk about this later. I think the Muians are about to start."

From the colonial side a trumpet blew. Bolts from the scorpions flew upward and outward. Most fell short. A few however, struck their marks and natives dropped.

Astride his elephant, Gar-el observed in boredom.

"This is getting us nowhere fast," he called down to his general in charge. "Those yips do not have the brains to retreat. We'll be here all day picking these natives off one by one." He yawned.

"But Governor, attacking long distance is much safer," replied the officer, trying to sound as reasonable as possible. "What does it matter if shooting bolts takes a few more minutes—?"

Gar-el glared at the man. "If you cannot finish off these creatures in a timely manner, sir, then I will. Send out the cavalry and make those savages jump—break their line in half and we'll get this farce over in a hurry."

The officer's jaws worked but he nodded and signaled to his bugler. Two short notes sounded and mounted warriors with lances advanced. There was another moment of silence and then another blare from the horn. The riders tensed.

From the back of the natives, on a raised platform

on top of a hill, Gail called down to Pontus.

"It's time for our men to advance—good luck!"

Pontus waved that he understood and the hunters moved out in a long line.

Another long bugle blast rang out from the colonial side followed by two short ones. The riders charged.

The two lines moved toward each other. Pontus waved a red flag over his head and the center of his line halted, dropped to the ground on their knees, and raised the long, sharpened poles. The two flanks continued their slow advance.

The colonial commanders, seeing the middle of the natives stopping and falling, decided the hunters were surrendering and directed their charge in that direction. When they realized their mistake, and saw what the warriors carried, mass confusion erupted.

Some tried to angle back toward the flanks; others attempted to halt only to disrupt the charge of those behind who were still riding forward. A few, either unaware of what the natives held, or too foolish to realize the consequences, continued their headlong attack. The stakes impaled their horses.

The colonial charge disintegrated into a mass of cursing men and screaming animals.

Pontus waved his red flag and his center advanced again. This time the native line had a distinct bow to it.

Gail, Amber, Jankus, and the rest of the elders watched the battle from their knoll.

"Is it time to send our horsemen in?" asked an apprehensive Jankus.

"No. We wait until the colonists send in the infantry and reserves." Gail pointed across the plain to the elephant and the remaining colonial troops. "I think they're getting ready."

Gar-el watched his cavalry charge fall apart. "What are they doing out there?" he sputtered to the general.

"Why did they stop? Why don't those fools attack?"

"Uh—I am not sure, sir." The commander studied the field of combat. "It appears the yips have put up stakes in the ground."

"Stakes, is it," snarled Gar-el, rising high on his mount to get a better look. "They want to play tricks? I'll show them tricks—send in the infantry."

"But sir—" the general protested, "— our riders—"

"Send them in *now!*"

The officer shook his head in disgust, and appeared to be ready to argue. He growled under his breath and changed his mind, signaling to his trumpeter instead.

More bugles blew and the colonial foot soldiers marched out. They started at a slow walk, but then fell into a trot, yelling and screaming as they advanced. They hit the milling cavalry, became tangled up in the confusion, and disappeared from view. A few managed to emerge from the other side and started for the native line in a ragged mass. The center of Pontus's troops began a slow retreat, their long spears still pointed before them, making it impossible for the Muians to attack them directly.

The natives drew the colonials deeper into the battlefield.

"That's it! That's it!" Gar-el gave a jubilant shout. "The center is crumbling, the yips are falling back. Send in our reserves and we can sweep the field."

His general watched with growing apprehension. "The natives do not appear to be crumbling, sire," he replied. "In fact, they are retreating in an orderly manner. I think—"

"Do it *now*, you dolt!" Gar-el screamed, pointing.

The officer ground his teeth in silent rage, looking first at the governor, and then at his aides, who shuffled their feet and refused to return his gaze. With a shrug, he waved his hand and the balance of the troops swept into the fight, attacking Pontus's centerline.

"Okay—he's committed," Gail said. She signaled to her reserves and horsemen. "Let's slam the door and close the trap." She waved and pointed. *"Go!"*

The remaining tribesmen surged forward, bracing the middle of the native's centerline. Two bands of cavalry led by Chron swept out on either side of the natives, raced along the outside of the fighting, and closed on the colonial rear.

The insurgent flanks turned inward.

The tribal warriors, reinforced by their reserves, stopped their retreat and started a slow advance, prodding the colonial forces with their long spears as they marched ahead.

The edges of Gail's line continued to swing shut, pressing ever tighter against the enemy.

Chron and his horsemen swept in behind, cutting off any possible line of retreat for the colonial soldiers.

Gail had created a box of death.

The Muians found themselves encircled. Trapped, most clustered in a swirling sea of men with no one to attack. Their comrades on the perimeter fought for their lives and died under the swords of the natives. The tribesmen kept pressing inward like a fist squeezing a rotten orange.

Gar-el's jaw dropped. He sputtered in bewilderment, "What is happening? What are those yips doing?"

The general watched in horror, unable to order a retreat, and with no reserves at his command to commit for another attack. "They've surrounded us, sir. We are losing."

The Gar-el turned white. "We cannot be losing—do something!"

The commander drew in a deep breath and let it escape. "There is nothing we can do, sir." He raised his hands in helpless rage. "The best thing to do is flee from here before we are captured."

"But—" The governor's son looked around for someone to help him. When he glanced back down at his general, he found the man and his staff already riding away toward the safety of the town.

With a moan of helpless terror, Gar-el watched a moment longer as his army was hacked to pieces and disappeared beneath the swords and spears of the natives. He struck his elephant and raced after his officers.

By the end of the day, the battle was over. Ravens circled the battlefield, on occasion diving to earth to settle on the bodies and pick the flesh of the dead.

The natives wandered among the fallen, rescuing their friends, or finishing off the enemy. No captives were taken. The colonists had waited too long to surrender, and by the time they did, the natives had fallen into a bloodlust.

Pontus, Chron, and Typhon rejoined Gail on her hill, blood-covered and exhausted, the horrors of battle etched in their faces.

"I could not stop," gasped Pontus, wiping dirt and gore off his face. "The men behind would not let me. They kept pushing forward. I had no choice but to keep fighting until I found no one else to kill."

"I tried," breathed Chron, sitting on the grass, his face in his hands. "I tried, when they began to surrender; but I could not. Something—" He looked at the rest and shook his head, still not believing what he had done, "— kept my sword stabbing. It was as if I had no control over myself." He stared at his right hand, still frozen in the grip of an imaginary sword.

Gail had tried to stop the slaughter when it became apparent the colonists were surrendering. "Jankus," she climbed down from her platform and grabbed the old man's hand. "We must do something, quick. This must be halted at once— those men are trying to give up." She had seen colonials fall to their knees and throw away their swords, only to have her men cut them down in cold blood.

"What can we do, Gaela?" The chief stood and waved to the churning men in the distance. "There is no stopping our people now. We must wait until this is over." He gave her a curious look. "You did not foresee this in the futures?"

Gail had. She hadn't realized the clashing of steel, the screaming of the dying, or the smell of the blood would be so real. "Oh, God, I never thought—" She grabbed Amber and held him tight, "Come here." *It was necessary,* she kept thinking. *This is the only way. Oh, God, forgive me— I had to!* For the remainder of the battle she buried her face in Amber's fur and covered her ears, hiding underneath her stand so she did not have to watch the massacre.

"It is over," Pontus said with a note of finality. "The colonists have been defeated and will not bother us again. They know our strength now and would be fools to do so."

"No, you are wrong," Gail replied, scrubbing at her eyes and wishing the fighting was over. "The worst is still to come." She gazed at the dark blotches on the battlefield with ravens landing on them. "We still have to take the town. No siege machines—not enough warriors—I saw more battles on the horizon."

She stood up with a sigh. "I'd better get down there and help with the wounded."

"Wait." Pontus grabbed her hand and pulled her back. "When was the last time you gazed at the future? Was there any change?"

Gail untied Amber and held tight to the leather thong as the Oslo tugged. "Yes, after the battle started and we were assured of winning." Her voice took on a darker tone. "The futures are crystalizing and the odds are now even that we will win in the end, but I see ships on the horizon, troops from Bethand coming. The hardest choices are still before us."

Pontus, Typhon, and Chron stared back at her, fatigue etched in their faces.

Yes, there is more. We are not done yet— not by a long shot.

She thought of one other thing she had to do before she walked the horror of the battlefield, or maybe she was making excuses not to go. "Pontus, take a hundred of your men and go to the town of the Hausa Chief. I want him brought here today." Gail swung to Chron and addressed him. "Take a hundred of your people and go to the Batu village and bring their headman back, also."

Both men glared at Gail in disbelief. "The warriors are exhausted, and it is late—" began Pontus.

Gail cut him off. "I know—I want both here today."

Chron shook his head as if he could not believe what she had said and asked, "Why? Tomorrow will be soon enough—"

"By tomorrow, those corpses will start to rot and stink," snapped Gail, her temper kept in check by will alone. "I don't want to be anywhere near this place when that happens." Gail scanned the plain before her in dismay. "But the Hausa and Batu must see what we did to the colonists. I want them to see those," she waved a hand at the battlefield, "with our men standing here victorious. Understand?"

Both men nodded their heads in resignation. "Yes, Gaela, it shall be done."

"Go."

Pontus and Chron collected their men and trotted off. Gail resumed her seat on her stand. Amber curled up at her feet.

As the sun reached the horizon, the warriors returned escorting the two headmen.

The Batu chief's eyes kept darting left and right as he gazed at the dead bodies lying across the plain. He licked his thin lips as Chron brought him in front of Gail, and stood twisting, first surveying at the battlefield, and then at the warriors lined up behind her.

The Hausa chief arrived moments later, surrounded by his councilors, his body covered in sweat from the unaccustomed trek. He glared at Pontus, making it plain he had not wanted to come. When he saw Gail, he stalked up before her, his heavyset body quivering with rage.

"Why have you brought me here?" he demanded. "We have done nothing." He waved to the battlefield. "This is none of our concern. The Hausa have remained neutral in this fight. I demand—"

"You demand?" Gail stared down at him in scorn. "Who are you to demand from *me!*"

The Batu leader spoke up. "People say you are not even one of us. You are a—"

"SILENCE."

Both men quailed back from her blast.

"I am the Spirit Goddess Gaela," Gail shouted, half rising from her seat. Amber sprang up in alarm and let out a low growl. "You have allied yourselves with the colonists in the past. This shall end. I do not want your neutrality, I expect your loyalty, otherwise—" she gestured to the plain. Birds still circled in the sky against the red clouds. "—this shall be the fate of your people as well." She sat back down in a huff, eyes blazing, and said, "What will you choose?"

The Batu chieftain followed her hand and then fell on his knees. He bowed his head and exclaimed, "My people are yours to command, Spirit Goddess," he choked out between clenched teeth.

The Hausa leader was slower. First, he glanced at his councilors, some already falling in homage, and then at the dead. His body slumped and with a low groan, he too dropped to his knees. "We will follow you, Gaela, wherever you may lead."

"Good." Gail took a deep breath and nodded in satisfaction. "You may go now," she said and waved her hand in dismissal. "In a few days I shall dispatch a runner to you with instructions. I will have need of your warriors."

The two chiefs hurried off with low mutters under their breath. Gail climbed off her stand and watched the pair go, stone-faced.

Pontus, Typhon, and Chron crowded around her. "I thought you did not want to be called the Spirit Goddess?" Pontus said, a puzzled look on his face. "Now you are calling yourself that."

Gail shrugged and looked grim. "They're already doing it, so I might as well use the fact." She gave each a stern look in turn. "But if I hear it out of any of you three, I'll take this sword and paddle you good, understand me?" She touched her short sword for emphasis. "That goes for our men too, I don't care what they think, but they'd better not call me Spirit Goddess where I can hear it."

Pontus grinned and said, "Yes, Gaela, as you will."

"It's getting dark." Gail said. Her legs felt weak, sweat and dirt covered every inch of her body. *I would love a hot bath,* she thought with a sigh, *but I can't put this off any longer. I have to do this so the men can see me—know I'm not afraid.*

"I'm going to walk in the battlefield," she said, tugging on Amber's leash, "and see if there is anyone I can help that we missed." The tribesmen parted as she and the Oslo left.

In the building darkness, crows and vultures flapped into the sky, disturbed by the passing of Amber and Gail as they moved among the dead. A few warriors were still busy stripping the bodies of weapons; a low rumble of distant thunder echoed behind her from their voices. As Gail wandered across the battlefield, she heard the hunters whisper, *"Spirit Goddess."*

She said nothing.

Chapter Seventeen

The Bethish fleet landed. Alak-an sat on the dock and watched as a hundred transport and supply ships unloaded men and crates in a continuing stream. He pushed himself erect with a grunt and wandered back to the Smokestack Inn. He was one of the lucky ones, he guessed, pushing through the crowded streets. With the colony under siege, and the plantation owners fleeing into the security of the town as their crops and homes burned, places to sleep were scarce. His men had set up their tents on the beach – he at least had managed to secure a room until the fighting was over.

Farmers with no harvest to reap and merchants with no cargo to carry packed the inn, the low babble of voices rose and fell like a snoring lion. Alak-an surveyed the room with disdain, and seeing no place to sit, was about ready to go to his room when two planters rose and left a small corner table vacant. He hastened to it before anyone else noticed and dropped into an empty chair, making himself comfortable.

Adiana hustled over and banged a tankard of ale down in front of him before he said anything. "Crazy in here tonight," she said. "All these soldiers and sailors off those ships." She looked toward the bar. Her father was conducting his own battle like a field marshal, directing cooks and serving girls. He beckoned to her urgently and pointed to a tray of food. "Be right back to take your order." She hurried away.

"Take yer time, honey," the trader called back and settled down to sip his drink, watching the people coming and going. A tall soldier strode in, stood irresolute by the door. His eyes fell on the lone chair opposite Alak-an, his brows rose in a question.

Alak-an waved him over. "Com'on, always room for one more," he boomed as the man sauntered to the table and sat. "Glad fer the company."

The man let out a sigh of relief, and looked Alak-an over. "Thanks. I was out walking, smelled the smoke, and decided I was hungry." He glanced around at all the people. "Always this busy in here?"

"Na, just since the war." Alak-an waved at Adiana as she hurried by carrying a tray. "Hey, girl, you're slowin' down. Two more tankard of ale here," he turned back to the soldier, "what ya having mate?"

"A steak would be good."

"Steak it is," he agreed. "Hey, Adiana, two steaks here, too. Rare—I want them to say moo when I stick a knife in them." Alak-an smirked as he watched the harried serving girl hurry to her father with their order. "She'll be a bit." He eyed the other. "You off one of those ships?"

Two more tankards of ale banged down in front of the pair. Moments later their steaks appeared.

"Twenty silver," Adiana say, glancing over her shoulder at her father.

"How much?" Alak-an replied, outraged. "Yesterday it was five for a tankard and steak. What happened?"

"Price has gone up," the serving girl replied impatiently, looking at her father who was waving to her frantically. "Beef's getting scarce. Better enjoy those. Tomorrow all you may get is fish."

Grumbling, Alak-an reached for his purse, but the soldier held up his hand. "My treat." When Alak-an protested the man added, "For the chair." He flipped Adiana over a fat gold Bethish round.

She grabbed it and gave him a wink. "For you we might find more steak."

The soldier chuckled and looked back to Alak-an. "Came in this morning," he said to Alak-an. "Been out ever since checking the stockade and fortifications." He surveyed the crowd as he took a bite. "All these refugees?"

Alak-an nodded and said between bites, "Yep. Could say Gar-el messed everything up good, 'cept'n it was messed up all ready."

"Yea?" The soldier sipped his ale and leaned back in his chair. "How so?"

Alak-an studied him closely, debating how much complaining this soldier would accept before arresting him. "Well, I'll tell ya," he said at last, deciding this newcomer was truly curious, "these colonists have been stealing the natives blind fer years—first in little ways. Now its worst'en ever." He gave the man a knowing nod. "I'm a free trader, have been for years, know the back country like the roof of my mouth. Probably know half the natives out there." He gestured toward the east.

"Now I'm not saying I don't drive a hard bargain," he continued, rubbing his hands together, "mind ya, sometimes I make a little more, sometimes a little less, but I ain't no thief." He leaned back in his chair and took a long draft of ale, watching the other to see what his reaction would be.

"You wouldn't know who these insurgents leaders are, do you? Like this Gaela, their spirit woman?" the soldier asked.

Alak-an took on a guarded look. He replied carefully, "Well, I couldn't say fer certain—closed-mouth group back there—could be any of a bunch of people."

The man fished around in his pouch, and this time pulled out a handful of gold Bethish rounds. He placed a stack on the table in front of Alak-an.

"Do you think you might take a message to any of these natives?"

Alak-an mouth dropped open and he rubbed his chin, looking from the gold to the soldier. "I—er—like I told ya, could be a bunch a different—"

The soldier took out another handful of coins and spilled them on top of the first stack. "But you have some idea? A message, nothing—"

"Put that away!" Alak-an whispered, cupping the pile and pushing it back toward the other. "Somebody sees that much gold and we'll both get our throats cut."

The man chuckled and scooped up the coins, shoving them into Alak-an's belly. "They're yours—a message to the leaders, nothing more, and three times that amount when you come back with a reply."

Alak-an swept the coins into his own purse with a furtive glance. "I ain't makin' no promises, I can't," he whispered. "The people you want could be anywhere in the outback. these folks don't stay in one place too long, if ya know what I mean. I'm taking a risk just going out there—those yips are riled up. I know the leaders, yea, but I don't know all the natives. If'n I run into the wrong bunch—" He ran his thumb across his throat.

"Well, if you were just blowing smoke, I suppose--"

"I didn't say that," replied Alak-an, "but this ain't no stroll in the park, I gotta tell ya that upfront. Gotta find supplies, too." He thought for a moment, estimating. "Pack mules, provision, and a horse. Maybe take me a couple of days, sold all my animals when I had to come here, needed the money, in case—don't know if we got that much time before things start to pop, anyway."

The soldier suddenly looked alert. "Why do you say that?"

Alak-an checked the dining room to make sure no one was listening and said in a low voice, "You said ya was out inspecting the stockade. How did it seem to you?"

"Looked strong enough to me," the man replied. "Have to reinforce it in places, but nothing major. Why?"

"See any holes dug underneath?" replied the trader.

The other laughed. "Oh, yes, I asked about that. The guards said pigs and dogs dig them at night. They fill whatever they find in the morning. No problem."

"Ain't many dogs and pigs running around anymore," Alak-an replied with a nod. "You heard Adiana, meat's getting scarce, but the half-breeds in town have relatives back in the bush, if ya know what I mean."

"You are not saying—"

Alak-an shrugged. "Told the authorities what I thought of course. Didn't want ta get caught up fighting in the colony. Nothing's been done about it that I know of."

"Well, something will be done now," the soldier replied, his voice grim. "You can be sure of it."

Alak-an looked the stranger over again and asked suspiciously, "Who are you anyway, I never got ya name?"

"My name is Ted," the soldier replied, sticking his arm out in greeting.

"Mine's Alak-an." He reached across the table and gasped the other's hand. "Well, if ya want me to go, I'll go— might stop this war before it goes on any farther, and it's better than sitting around here anyway doing nothing. Where can I find you when I come back?"

The stranger laughed and finished his steak, standing up. "It won't be hard. I'm the general in charge of this mess. Right now, I'm up in the governor's house. Stop by later and we will see what we can find for those supplies, and get you started – the sooner the better, I think. After that, I'll be with the army, camped out on that plain trying to figure out some way to stop this war." He gestured to the savannah. "Look for the tents."

***

Gail and Pontus argued.

"We attack now." Pontus's pacing took him back and forth in front of Chron and Typhon, who sat on the grass watching the two fight over when to start their final assault. The native glared at Gail in exasperation and exclaimed, "We have been waiting for this day. Everything we have done is for this moment. What is the problem now?"

"Now?" Gail understood his disappointment. They had fought so hard, so long. "Something has changed—the futures are different. If we—"

"Yes, of course—the future is different." Pontus pointed his finger and kicked the grass in frustration. "We have an army in front of us, and our runners tell me another is closing in from behind, marching from Bionx. They are loading on rafts now at the Ubo River. If we do not act soon—" He pressed his thumb and forefinger together before Gail's eyes "—we will get squished like bugs." He turned to Typhon. "Are our men still ready inside the colony?"

Typhon replied at once. "Yes, for the last two weeks since the new Muians arrived. The soldiers are guarding the gates and walls better, but our men say they can still breach them when the time comes."

Chron spoke up. "We had better do something soon. I cannot hold my people here forever. Soon the rains will start. They must go home and take in their crops, hunt and store food. Even the presences of the Spirit Goddess Gaela will not keep them here if their families are faced with starvation."

Pontus turned to Gail. "You see, it must be done now. What is the matter? Have the futures changed against us?"

"No, it's not that." Gail rose and placed her hands on his shoulders. "I know it's strange, but the futures tell me that if we wait, we will win. If we attack, we lose."

"What do you mean? That does not make any sense!" Pontus exclaimed in confusion.

Gail sat down. "I know it doesn't. It makes no sense to me either, but I see—" She closed her eyes. "A man, happy, bouncing a baby girl on his knee. '*Ride the pony, ride to town. Ride the pony, don't fall down*'," she recited, gazing at the scene that was so clear in her mind.

Pontus, Typhon, and Chron watched her in awe, not saying anything, afraid to disrupt whatever vision she had.

Gail still watched the scenes unfold before her in a kaleidoscope of changing images. "In another future I see the same man, but he is haggard, bloody. He wears the face of a mule that must toil but is too old to work." She continued in a small voice, *"There is no joy in him, no hope."*

Gail opened her eyes and started, having forgotten the three still stood before her. "Our future depends on which of these two men we meet."

"What do the futures show about us?" Typhon asked.

Gail shook her head. "That's the thing. They show nothing. This war revolves around him right now, what he does or doesn't do. Events have been taken out of our hands."

Their discussion was interrupted by the approach of two scouts, prodding a disheveled Alak-an before them and leading a string of pack mules.

"All right, boys—all right!" Alak-an tried hard to look behind at his guards, and still watch where he was going. When he saw Gail, Pontus, Chron, and Typhon, he broke out in a grin and quickened his pace.

"Told ya I knew the chiefs, didn't I?" he said to his captors. He pushed aside a spear point in his back. "You can stop sticking me now."

"Alak-an!" Gail waved the two warriors away. "What are you doing here?"

The trader stopped in front of the four, out of breath. "There ya are. Been lookin' all over the back country fer you bunch." He searched each face and settled on Gail. "Got news. Army wants to parley."

Pontus strode forward and swung the trader to look at him. "What? What do you mean?"

"Met a man in the Smokestack," Alak-an explained

in a rush, "said he was the commander of the army. I guess so, he had a lot of money. Asked me to get a message to ya—said he wanted to talk."

"You talked to the general of the Bethish force?" Gail gave him a skeptical look. "Are you sure?"

Alak-an screwed up his face and looked puzzled. "Yea, I think so, anyway. Told me to come up to the governor's house to get fitted out with supplies to come find ya. When I got there, he was sitting in Gar-el's chair. Didn't see that jerk anywhere around. I guess he's in charge now."

"That explains the change in the colonial tactics," said Pontus. "He must be in charge of the Bionx forces too. Bethand and Ambos have united against us. That is why they finally dispatched an army."

"Don't know about that," replied Alak-an, scratching his beard. "All I know is that the army wanted to talk. He sent me out ta tell ya that and get a reply." He glanced at the Gail and the hunters surrounding him. "Well?"

Gail had an otherworld look. Pontus studied her face and then realized the hunters were looking at him. "I guess it would not hurt. I hope this is not a ploy to buy the Muians more time. Chron, what do you think?"

"Me?" the native replied, startled. "I am all for talking—but like you said, I hope it is not a trap."

"If we wait too long that army will be behind us, and we will have no other choice but to talk," put in Typhon. "Act quick or not at all."

Gail finally spoke up. "Okay, Alak-an," she said, "Tell this general we'll meet him. Wait—" she paused, "we'll meet with him *after* that army behind us stops. Understand me?"

Alak-an smiled at her forethought. "Gottcha. Lost my ride when your men grabbed me. It'll take four-five day to get back to the colony—"

"We have horses," said Pontus. "We will have you back there in two."

"Sounds good. Maybe we can finish this and get back to normal," Alak-an replied. "Man can't make no money in times like this."

"Let's hope this general is an honest man," Gail replied. "Alak-an, I want you to be our official go-between," She nodded at the others, "if that is okay with you. I trust this man, but in this matter all must agree."

Pontus spoke up. "Alak-an has always been honest with us. I see no problem with him as our herald."

Chon and Typhon shook their heads in agreement.

"W-why, thank ya," Alak-an stammered, turning a faint pink under his sunburnt skin. "I'll try and do my best."

"And Alak-an, I have one more job for you." Gail fished around in her pouch. She had stopped carrying around a sack of gold nuggets, but still had a few in case the need arose. She found one and handed it over to the trader.

Alak-an's eyes widened as he took the rock. "Now, Gaela, ya know I can't be bringin' any more—"

"Not that," Gail said. "Remember at one time I told knowledge can be a weapon? I want you to learn about this general."

The trader still appeared hesitant. "Well, ya know, tryin' to get military secrets outta people ain't—"

"No, nothing like that," Gail replied. "I don't need information he will not tell you of his own free will. What I mean is, find out his likes, dislikes, little things. Does he enjoy being a soldier and fighting in battles? Travel? Does he have a wife and family? That sort of knowledge I need to know."

"That I can do," Alak-an said. "Anything else?"

"No, I don't think so. Why don't you go get something to eat?" Gail suggested. "You must be famished."

"Uh, okay, thanks," he replied, startled by the sudden dismissal. "I could go fer something, haven't eaten all day." He wandered off to an open-air kitchen where a cook was stirring a kettle of stew.

After the trader was out of earshot, Gail said to Pontus. "This general that Alak-an speaks of, he is the one I saw in our future."

"Are you sure?"

"Yes, the father, the one who is worn out from war."

"Then you know how to defeat him, right?" Typhon asked eagerly, hope on his face. "You must, you have seen him in your visions."

Gail closed her eyes, concentrating on the events to come. "No, but when we meet I will."

Chapter Eighteen

G ail, Amber, and Pontus stood waiting. They had strolled out into the no-man's-land between the armies the night before and started a campfire. In the early morning, the smoke curling to the sky acted as a signal of their location to the Bethish troops.

Chron and Typhon had stayed behind with the insurgent army. Gail had left strict instructions.

"If we're not back in two days, or if either one of those armies move, scatter our forces and regroup behind the Ubo River. After that, do whatever you have to do. Don't wait on us."

"It will not be long now," said Pontus, scratching Amber behind his ears.

Gail scrutinized the plain in the direction of the Bethish army. "No, it won't. I see three riders coming this way now."

Alak-an kept busy racing back and forth between the two forces, passing messages and setting up this meeting. On one such trip, he had reported to Gail, "This soldier fella is important back in Mu. He's a baron in Ambos, his brother-in-law is a prince there, and his father-in-law is an important senator in Bethand."

Pontus's eyes lit up. "That is why he was placed in charge of both the New Bethand and Ambos forces."

"Reckon so," Alak-an agreed. "He has complete control of this whole operation. Whatever he says, goes."

On another visit, Alak-an had arranged the exchange of prisoners, and an agreement to let the planters return to their farms. Pontus and the others were hesitant at first. "The idea is to keep the pressure on the colony as long as we can—the planters are part of this," said Pontus, with a shake of his head. "The more complaints this general gets, the quicker we can force the colonists into an agreement."

Alak-an nodded. "I expect you're right." He casually remarked, "Ya know, they're starving in there. Don't see any dogs, didn't see many rats, either. The half-breeds and native prisoners are suffering the most. They get fed last."

When Gail heard this, she gave a sigh. Without looking at Pontus, she replied, "Tell the general the planters can go home to their farms."

On his last visit before this meeting, the trader brought Gail the information she was looking for.

"Got to talking with that general over a tankard of ale before I left," he said. Gail, Pontus and Alak-an sat around their campfire discussing the coming negotiations. "He always wanted to be a soldier, fought in both the Bethand-Caragon war and the Ambos civil war."

"That means he's been fighting nonstop for three years," exclaimed Gail.

"Yea, says he tired," agreed Alak-an. "Mentioned he rescued his wife in the Ambos civil war."

"He's married, huh?" Gail nodded thoughtfully. "Did he say if he had any children?"

"As a matter-of-fact, he said she was expecting a baby when he was ordered here." Alak-an chuckled. "Wasn't happy to leave home, but he came."

The happy father bouncing the baby girl on his knee—the tired warrior still fighting long after he should stop. Gail peered into the futures and saw the two, side by side.

Gail watched as the three horsemen came closer, Alak-an in the lead. She tried a tentative mind touch on the two Muians following, but the riders held themselves closed. As they drew closer, even their faces were impassive, blank masks that gave nothing away.

The two soldiers dismounted and strolled to the fire

with confidence. The trader stood to one side, arms folded, a silent witness to what was happening.

"I'm glad you decided to come," said the taller of the two men. He smiled at Gail and Pontus and said, "We have much to discuss, and I hope we can solve our old problems here today." He opened his mind and beamed good will to the natives to make his point.

"I hope you are right. I wouldn't want to beat you in a battle, Ted," Gail thought back.

"What the...? Who?" The soldier peered at the two before him. His eyes widened in recognition. "Gail, is that you?" He broke out into a smile, and grabbed her around the waist in a hug. "It is! How?"

She grinned back and returned his hug. "Yes, I'm me. I'll explain everything later—but right now we have more serious problems, like for one, we are people and should be treated as such."

Ted recovered and gave a shrewd nod. "Let me start over again. I am General Ted Cole of the combined Bethish-Bionx forces. This is my aide Fredrick Von Braun from Ambos." He nodded to Pontus. You are—?"

The native spoke up. Gail had coached him on how to respond to the Muians. She wanted their party to sound as impressive as possible. "I am *Prince* Pontus, *General* of the central and northern forces." He made a sweeping wave to Gail. "This is the Seeress Gaela, Commander of all the native tribes."

The general did a double take and scrutinized Gail closer this time, taking in her full measure. "So you're the one. 'Spirit Goddess of the plains and forest'." He nodded to himself with a grin of understanding and got down on his knees, offering his hand to Amber for a sniff. "This must be the 'savage lion that follows', huh?" The Oslo responded by shoving his head under the fingers of Ted to get a scratch behind the ears.

Gail made a chuckling sound and knelt beside the

cat. "It seems you have already subverted one of our party to your cause. Let's get down to business."

Their eyes met. "You are not what you were before," Ted muttered more to himself than to Gail as he rose. "You have learned things."

He knows, Gail thought. *It doesn't matter.*

She stood also and brushed off her hands. "That can be discussed later; it has no bearing on this meeting." Gail said to Pontus, "Do you want to tell Ted what's been going on, and what we want?"

"You have been in charge of this from the first," Pontus replied. "The tribes trust you to talk for us."

"I'll do my best," Gail replied with a smile. She walked over to the signal fire and sat cross-legged on the grass, motioning for the others to do the same in a circle. "This is what has happened…"

At the end of an hour, Gail concluded, "…so you see? We had no choice. We want to trade, but in an honest way. We're not looking for anything special, or to get rich, but we don't want people getting wealthy off of us either, nor do we want to be treated like slaves. If that's going to be the attitude of the Bethish government, we'll take this rebellion into the hills for a thousand years and never stop."

Ted was silent, thinking. "Well, we cannot have that, can we? Too many of our people on both sides would die."

Gail searched his face. "You would be here for many years. It's a shame to be away from your family for so long."

Ted gave a short laugh. "I got married right after the Ambos civil war, had to search for her through two different countries. We are going to have a baby." His eyes got a faraway look in them, thinking.

"It's terrible to be away from someone you love during a time like that," Gail said, softly, reaching over and touching his arm for a moment. "You should be with her."

"You are right." Ted slapped his hands on his knees. "What is it that the natives want?"

"At least one seat on the colonial council," Gail said at once. "That way we can air our complaints and resolve them before they get blown out of proportion."

"Done," Ted replied at once. "What else?"

"Fair prices for our ivory and other goods we bring into the colony to sell. No more arbitrary price changes at the whims of the merchants."

The general nodded. "That seems reasonable, but you must understand, the merchants here are subject to the demand back in Mu. There will be changes occasionally."

"I realize that," Gail replied, "but right now prices go down here when prices in Bethand go up. That's stealing."

"Okay, I can agree on that. It would be taken care of by the council anyway." He chuckled and joked, "Anything else, appoint the new governor, too?"

Gail thought about it. "Sure, why not. That would solve all our problems."

For a moment, her remark set Ted aback, and then he replied cautiously, "Any appointment I make here would be temporary, subject to the approval of the senate in Bethand and the Council of Commons in Ambos. I can make no guarantee that whoever is put in charge would remain so."

Gail pressed her point, "This would fix everything, and—" she looked the general in the eye—" I wouldn't want you to be stuck here putting down rebellions, when you should be home with your wife and child."

Ted gave her a smirk and said in resignation, "I guess you have a point. It looks like a change in management is in order," he said to Fredrick. "What do you think?"

"'Tis true," he agreed, "but who do we get to be the new governor who is acceptable to both the natives and the colonists?"

"That's the trouble," Ted said to Gail and Pontus. "Any suggestions?"

Gail scowled and looked startled. She hadn't expected they would really let the natives appoint the next governor. For a moment, she was lost in thought.

When she did not reply, Ted turned to Pontus. "Do you have anyone in mind?"

"Uh, no," Pontus stammered and looked back at Gail in confusion. "Gaela—"

She thought hard. *It's all up to me, and I don't know anyone.* "There's the trader, Alak-an, but—"

"Him?" Ted's eyebrows shot up. Alak-an, who had been listening to the conversation in silence, suddenly came alert and took a few steps closer.

"Yes, him," Gail replied. "He is the perfect choice for the job."

"Well, why not." The general threw his hands in the air in resignation. He gave Alak-an a nod and waved him over. "He knows the natives, he knows the merchants— probably have to leave someone here to advise him, though, but I would have to do that in any case with whomever I appoint. Don't even know if he wants the job." He looked at the trader. "Well?"

Alak-an swung from the general to Gail in confusion. "Ah—er, yea, I guess so," he stammered out. "Sure, why not."

Ted smirked and stuck out his hand to Gail. "Done!"

She took it, her mind in a daze. It was over. They had won.

***

The exchange of prisoners finished—the few the natives held, and the hundreds that the colonists had kept for their labor gangs. Life returned to normal. Gail disbanded her army while first extracting pledges of support and loyalty from the northern, southern and coastal tribes.

Ted dispatched his aide, Fredrick, to Bionx to stay as the acting magistrate until a suitable replacement arrived from Ambos. After a reluctant Alak-an was installed as the new governor in New Bethand, Gail had time to tell her story. Ted escorted Pontus and Gail back to their village, as much to hear what she had to say, as to see the savannah first hand.

"And I thought I had adventures in this time." Ted shook his head in wonder. "You can't be happy here in the past, especially in the back country – everything must be so strange and primitive." He thought for a moment. "Tell you what, do you want to return to Bethand with me? It's not much, but you could settle down, have a nice place to live, even have running water and real stores to shop in. With your skills, you would have no problem making a living. It's better than trying to survive here in the wilderness." He paused. "With my influence, I could even get you a job in the government – liaison to the natives or something if you wished."

Gail thought over what he had said. She remembered what her old life had been, and what it was now.

They rode up the trail and the village came into view. Jankus, Malta and the rest of the villagers streamed out to greet Gail and Pontus. Amber bounded off to investigate their hut and then made himself comfortable in the shade of a tree for a nap.

"So what do you say?"

"I think I'll stay here," Gaela replied.

About the Author:

Army Veteran, graduate of Florida State University, former police officer and plant manager. Native Long Islander now living in Florida was wife, two puppies and SnoopyCat. (and yes, a coffee drinker!)

Acknowledgements:

Summer Solstice, K.C. Sprayberry, and all the other wonderful people at Solstice Publishing.

I would like to thank my former boss and friend C. Baldi for asking, "What happened to Gail," and giving me the idea for this book.

Social Media Links:

Twitter: https://twitter.com/artyny59

Facebook/Author Page:
https://www.facebook.com/pages/Arthur-Butt-The-Fantasy-SyFi-Author/1528729850734703